Greatest Short Stories

VOLUME V

FOREIGN

P. F. COLLIER & SON CORPORATION

NEW YORK

CONTENTS

PAGE

1. THE QUEEN OF SPADES 7
   Alexander Sergeievitch Pushkin

2. THE UNKNOWN MASTERPIECE 25
   Honoré de Balzac

3. MY FRIEND THE MURDERER 71
   A. Conan Doyle

4. THE DEAD ARE SILENT 103
   Arthur Schnitzler

5. HOW THE REDOUBT WAS TAKEN 131
   Prosper Mérimée

6. THE SLANDERER 141
   Anton Pavlovitch Chekhov

7. THE NECKLACE 149
   Guy de Maupassant

8. PUTOIS 165
   Anatole France

9. THE COURTING OF T'NOWHEAD'S BELL . . 187
   James Matthew Barrie

10. THE ROLL-CALL OF THE REEF 219
    A. T. Quiller-Couch

CONTENTS

PAGE

11. THE RENDEZVOUS 247
Ivan Turgenev

12. A BAL MASQUÉ 265
Alexandre Dumas

13. VALIA 281
Leonid Andreiev

14. THE LOST CHILD 303
François Edouard Joachim Coppée

15. THE MAN WHO WOULD BE KING 329
Rudyard Kipling

THE QUEEN OF SPADES

BY ALEXANDER SERGEIEVITCH PUSHKIN

THE QUEEN OF SPADES

BY ALEXANDER SERGEIEVITCH PUSHKIN

AT the house of Naroumov, a cavalry officer, the long winter night had been passed in gambling. At five in the morning break-fast was served to the weary players. The win-ners ate with relish; the losers, on the contrary, pushed back their plates and sat brooding gloomily. Under the influence of the good wine, however, the conversation then became general.

"Well, Sourine?" said the host inquiringly.

"Oh, I lost as usual. My luck is abominable. No matter how cool I keep, I never win."

"How is it, Herman, that you never touch a card?" remarked one of the men, addressing a young officer of the Engineering Corps. "Here you are with the rest of us at five o'clock in the morning, and you have neither played nor bet all night."

"Play interests me greatly," replied the person addressed, "but I hardly care to sacrifice the necessaries of life for uncertain superfluities."

"Herman is a German, therefore economical; that explains it," said Tomsky. "But the person

Translated by H. Twitchell. Copyright, 1901, by The Current Litera-ture Publishing Company.

I can't quite understand is my grandmother, the Countess Anna Fedorovna."

"Why?" inquired a chorus of voices.

"I can't understand why my grandmother never gambles."

"I don't see anything very striking in the fact that a woman of eighty refuses to gamble," objected Naroumov.

"Have you never heard her story?"

"No."

"Well, then, listen to it. To begin with, sixty years ago my grandmother went to Paris, where she was all the fashion. People crowded each other in the streets to get a chance to see the 'Muscovite Venus,' as she was called. All the great ladies played faro, then. On one occasion, while playing with the Duke of Orleans, she lost an enormous sum. She told her husband of the debt, but he refused outright to pay it. Nothing could induce him to change his mind on the subject, and grandmother was at her wits' ends. Finally, she remembered a friend of hers, Count Saint-Germain. You must have heard of him, as many wonderful stories have been told about him. He is said to have discovered the elixir of life, the philosopher's stone, and many other equally marvelous things. He had money at his disposal, and my grandmother knew it. She sent him a note asking him to come to see her. He obeyed her summons and found her in great distress. She painted the cruelty of her husband in the darkest colors, and ended by telling the Count that she depended upon his friendship and generosity.

" 'I could lend you the money,' replied the Count, after a moment of thoughtfulness, 'but I know that you would not enjoy a moment's rest until you had returned it; it would only add to your embarrassment. There is another way of freeing yourself.'

" 'But I have no money at all,' insisted my grandmother.

" 'There is no need of money. Listen to me.'

"The Count then told her a secret which any of us would give a good deal to know."

The young gamesters were all attention. Tomsky lit his pipe, took a few whiffs, then continued:

"The next evening, grandmother appeared at Versailles at the Queen's gaming-table. The Duke of Orleans was the dealer. Grandmother made some excuse for not having brought any money, and began to punt. She chose three cards in succession, again and again, winning every time, and was soon out of debt."

"A fable," remarked Herman; "perhaps the cards were marked."

"I hardly think so," replied Tomsky, with an air of importance.

"So you have a grandmother who knows three winning cards, and you haven't found out the magic secret."

"I must say I have not. She had four sons, one of them being my father, all of whom are devoted to play; she never told the secret to one of them. But my uncle told me this much, on his word of honor. Tchaplitzky, who died in poverty after having squandered millions, lost at one time, at play, nearly three hundred thousand rubles. He was desperate and grandmother took pity on him. She told him the three cards, making him swear never to use them again. He returned to the game, staked fifty thousand rubles on each card, and came out ahead, after paying his debts."

As day was dawning the party now broke up, each one draining his glass and taking his leave.

.   .   .   .

The Countess Anna Fedorovna was seated before her mirror in her dressing-room. Three women were assisting at her toilet. The old Countess no longer made the slightest pretensions to beauty, but she still clung to all the habits of her youth, and spent as much time at her toilet as she had done sixty years before. At the window a young girl, her ward, sat at her needlework.

"Good afternoon, grandmother," cried a young officer, who had just entered the room. "I have come to ask a favor of you."

"What, Pavel?"

"I want to be allowed to present one of my

friends to you, and to take you to the ball on Tuesday night."

"Take me to the ball and present him to me there."

After a few more remarks the officer walked up to the window where Lisaveta Ivanovna sat.

"Whom do you wish to present?" asked the girl.

"Naroumov; do you know him?"

"No; is he a soldier?"

"Yes."

"An engineer?"

"No; why do you ask?"

The girl smiled and made no reply.

Pavel Tomsky took his leave, and, left to herself, Lisaveta glanced out of the window. Soon, a young officer appeared at the corner of the street; the girl blushed and bent her head low over her canvas.

This appearance of the officer had become a daily occurrence. The man was totally unknown to her, and as she was not accustomed to coquetting with the soldiers she saw on the street, she hardly knew how to explain his presence. His persistence finally roused an interest entirely strange to her. One day, she even ventured to smile upon her admirer, for such he seemed to be.

The reader need hardly be told that the officer was no other than Herman, the would-be gambler, whose imagination had been strongly excited by the story told by Tomsky of the three magic cards.

"Ah," he thought, "if the old Countess would only reveal the secret to me. Why not try to win her good-will and appeal to her sympathy?"

With this idea in mind, he took up his daily station before the house, watching the pretty face at the window, and trusting to fate to bring about the desired acquaintance.

One day, as Lisaveta was standing on the pavement about to enter the carriage after the Countess, she felt herself jostled and a note was thrust into her hand. Turning, she saw the young officer at her elbow. As quick as thought, she put the note in her glove and entered the carriage. On her return from the drive, she hastened to her chamber to read the missive, in a state of excitement mingled with fear. It was a tender and respectful declaration of affection, copied word for word from a German novel. Of this fact, Lisa was, of course, ignorant.

The young girl was much impressed by the missive, but she felt that the writer must not be encouraged. She therefore wrote a few lines of explanation and, at the first opportunity, dropped it, with the letter, out of the window. The officer hastily crossed the street, picked up the papers and entered a shop to read them.

In no wise daunted by this rebuff, he found the opportunity to send her another note in a few days. He received no reply, but, evidently understanding the female heart, he presevered, begging for an interview. He was rewarded at last by the following:

"To-night we go to the ambassador's ball. We shall remain until two o'clock. I can arrange for a meeting in this way. After our departure, the servants will probably all go out, or go to sleep. At half-past eleven enter the vestibule boldly, and if you see any one, inquire for the Countess; if not, ascend the stairs, turn to the left and go on until you come to a door, which opens into her bedchamber. Enter this room and behind a screen you will find another door leading to a corridor; from this a spiral staircase leads to my sitting-room. I shall expect to find you there on my return."

Herman trembled like a leaf as the appointed hour drew near. He obeyed instructions fully, and, as he met no one, he reached the old lady's bedchamber without difficulty. Instead of going out of the small door behind the screen, however, he concealed himself in a closet to await the return of the old Countess.

The hours dragged slowly by; at last he heard the sound of wheels. Immediately lamps were lighted and servants began moving about. Finally the old woman tottered into the room, completely exhausted. Her women removed her wraps and proceeded to get her in readiness for the night. Herman watched the proceedings with a curiosity not unmingled with superstitious

13

fear. When at last she was attired in cap and gown, the old woman looked less uncanny than when she wore her ball-dress of blue brocade.

She sat down in an easy chair beside a table, as she was in the habit of doing before retiring, and her women withdrew. As the old lady sat swaying to and fro, seemingly oblivious to her surroundings, Herman crept out of his hiding-place.

At the slight noise the old woman opened her eyes, and gazed at the intruder with a half-dazed expression.

"Have no fear, I beg of you," said Herman, in a calm voice. "I have not come to harm you, but to ask a favor of you instead."

The Countess looked at him in silence, seemingly without comprehending him. Herman thought she might be deaf, so he put his lips close to her ear and repeated his remark. The listener remained perfectly mute.

"You could make my fortune without its costing you anything," pleaded the young man; "only tell me the three cards which are sure to win, and—"

Herman paused as the old woman opened her lips as if about to speak.

"It was only a jest; I swear to you, it was only a jest," came from the withered lips.

"There was no jesting about it. Remember Tchaplitzky, who, thanks to you, was able to pay his debts."

An expression of interior agitation passed over the face of the old woman; then she relapsed into her former apathy.

"Will you tell me the names of the magic cards, or not?" asked Herman after a pause.

There was no reply.

The young man then drew a pistol from his pocket, exclaiming: "You old witch, I'll force you to tell me!"

At the sight of the weapon the Countess gave a second sign of life. She threw back her head and put out her hands as if to protect herself; then they dropped and she sat motionless.

Herman grasped her arm roughly, and was about to renew his threats, when he saw that she was dead!

.   .   .   .

Seated in her room, still in her ball-dress, Lisaveta gave herself up to her reflections. She had expected to find the young officer there, but she felt relieved to see that he was not.

Strangely enough, that very night at the ball, Tomsky had rallied her about her preference for the young officer, assuring her that he knew more than she supposed he did.

"Of whom are you speaking?" she had asked in alarm, fearing her adventure had been discovered.

"Of the remarkable man," was the reply. "His name is Herman."

Lisa made no reply.

"This Herman," continued Tomsky, "is a romantic character; he has the profile of a Napoleon
and the heart of a Mephistopheles. It is said he
has at least three crimes on his conscience. But
how pale you are."

"It is only a slight headache. But why do you
talk to me of this Herman?"

"Because I believe he has serious intentions
concerning you."

"Where has he seen me?"

"At church, perhaps, or on the street."

The conversation was interrupted at this point,
to the great regret of the young girl. The words
of Tomsky made a deep impression upon her,
and she realized how imprudently she had acted.
She was thinking of all this and a great deal
more when the door of her apartment suddenly
opened, and Herman stood before her. She drew
back at sight of him, trembling violently.

"Where have you been?" she asked in a frightened whisper.

"In the bedchamber of the Countess. She is
dead," was the calm reply.

"My God! What are you saying?" cried the
girl.

"Furthermore, I believe that I was the cause
of her death."

The words of Tomsky flashed through Lisa's
mind.

Herman sat down and told her all. She listened with a feeling of terror and disgust. So

16

those passionate letters, that audacious pursuit were not the result of tenderness and love. It was money that he desired. The poor girl felt that she had in a sense been an accomplice in the death of her benefactress. She began to weep bitterly. Herman regarded her in silence.

"You are a monster!" exclaimed Lisa, drying her eyes.

"I didn't intend to kill her; the pistol was not even loaded."

"How are you going to get out of the house?" inquired Lisa. "It is nearly daylight. I intended to show you the way to a secret staircase, while the Countess was asleep, as we would have to cross her chamber. Now I am afraid to do so."

"Direct me, and I will find the way alone," replied Herman.

She gave him minute instructions and a key with which to open the street door. The young man pressed the cold, inert hand, then went out.

The death of the Countess had surprised no one, as it had long been expected. Her funeral was attended by every one of note in the vicinity. Herman mingled with the throng without attracting any especial attention. After all the friends had taken their last look at the dead face, the young man approached the bier. He prostrated himself on the cold floor, and remained motionless for a long time. He rose at last with a face almost as pale as that of the corpse itself, and went up the steps to look into the casket. As he looked down it seemed to him that the rigid face returned his glance mockingly, closing one eye. He turned abruptly away, made a false step, and fell to the floor. He was picked up, and, at the same moment, Lisaveta was carried out in a faint.

Herman did not recover his usual composure during the entire day. He dined alone at an out-of-the-way restaurant, and drank a great deal, in the hope of stifling his emotion. The wine only served to stimulate his imagination. He returned home and threw himself down on his bed without undressing.

During the night he awoke with a start; the moon shone into his chamber, making everything plainly visible. Some one looked in at the window, then quickly disappeared. He paid no attention to this, but soon he heard the vestibule door open. He thought it was his orderly, returning late, drunk as usual. The step was an unfamiliar one, and he heard the shuffling sound of loose slippers.

The door of his room opened, and a woman in white entered. She came close to the bed, and the terrified man recognized the Countess.

"I have come to you against my will," she said abruptly; "but I was commanded to grant your request. The tray, seven, and ace in succession are the magic cards. Twenty-four hours

18

must elapse between the use of each card, and after the three have been used you must never play again."

The phantom then turned and walked away. Herman heard the outside door close, and again saw the form pass the window.

He rose and went out into the hall, where his orderly lay asleep on the floor. The door was closed. Finding no trace of a visitor, he returned to his room, lit his candle, and wrote down what he had just heard.

Two fixed ideas cannot exist in the brain at the same time any more than two bodies can occupy the same point in space. The tray, seven, and ace soon chased away the thoughts of the dead woman, and all other thoughts from the brain of the young officer. All his ideas merged into a single one: how to turn to advantage the secret paid for so dearly. He even thought of resigning his commission and going to Paris to force a fortune from conquered fate. Chance rescued him from his embarrassment.

Tchekalinsky, a man who had passed his whole life at cards, opened a club at St. Petersburg. His long experience secured for him the confidence of his companions, and his hospitality and genial humor conciliated society.

The gilded youth flocked around him, neglecting society, preferring the charms of faro to those of their sweethearts. Naroumov invited Herman to accompany him to the club, and the

young man accepted the invitation only too will·
ingly.

The two officers found the apartments full.
Generals and statesmen played whist; young men
lounged on sofas, eating ices or smoking. In the
principal salon stood a long table, at which about
twenty men sat playing faro, the host of the
establishment being the banker.

He was a man of about sixty, gray-haired and
respectable. His ruddy face shone with genial
humor; his eyes sparkled and a constant smile
hovered around his lips.

Naroumov presented Herman. The host gave
him a cordial handshake, begged him not to stand
upon ceremony, and returned to his dealing.
More than thirty cards were already on the table.
Tchekalinsky paused after each coup, to allow
the punters time to recognize their gains or losses,
politely answering all questions and constantly
smiling.

After the deal was over, the cards were shuffled
and the game began again.

"Permit me to choose a card," said Herman,
stretching out his hand over the head of a portly
gentleman, to reach a livret. The banker bowed
without replying.

Herman chose a card, and wrote the amount
of his stake upon it with a piece of chalk.

"How much is that?" asked the banker; "excuse me, sir, but I do not see well."

"Forty thousand rubles," said Herman coolly.

All eyes were instantly turned to the speaker.

"He has lost his wits," thought Naroumov.

"Allow me to observe," said Tchekalinsky, with his eternal smile, "that your stake is excessive."

"What of it?" replied Herman, nettled. "Do you accept it or not?"

The banker nodded in assent. "I have only to remind you that the cash will be necessary; of course your word is good, but to keep the confidence of my patrons, I prefer the ready money."

Herman took a bank-check from his pocket and handed it to his host. The latter examined it attentively, then laid it on the card chosen.

He began dealing: to the right, a nine; to the left, a tray.

"The tray wins," said Herman, showing the card he held—a tray.

A murmur ran through the crowd. Tchekalinsky frowned for a second only, then his smile returned. He took a roll of bank-bills from his pocket and counted out the required sum. Herman received it and at once left the table.

The next evening saw him at the place again. Every one eyed him curiously, and Tchekalinsky greeted him cordially.

He selected his card and placed upon it his fresh stake. The banker began dealing: to the right, a nine; to the left, a seven.

Herman then showed his card—a seven spot. The onlookers exclaimed, and the host was visibly disturbed. He counted out ninety-four-thousand rubles and passed them to Herman, who accepted them without showing the least surprise and at once withdrew.

The following evening he went again. His appearance was the signal for the cessation of all occupation, every one being eager to watch the development of events. He selected his card— an ace.

The dealing began: to the right, a queen; to the left, an ace.

"The ace wins," remarked Herman, turning up his card without glancing at it.

"Your queen is killed," remarked Tchekalinsky quietly.

Herman trembled; looking down, he saw, not the ace he had selected, but the queen of spades. He could scarcely believe his eyes. It seemed impossible that he could have made such a mistake. As he stared at the card it seemed to him that the queen winked one eye at him mockingly.

"The old woman!" he exclaimed involuntarily.

The croupier raked in the money while he looked on in stupid terror. When he left the table, all made way for him to pass; the cards were shuffled, and the gambling went on.

Herman became a lunatic. He was confined at the hospital at Oboukov, where he spoke to no one, but kept constantly murmuring in a monotonous tone: "The tray, seven, ace! The tray, seven, queen!"

THE UNKNOWN MASTERPIECE

BY HONORE DE BALZAC

THE UNKNOWN MASTERPIECE

TO A LORD

BY HONORÉ DE BALZAC

1845

I

GILLETTE

ON a cold December morning in the year 1612, a young man, whose clothing was somewhat of the thinnest, was walking to and fro before a gateway in the Rue des Grands-Augustins in Paris. He went up and down the street before this house with the irresolution of a gallant who dares not venture into the presence of the mistress whom he loves for the first time, easy of access though she may be; but after a sufficiently long interval of hesitation, he at last crossed the threshold and inquired of an old woman, who was sweeping out a large room on the ground floor, whether Master Porbus was within. Receiving a reply in the affirmative, the young man went slowly up the staircase, like a gentleman but newly come to court, and doubtful as to his reception by the king. He came to a stand once more on the landing at the head of the stairs, and again he hesitated before raising

25

his hand to the grotesque knocker on the door of the studio, where doubtless the painter was at work—Master Porbus, sometime painter in ordinary to Henri IV till Mary de' Medici took Rubens into favor.

The young man felt deeply stirred by an emotion that must thrill the hearts of all great artists when, in the pride of their youth and their first love of art, they come into the presence of a master or stand before a masterpiece. For all human sentiments there is a time of early blossoming, a day of generous enthusiasm that gradually fades until nothing is left of happiness but a memory, and glory is known for a delusion. Of all these delicate and short-lived emotions, none so resemble love as the passion of a young artist for his art, as he is about to enter on the blissful martyrdom of his career of glory and disaster, of vague expectations and real disappointments.

Those who have missed this experience in the early days of light purses; who have not, in the dawn of their genius, stood in the presence of a master and felt the throbbing of their hearts, will always carry in their inmost souls a chord that has never been touched, and in their work an indefinable quality will be lacking, a something in the stroke of the brush, a mysterious element that we call poetry. The swaggerers, so puffed up by self-conceit that they are confident oversoon of their success, can never be taken for men of talent save by fools. From this point of view, if youthful modesty is the measure of youthful genius, the stranger on the staircase might be allowed to have something in him; for he seemed to possess the indescribable diffidence, the early timidity that artists are bound to lose in the course of a great career, even as pretty women lose it as they make progress in the arts of co-quetry. Self-distrust vanishes as triumph succeeds to triumph, and modesty is, perhaps, distrust of itself.

The poor neophyte was so overcome by the consciousness of his own presumption and insignificance, that it began to look as if he was hardly likely to penetrate into the studio of the painter, to whom we owe the wonderful portrait of Henri IV. But fate was propitious; an old man came up the staircase. From the quaint costume of this newcomer, his collar of magnificent lace, and a certain serene gravity in his bearing, the first arrival thought that this personage must be either a patron or a friend of the court painter. He stood aside therefore upon the landing to allow the visitor to pass, scrutinizing him curiously the while. Perhaps he might hope to find the good nature of an artist or to receive the good offices of an amateur not unfriendly to the arts; but besides an almost diabolical expression in the face that met his gaze, there was that indescribable something which has an irresistible attrac-tion for artists.

Picture that face. A bald high forehead and rugged jutting brows above a small flat nose turned up at the end, as in the portraits of Socrates and Rabelais; deep lines about the mocking mouth; a short chin, carried proudly, covered with a grizzled pointed beard; sea-green eyes that age might seem to have dimmed were it not for the contrast between the iris and the surrounding mother-of-pearl tints, so that it seemed as if under the stress of anger or enthusiasm there would be a magnetic power to quell or kindle in their glances. The face was withered beyond wont by the fatigue of years, yet it seemed aged still more by the thoughts that had worn away both soul and body. There were no lashes to the deep-set eyes, and scarcely a trace of the arching lines of the eyebrows above them. Set this head on a spare and feeble frame, place it in a frame of lace wrought like an engraved silver fish-slice, imagine a heavy gold chain over the old man's black doublet, and you will have some dim idea of this strange personage, who seemed still more fantastic in the sombre twilight of the staircase. One of Rembrandt's portraits might have stepped down from its frame to walk in an appropriate atmosphere of gloom, such as the great painter loved. The older man gave the younger a shrewd glance, and knocked thrice at the door. It was opened by a man of forty or thereabout, who seemed to be an invalid.

"Good day, Master."

Porbus bowed respectfully, and held the door open for the younger man to enter, thinking that the latter accompanied his visitor; and when he saw that the neophyte stood a while as if spellbound, feeling, as every artist-nature must feel, the fascinating influence of the first sight of a studio in which the material processes of art are revealed, Porbus troubled himself no more about this second comer.

All the light in the studio came from a window in the roof, and was concentrated upon an easel, where a canvas stood untouched as yet save for three or four outlines in chalk. The daylight scarcely reached the remoter angles and corners of the vast room; they were as dark as night, but the silver ornamented breastplate of a Reiter's corselet, that hung upon the wall, attracted a stray gleam to its dim abiding-place among the brown shadows; or a shaft of light shot across the carved and glistening surface of an antique sideboard covered with curious silver-plate, or struck out a line of glittering dots among the raised threads of the golden warp of some old brocaded curtains, where the lines of the stiff, heavy folds were broken, as the stuff had been flung carelessly down to serve as a model.

Plaster *écorchés* stood about the room; and here and there, on shelves and tables, lay fragments of classical sculpture—torsos of antique goddesses. worn smooth as though all the years of the centuries that had passed over them had been lovers' kisses. The walls were covered, from floor to ceiling, with countless sketches in charcoal, red chalk, or pen and ink. Amid the litter and confusion of color boxes, overturned stools, flasks of oil, and essences, there was just room to move so as to reach the illuminated circular space where the easel stood. The light from the window in the roof fell full upon Porbus's pale face and on the ivory-tinted forehead of his strange visitor. But in another moment the younger man heeded nothing but a picture that had already become famous even in those stormy days of political and religious revolution, a picture that a few of the zealous worshipers, who have so often kept the sacred fire of art alive in evil days, were wont to go on pilgrimage to see. The beautiful panel represented a Saint Mary of Egypt about to pay her passage across the seas. It was a masterpiece destined for Mary de' Medici, who sold it in later years of poverty.

"I like your saint," the old man remarked, addressing Porbus. "I would give you ten golden crowns for her over and above the price the Queen is paying; but as for putting a spoke in that wheel—the devil take it!"

"It is good then?"

"Hey! hey!" said the old man; "good, say you?— Yes and no. Your good woman is not badly done, but she is not alive. You artists fancy that when a figure is correctly drawn, and everything in its place according to the rules of anatomy, there is nothing more to be done. You make up the flesh tints beforehand on your palettes according to your formulæ, and fill in the outlines with due care that one side of the face shall be darker than the other; and because you look from time to time at a naked woman who stands on the platform before you, you fondly imagine that you have copied nature, think yourselves to be painters, believe that you have wrested His secret from God. Pshaw! You may know your syntax thoroughly and make no blunders in your grammar, but it takes that and something more to make a great poet. Look at your saint, Porbus! At a first glance she is admirable; look at her again, and you see at once that she is glued to the background, and that you could not walk round her. She is a silhouette that turns but one side of her face to all beholders, a figure cut out of canvas, an image with no power to move nor change her position. I feel as if there were no air between that arm and the background, no space, no sense of distance in your canvas. The perspective is perfectly correct, the strength of the coloring is accurately diminished with the distance; but, in spite of these praiseworthy efforts, I could never bring myself to believe that the warm breath of life comes and goes in that beautiful body. It seems to me that if I laid my hand on the firm, rounded throat, it would be cold as marble to the touch.

No, my friend, the blood does not flow beneath
that ivory skin, the tide of life does not flush
those delicate fibres, the purple veins that trace
a network beneath the transparent amber of her
brow and breast. Here the pulse seems to beat,
there it is motionless, life and death are at strife
in every detail; here you see a woman, there a
statue, there again a corpse. Your creation is
incomplete. You had only power to breathe a
portion of your soul into your beloved work.
The fire of Prometheus died out again and again
in your hands; many a spot in your picture has
not been touched by the divine flame."

"But how is it, dear master?" Porbus asked
respectfully, while the young man with difficulty
repressed his strong desire to beat the critic.

"Ah!" said the old man, "it is this! You have
halted between two manners. You have hesitated
between drawing and color, between the dogged
attention to detail, the stiff precision of the German masters and the dazzling glow, the joyous
exuberance of Italian painters. You have set
yourself to imitate Hans Holbein and Titian,
Albrecht Dürer and Paul Veronese in a single
picture. A magnificent ambition truly, but what
has come of it? Your work has neither the
severe charm of a dry execution nor the magical
illusion of Italian *chiaroscuro*. Titian's rich
golden coloring poured into Albrecht Dürer's
austere outlines has shattered them, like molten
bronze bursting through the mold that is not

strong enough to hold it. In other places the outlines have held firm, imprisoning and obscuring the magnificent, glowing flood of Venetian color. The drawing of the face is not perfect, the coloring is not perfect; traces of that unlucky indecision are to be seen everywhere. Unless you felt strong enough to fuse the two opposed manners in the fire of your own genius, you should have cast in your lot boldly with the one or the other, and so have obtained the unity which simulates one of the conditions of life itself. Your work is only true in the centres; your outlines are false, they project nothing, there is no hint of anything behind them. There is truth here," said the old man, pointing to the breast of the Saint, "and again here," he went on, indicating the rounded shoulder. "But there," once more returning to the column of the throat, "everything is false. Let us go no further into detail; you would be disheartened."

The old man sat down on a stool, and remained a while without speaking, with his face buried in his hands.

"Yet I studied that throat from the life, dear master," Porbus began; "it happens sometimes, for our misfortune, that real effects in nature look improbable when transferred to canvas—"

"The aim of art is not to copy nature, but to express it. You are not a servile copyist, but a poet!" cried the old man sharply, cutting Porbus short with an imperious gesture. "Otherwise a sculptor might make a plaster cast of a living woman and save himself all further trouble. Well, try to make a cast of your mistress's hand, and set up the thing before you. You will see a monstrosity, a dead mass, bearing no resemblance to the living hand; you would be compelled to have recourse to the chisel of a sculptor who, without making an exact copy, would represent for you its movement and its life. We must detect the spirit, the informing soul in the appearances of things and beings. Effects! What are effects but the accidents of life, not life itself? A hand, since I have taken that example, is not only a part of a body, it is the expression and extension of a thought that must be grasped and rendered. Neither painter nor poet nor sculptor may separate the effect from the cause, which are inevitably contained the one in the other. There begins the real struggle! Many a painter achieves success instinctively, unconscious of the task that is set before art. You draw a woman, yet you do not see her! Not so do you succeed in wresting Nature's secrets from her! You are reproducing mechanically the model that you copied in your master's studio. You do not penetrate far enough into the inmost secrets of the mystery of form; you do not seek with love enough and perseverance enough after the form that baffles and eludes you. Beauty is a thing severe and unapproachable, never to be won by

a languid lover. You must lie in wait for her
coming and take her unawares, press her hard
and clasp her in a tight embrace, and force her
to yield. Form is a Proteus more intangible and
more manifold than the Proteus of the legend;
compelled, only after long wrestling, to stand
forth manifest in his true aspect. Some of you
are satisfied with the first shape, or at most by
the second or the third that appears. Not thus
wrestle the victors, the unvanquished painters
who never suffer themselves to be deluded by all
those treacherous shadow-shapes; they persevere
till Nature at the last stands bare to their gaze,
and her very soul is revealed.

"In this manner worked Rafael," said the old
man, taking off his cap to express his reverence
for the King of Art. "His transcendent great-
ness came of the intimate sense that, in him,
seems as if it would shatter external form.
Form in his figures (as with us) is a symbol, a
means of communicating sensations, ideas, the
vast imaginings of a poet. Every face is a whole
world. The subject of the portrait appeared for
him bathed in the light of a divine vision; it was
revealed by an inner voice, the finger of God laid
bare the sources of expression in the past of a
whole life.

"You clothe your women in fair raiment of
flesh, in gracious veiling of hair; but where is the
blood, the source of passion and of calm, the
cause of the particular effect? Why, this brown

Egyptian of yours, my good Porbus, is a color-
less creature! These figures that you set before
us are painted bloodless fantoms; and you call
that painting, you call that art!

"Because you have made something more like
a woman than a house, you think that you have
set your fingers on the goal; you are quite proud
that you need not to write *currus venustus* or
pulcher homo beside your figures, as early
painters were wont to do and you fancy that you
have done wonders. Ah! my good friend, there
is still something more to learn, and you will use
up a great deal of chalk and cover many a canvas before you will learn it. Yes, truly, a woman
carries her head in just such a way, so she holds
her garments gathered into her hand; her eyes
grow dreamy and soft with that expression of
meek sweetness, and even so the quivering
shadow of the lashes hovers upon her cheeks.
It is all there, and yet it is not there. What
is lacking? A nothing, but that nothing is
everything.

"There you have the semblance of life, but you
do not express its fulness and effluence, that indescribable something, perhaps the soul itself,
that envelopes the outlines of the body like a
haze; that flower of life, in short, that Titian
and Rafael caught. Your utmost achievement
hitherto has only brought you to the starting-
point. You might now perhaps begin to do excellent work, but you grow weary all too soon;

and the crowd admires, and those who know smile.

"Oh, Mabuse! oh, my master!" cried the strange speaker, "thou art a thief! Thou hast carried away the secret of life with thee!"

"Nevertheless," he began again, "this picture of yours is worth more than all the paintings of that rascal Rubens, with his mountains of Flemish flesh raddled with vermilion, his torrents of red hair, his riot of color. You, at least have color there, and feeling and drawing—the three essentials in art."

The young man roused himself from his deep musings.

"Why, my good man, the Saint is sublime!" he cried. "There is a subtlety of imagination about those two figures, the Saint Mary and the Shipman, that can not be found among Italian masters; I do not know a single one of them capable of imagining the Shipman's hesitation."

"Did that little malapert come with you?" asked Porbus of the older man.

"Alas! master, pardon my boldness," cried the neophyte, and the color mounted to his face. "I am unknown—a dauber by instinct, and but lately come to this city—the fountain-head of all learning."

"Set to work," said Porbus, handing him a bit of red chalk and a sheet of paper.

The new-comer quickly sketched the Saint Mary line for line.

"Aha!" exclaimed the old man. "Your name?" he added.

The young man wrote "Nicolas Poussin" below the sketch.

"Not bad that for a beginning," said the strange speaker, who had discoursed so wildly. "I see that we can talk of art in your presence. I do not blame you for admiring Porbus's saint. In the eyes of the world she is a masterpiece, and those alone who have been initiated into the inmost mysteries of art can discover her shortcomings. But it is worth while to give you the lesson, for you are able to understand it, so I will show you how little it needs to complete this picture. You must be all eyes, all attention, for it may be that such a chance of learning will never come in your way again—Porbus! your palette."

Porbus went in search of palette and brushes. The little old man turned back his sleeves with impatient energy, seized the palette, covered with many hues, that Porbus handed to him, and snatched rather than took a handful of brushes of various sizes from the hands of his acquaintance. His pointed beard suddenly bristled—a menacing movement that expressed the prick of a lover's fancy. As he loaded his brush, he muttered between his teeth, "These paints are only fit to fling out of the window, together with the fellow who ground them, their crudeness and falseness are disgusting! How can one paint with this?"

He dipped the tip of the brush with feverish eagerness in the different pigments, making the circuit of the palette several times more quickly than the organist of a cathedral sweeps the octaves on the keyboard of his clavier for the "O Filii" at Easter.

Porbus and Poussin, on either side of the easel, stood stock-still, watching with intense interest.

"Look, young man," he began again, "see how three or four strokes of the brush and a thin glaze of blue let in the free air to play about the head of the poor Saint, who must have felt stifled and oppressed by the close atmosphere! See how the drapery begins to flutter; you feel that it is lifted by the breeze! A moment ago it hung as heavily and stiffly as if it were held out by pins. Do you see how the satin sheen that I have just given to the breast rends the pliant, silken softness of a young girl's skin, and how the brown-red, blended with burnt ochre, brings warmth into the cold gray of the deep shadow where the blood lay congealed instead of coursing through the veins? Young man, young man, no master could teach you how to do this that I am doing before your eyes. Mabuse alone possessed the secret of giving life to his figures; Mabuse had but one pupil—that was I. I have had none, and I am old. You have sufficient intelligence to imagine the rest from the glimpses that I am giving you."

While the old man was speaking, he gave a touch here and there; sometimes two strokes of the brush, sometimes a single one; but every stroke told so well, that the whole picture seemed transfigured—the painting was flooded with light. He worked with such passionate fervor that beads of sweat gathered upon his bare forehead; he worked so quickly, in brief, impatient jerks, that it seemed to young Poussin as if some familiar spirit inhabiting the body of this strange being took a grotesque pleasure in making use of the man's hands against his own will. The unearthly glitter of his eyes, the convulsive movements that seemed like struggles, gave to this fancy a semblance of truth which could not but stir a young imagination. The old man continued, saying as he did so—

"Paf! paf! that is how to lay it on, young man!— Little touches! come and bring a glow into those icy cold tones for me! Just so! Pon! pon! pon!" and those parts of the picture that he had pointed out as cold and lifeless flushed with warmer hues, a few bold strokes of color brought all the tones of the picture into the required harmony with the glowing tints of the Egyptian, and the differences in temperament vanished.

"Look you, youngster, the last touches make the picture. Porbus has given it a hundred strokes for every one of mine. No one thanks us for what lies beneath. Bear that in mind."

At last the restless spirit stopped, and turning to Porbus and Poussin, who were speechless with admiration, he spoke—

"This is not as good as my 'Belle Noiseuse'; still one might put one's name to such a thing as this.— Yes, I would put my name to it," he added, rising to reach for a mirror, in which he looked at the picture.— "And now," he said, "will you both come and breakfast with me? I have a smoked ham and some very fair wine! . . . Eh! eh! the times may be bad, but we can still have some talk about art! We can talk like equals. . . . Here is a little fellow who has aptitude," he added, laying a hand on Nicolas Poussin's shoulder.

In this way the stranger became aware of the threadbare condition of the Norman's doublet. He drew a leather purse from his girdle, felt in it, found two gold coins, and held them out.

"I will buy your sketch," he said.

"Take it," said Porbus, as he saw the other start and flush with embarrassment, for Poussin had the pride of poverty. "Pray, take it; he has a couple of king's ransoms in his pouch!"

The three came down together from the studio, and, talking of art by the way, reached a picturesque wooden house hard by the Pont Saint-Michel. Poussin wondered a moment at its ornament, at the knocker, at the frames of the casements, at the scroll-work designs, and in the next he stood in a vast low-ceiled room. A table, covered with tempting dishes, stood near the blazing fire, and (luck unhoped for) he was in the company of two great artists full of genial good humor.

"Do not look too long at that canvas, young man," said Porbus, when he saw that Poussin was standing, struck with wonder, before a painting. "You would fall a victim to despair."

It was the "Adam" painted by Mabuse to purchase his release from the prison, where his creditors had so long kept him. And, as a matter of fact, the figure stood out so boldly and convincingly, that Nicolas Poussin began to understand the real meaning of the words poured out by the old artist, who was himself looking at the picture with apparent satisfaction, but without enthusiasm. "I have done better than that!" he seemed to be saying to himself.

"There is life in it," he said aloud; "in that respect my poor master here surpassed himself, but there is some lack of truth in the background. The man lives indeed; he is rising, and will come toward us; but the atmosphere, the sky, the air, the breath of the breeze—you look and feel for them, but they are not there. And then the man himself is, after all, only a man! Ah! but the one man in the world who came direct from the hands of God must have had a something divine about him that is wanting here. Mabuse himself would grind his teeth and say so when he was not drunk."

Poussin looked from the speaker to Porbus,

and from Porbus to the speaker, with restless curiosity. He went up to the latter to ask for the name of their host; but the painter laid a finger on his lips with an air of mystery. The young man's interest was excited; he kept silence, but hoped that sooner or later some word might be let fall that would reveal the name of his entertainer. It was evident that he was a man of talent and very wealthy, for Porbus listened to him respectfully, and the vast room was crowded with marvels of art.

A magnificent portrait of a woman, hung against the dark oak panels of the wall, next caught Poussin's attention.

"What a glorious Giorgione!" he cried.

"No," said his host, "it is an early daub of mine—"

"Gramercy! I am in the abode of the god of painting, it seems!" cried Poussin ingenuously.

The old man smiled as if he had long grown familiar with such praise.

"Master Frenhofer!" said Porbus, "do you think you could spare me a little of your capital Rhine wine?"

"A couple of pipes!" answered his host; "one to discharge a debt, for the pleasure of seeing your pretty sinner, the other as a present from a friend."

"Ah! if I had my health," returned Porbus, "and if you would but let me see your 'Belle Noiseuse,' I would paint some great picture, with breadth in it and depth; the figures should be life-size."

"Let you see my work!" cried the painter in agitation. "No, no! it is not perfect yet; something still remains for me to do. Yesterday, in the dusk," he said, "I thought I had reached the end. Her eyes seemed moist, the flesh quivered, something stirred the tresses of her hair. She breathed! But though I have succeeded in reproducing Nature's roundness and relief on the flat surface of the canvas, this morning, by daylight, I found out my mistake. Ah! to achieve that glorious result I have studied the works of the great masters of color, stripping off coat after coat of color from Titian's canvas, analyzing the pigments of the king of light. Like that sovereign painter, I began the face in a slight tone with a supple and fat paste—for shadow is but an accident; bear that in mind, youngster!— Then I began afresh, and by half-tones and thin glazes of color less and less transparent, I gradually deepened the tints to the deepest black of the strongest shadows. An ordinary painter makes his shadows something entirely different in nature from the high lights; they are wood or brass, or what you will, anything but flesh in shadow. You feel that even if those figures were to alter their position, those shadow stains would never be cleansed away, those parts of the picture would never glow with light.

"I have escaped one mistake, into which the

most famous painters have sometimes fallen; in my canvas the whiteness shines through the densest and most persistent shadow. I have not marked out the limits of my figure in hard, dry outlines, and brought every least anatomical detail into prominence (like a host of dunces, who fancy that they can draw because they can trace a line elaborately smooth and clean), for the human body is not contained within the limits of line. In this the sculptor can approach the truth more nearly than we painters. Nature's way is a complicated succession of curve within curve. Strictly speaking, there is no such thing as drawing.—Do not laugh, young man; strange as that speech may seem to you, you will understand the truth in it some day.—A line is a method of expressing the effect of light upon an object; but there are no lines in Nature, everything is solid. We draw by modeling, that is to say, that we disengage an object from its setting; the distribution of the light alone gives to a body the appearance by which we know it. So I have not defined the outlines; I have suffused them with a haze of half-tints warm or golden, in such a sort that you can not lay your finger on the exact spot where background and contours meet. Seen from near, the picture looks a blur; it seems to lack definition; but step back two paces, and the whole thing becomes clear, distinct, and solid; the body stands out; the rounded form comes into relief; you feel that the air plays round it.

And yet—I am not satisfied; I have misgivings. Perhaps one ought not to draw a single line; perhaps it would be better to attack the face from the centre, taking the highest prominences first, proceeding from them through the whole range of shadows to the heaviest of all. Is not this the method of the sun, the divine painter of the world? Oh, Nature, Nature! who has surprised thee, fugitive? But, after all, too much knowledge, like ignorance, brings you to a negation. I have doubts about my work."

There was a pause. Then the old man spoke again. "I have been at work upon it for ten years, young man; but what are ten short years in a struggle with Nature? Do we know how long Sir Pygmalion wrought at the one statue that came to life?" The old man fell into deep musings, and gazed before him with unseeing eyes, while he played unheedingly with his knife.

"Look, he is in conversation with his *dæmon*!" murmured Porbus.

At the word, Nicolas Poussin felt himself carried away by an unaccountable accession of artist's curiosity. For him the old man, at once intent and inert, the seer with the unseeing eyes, became something more than a man—a fantastic spirit living in a mysterious world, and countless vague thoughts awoke within his soul. The effect of this species of fascination upon his mind can no more be described in words than the passionate longing awakened in an exile's heart by the song that recalls his home. He thought of the scorn that the old man affected to display for the noblest efforts of art, of his wealth, his manners, of the deference paid to him by Porbus. The mysterious picture, the work of patience on which he had wrought so long in secret, was doubtless a work of genius, for the head of the Virgin which young Poussin had admired so frankly was beautiful even beside Mabuse's "Adam"—there was no mistaking the imperial manner of one of the princes of art. Everything combined to set the old man beyond the limits of human nature.

Out of the wealth of fancies in Nicolas Poussin's brain an idea grew, and gathered shape and clearness. He saw in this supernatural being a complete type of the artist nature, a nature mocking and kindly, barren and prolific, an erratic spirit intrusted with great and manifold powers which she too often abuses, leading sober reason, the Philistine, and sometimes even the amateur forth into a stony wilderness where they see nothing; but the white-winged maiden herself, wild as her fancies may be, finds epics there and castles and works of art. For Poussin, the enthusiast, the old man, was suddenly transfigured, and became Art incarnate, Art with its mysteries, its vehement passion and its dreams.

"Yes, my dear Porbus," Frenhofer continued. "hitherto I have never found a flawless model, a body with outlines of perfect beauty, the car-

nations—Ah! where does she live?" he cried,
breaking in upon himself, "the undiscoverable
Venus of the older time, for whom we have
sought so often, only to find the scattered gleams
of her beauty here and there? Oh! to behold
once and for one moment, Nature grown perfect
and divine, the Ideal at last, I would give all
that I possess. . . . Nay, Beauty divine, I
would go to seek thee in the dim land of the dead;
like Orpheus, I would go down into the Hades
of Art to bring back the life of art from among
the shadows of death."

"We can go now," said Porbus to Poussin.
"He neither hears nor sees us any longer."

"Let us go to his studio," said young Poussin,
wondering greatly.

"Oh! the old fox takes care that no one shall
enter it. His treasures are so carefully guarded
that it is impossible for us to come at them. I
have not waited for your suggestion and your
fancy to attempt to lay hands on this mystery
by force."

"So there is a mystery?"

"Yes," answered Porbus. "Old Frenhofer is
the only pupil Mabuse would take. Frenhofer
became the painter's friend, deliverer, and father;
he sacrificed the greater part of his fortune to
enable Mabuse to indulge in riotous extrava-
gance, and in return Mabuse bequeathed to him
the secret of relief, the power of giving to his
figures the wonderful life, the flower of Nature,

the eternal despair of art, the secret which Mabuse knew so well that one day when he had sold the flowered brocade suit in which he should have appeared at the Entry of Charles V, he accompanied his master in a suit of paper painted to resemble the brocade. The peculiar richness and splendor of the stuff struck the Emperor; he complimented the old drunkard's patron on the artist's appearance, and so the trick was brought to light. Frenhofer is a passionate enthusiast, who sees above and beyond other painters. He has meditated profoundly on color, and the absolute truth of line; but by the way of much research he has come to doubt the very existence of the objects of his search. He says, in moments of despondency, that there is no such thing as drawing, and that by means of lines we can only reproduce geometrical figures; but that is overshooting the mark, for by outline and shadow you can reproduce form without any color at all, which shows that our art, like Nature, is composed of an infinite number of elements. Drawing gives you the skeleton, the anatomical framework, and color puts the life into it; but life without the skeleton is even more incomplete than a skeleton without life. But there is something else truer still, and it is this—for painters, practise and observation are everything; and when theories and poetical ideas begin to quarrel with the brushes, the end is doubt, as has happened with our good friend, who is half crack-brained enthusiast, half painter. A sublime painter! but unlucky for him, he was born to riches, and so he has leisure to follow his fancies. Do not you follow his example! Work! painters have no business to think, except brush in hand."

"We will find a way into his studio!" cried Poussin confidently. He had ceased to heed Porbus's remarks. The other smiled at the young painter's enthusiasm, asked him to come to see him again, and they parted. Nicolas Poussin went slowly back to the Rue de la Harpe, and passed the modest hostelry where he was lodging without noticing it. A feeling of uneasiness prompted him to hurry up the crazy staircase till he reached a room at the top, a quaint, airy recess under the steep, high-pitched roof common among houses in old Paris. In the one dingy window of the place sat a young girl, who sprang up at once when she heard some one at the door; it was the prompting of love; she had recognized the painter's touch on the latch.

"What is the matter with you?" she asked.

"The matter is . . . is . . . Oh! I have felt that I am a painter! Until to-day I have had doubts, but now I believe in myself! There is the making of a great man in me! Never mind, Gillette, we shall be rich and happy! There is gold at the tips of those brushes—"

He broke off suddenly. The joy faded from his powerful and earnest face as he compared his vast hopes with his slender resources. The walls

were covered with sketches in chalk on sheets of
common paper. There were but four canvases
in the room. Colors were very costly, and the
young painter's palette was almost bare. Yet
in the midst of his poverty he possessed and was
conscious of the possession of inexhaustible treasures of the heart, of a devouring genius equal to
all the tasks that lay before him.

He had been brought to Paris by a nobleman
among his friends, or perchance by the consciousness of his powers; and in Paris he had
found a mistress, one of those noble and generous souls who choose to suffer by a great man's
side, who share his struggles and strive to understand his fancies, accepting their lot of poverty
and love as bravely and dauntlessly as other
women will set themselves to bear the burden of
riches and make a parade of their insensibility.
The smile that stole over Gillette's lips filled the
garret with golden light, and rivaled the brightness of the sun in heaven. The sun, moreover,
does not always shine in heaven, whereas Gillette
was always in the garret, absorbed in her passion,
occupied by Poussin's happiness and sorrow,
consoling the genius which found an outlet in
love before art engrossed it.

"Listen, Gillette. Come here."

The girl obeyed joyously, and sprang upon
the painter's knee. Hers was perfect grace and
beauty, and the loveliness of spring; she was
adorned with all luxuriant fairness of outward

form, lighted up by the glow of a fair soul within.

"Oh! God," he cried; "I shall never dare to tell her—"

"A secret?" she cried; "I must know it!"

Poussin was absorbed in his dreams.

"Do tell it me!"

"Gillette . . . poor beloved heart! . . ."

"Oh! do you want something of me?"

"Yes."

"If you wish me to sit once more for you as I did the other day," she continued with playful petulance, "I will never consent to do such a thing again, for your eyes say nothing all the while. You do not think of me at all, and yet you look at me—"

"Would you rather have me draw another woman?"

"Perhaps—if she were very ugly," she said.

"Well," said Poussin gravely, "and if, for the sake of my fame to come, if to make me a great painter, you must sit to some one else?"

"You may try me," she said; "you know quite well that I would not."

Poussin's head sank on her breast; he seemed to be overpowered by some intolerable joy or sorrow.

"Listen," she cried, plucking at the sleeve of Poussin's threadbare doublet. "I told you, Nick, that I would lay down my life for you; but I

never promised you that I in my lifetime would
lay down my love."

"Your love?" cried the young artist.

"If I showed myself thus to another, you
would love me no longer, and I should feel myself unworthy of you. Obedience to your fancies
was a natural and simple thing, was it not?
Even against my own will, I am glad and even
proud to do thy dear will. But for another, out
upon it!"

"Forgive me, my Gillette," said the painter,
falling upon his knees; "I would rather be beloved than famous. You are fairer than success
and honors. There, fling the pencils away, and
burn these sketches! I have made a mistake. I
was meant to love and not to paint. Perish art
and all its secrets!"

Gillette looked admiringly at him, in an ecstasy
of happiness! She was triumphant; she felt
instinctively that art was laid aside for her
sake, and flung like a grain of incense at her
feet.

"Yet he is only an old man," Poussin continued; "for him you would be a woman, and
nothing more. You—so perfect!"

"I must love you indeed!" she cried, ready to
sacrifice even love's scruples to the lover who had
given up so much for her sake; "but I should
bring about my own ruin. Ah! to ruin myself,
to lose everything for you! . . . It is a very
glorious thought! Ah! but you will forget me.

Oh! what evil thought is this that has come to you?"

"I love you, and yet I thought of it," he said, with something like remorse. "Am I so base a wretch?"

"Let us consult Père Hardouin," she said.

"No, no! Let it be a secret between us."

"Very well; I will do it. But you must not be there," she said. "Stay at the door with your dagger in your hand; and if I call, rush in and kill the painter."

Poussin forgot everything but art. He held Gillette tightly in his arms.

"He loves me no longer!" thought Gillette when she was alone. She repented of her resolution already.

But to these misgivings there soon succeeded a sharper pain, and she strove to banish a hideous thought that arose in her own heart. It seemed to her that her own love had grown less already, with a vague suspicion that the painter had fallen somewhat in her eyes.

II

CATHERINE LESCAULT

Three months after Poussin and Porbus met, the latter went to see Master Frenhofer. The old man had fallen a victim to one of those profound and spontaneous fits of discouragement that are caused, according to medical logicians, by indigestion, flatulence, fever, or enlargement of the spleen; or, if you take the opinion of the Spiritualists, by the imperfections of our mortal nature. The good man had simply overworked himself in putting the finishing touches to his mysterious picture. He was lounging in a huge carved oak chair, covered with black leather, and did not change his listless attitude, but glanced at Porbus like a man who has settled down into low spirits.

"Well, master," said Porbus, "was the ultramarine bad that you sent for to Bruges? Is the new white difficult to grind? Is the oil poor, or are the brushes recalcitrant?"

"Alas!" cried the old man, "for a moment I thought that my work was finished, but I am sure that I am mistaken in certain details, and I can not rest until I have cleared my doubts. I am thinking of traveling. I am going to Turkey, to Greece, to Asia, in quest of a model, so as to compare my picture with the different living forms of Nature. Perhaps," and a smile of contentment stole over his face, "perhaps I have Nature herself up there. At times I am half afraid that a breath may waken her, and that she will escape me."

He rose to his feet as if to set out at once.

"Aha!" said Porbus, "I have come just in time to save you the trouble and expense of a journey."

"What?" asked Frenhofer in amazement.

"Young Poussin is loved by a woman of incomparable and flawless beauty. But, dear master, if he consents to lend her to you, at the least you ought to let us see your work."

The old man stood motionless and completely dazed.

"What!" he cried piteously at last, "show you my creation, my bride? Rend the veil that has kept my happiness sacred? It would be an infamous profanation. For ten years I have lived with her; she is mine, mine alone; she loves me. Has she not smiled at me, at each stroke of the brush upon the canvas? She has a soul—the soul that I have given her. She would blush if any eyes but mine should rest on her. To exhibit her! Where is the husband, the lover so vile as to bring the woman he loves to dishonor? When you paint a picture for the court, you do not put your whole soul into it; to courtiers you sell lay figures duly colored. My painting is no painting, it is a sentiment, a passion. She was born in my studio, there she must dwell in maiden solitude, and only when clad can she issue thence. Poetry and women only lay the last veil aside for their lovers Have we Rafael's model, Ariosto's Angelica, Dante's Beatrice? Nay, only their form and semblance. But this picture, locked away above in my studio, is an exception in our art. It is not a canvas, it is a woman—a woman with whom I talk. I share her thoughts, her tears, her laughter. Would you have me fling aside these ten years of happiness like a cloak? Would you have me cease at once to be father, lover, and creator? She is not a creature, but a creation.

"Bring your young painter here. I will give him my treasures; I will give him pictures by Correggio and Michelangelo and Titian; I will kiss his footprints in the dust; but make him my rival! Shame on me. Ah! ah! I am a lover first, and then a painter. Yes, with my latest sigh I could find strength to burn my 'Belle Noiseuse'; but—compel her to endure the gaze of a stranger, a young man and a painter!—Ah! no, no! I would kill him on the morrow who should sully her with a glance! Nay, you, my friend, I would kill you with my own hands in a moment if you did not kneel in reverence before her! Now, will you have me submit my idol to the careless eyes and senseless criticisms of fools? Ah! love is a mystery; it can only live hidden in the depths of the heart. You say, even to your friend, 'Behold her whom I love,' and there is an end of love."

The old man seemed to have grown young again; there was light and life in his eyes, and a faint flush of red in his pale face. His hands shook. Porbus was so amazed by the passionate vehemence of Frenhofer's words that he knew not what to reply to this utterance of an emotion as strange as it was profound. Was Frenhofer sane or mad? Had he fallen a victim to some freak of the artist's fancy? or were these ideas of his produced by the strange light-headedness

which comes over us during the long travail of
a work of art. Would it be possible to come to
terms with this singular passion?

Harassed by all these doubts, Porbus spoke—
"Is it not woman for woman?" he said. "Does
not Poussin submit his mistress to your gaze?"

"What is she?" retorted the other. "A mistress
who will be false to him sooner or later. Mine
will be faithful to me forever."

"Well, well," said Porbus, "let us say no more
about it. But you may die before you will find
such a flawless beauty as hers, even in Asia, and
then your picture will be left unfinished.

"Oh! it is finished," said Frenhofer. "Standing before it you would think that it was a living
woman lying on the velvet couch beneath the
shadow of the curtains. Perfumes are burning
on a golden tripod by her side. You would be
tempted to lay your hand upon the tassel of the
cord that holds back the curtains; it would seem
to you that you saw her breast rise and fall as she
breathed; that you beheld the living Catherine
Lescault, the beautiful courtezan whom men
called 'La Belle Noiseuse.' And yet—if I could
but be sure—"

"Then go to Asia," returned Porbus, noticing
a certain indecision in Frenhofer's face. And
with that Porbus made a few steps toward the
door. By that time Gillette and Nicolas Poussin
had reached Frenhofer's house. The girl drew
away her arm from her lover's as she stood on the

threshold, and shrank back as if some presentiment flashed through her mind.

"Oh! what have I come to do here?" she asked of her lover in low vibrating tones, with her eyes fixed on his.

"Gillette, I have left you to decide; I am ready to obey you in everything. You are my conscience and my glory. Go home again; I shall be happier, perhaps, if you do not——"

"Am I my own when you speak to me like that? No, no; I am a child.—Come," she added, seemingly with a violent effort; "if our love dies, if I plant a long regret in my heart, your fame will be the reward of my obedience to your wishes, will it not? Let us go in. I shall still live on as a memory on your palette; that shall be life for me afterward."

The door opened, and the two lovers encountered Porbus, who was surprised by the beauty of Gillette, whose eyes were full of tears. He hurried her, trembling from head to foot, into the presence of the old painter.

"Here!" he cried, "is she not worth all the masterpieces in the world!"

Frenhofer trembled. There stood Gillette in the artless and childlike attitude of some timid and innocent Georgian, carried off by brigands, and confronted with a slave merchant. A shamefaced red flushed her face, her eyes drooped, her hands hung by her side, her strength seemed to have failed her, her tears protested against this outrage. Poussin cursed himself in despair that he should have brought his fair treasure from its hiding-place. The lover overcame the artist, and countless doubts assailed Poussin's heart when he saw youth dawn in the old man's eyes, as, like a painter, he discerned every line of the form hidden beneath the young girl's vesture. Then the lover's savage jealousy awoke.

"Gillette!" he cried, "let us go."

The girl turned joyously at the cry and the tone in which it was uttered, raised her eyes to his, looked at him, and fled to his arms.

"Ah! then you love me," she cried; "you love me!" and she burst into tears.

She had spirit enough to suffer in silence, but she had no strength to hide her joy.

"Oh! leave her with me for one moment," said the old painter, "and you shall compare her with my Catherine . . . yes—I consent."

Frenhofer's words likewise came from him like a lover's cry. His vanity seemed to be engaged for his semblance of womanhood; he anticipated the triumph of the beauty of his own creation over the beauty of the living girl.

"Do not give him time to change his mind!" cried Porbus, striking Poussin on the shoulder. "The flower of love soon fades, but the flower of art is immortal."

"Then am I only a woman now for him?" said Gillette. She was watching Poussin and Porbus closely.

She raised her head proudly; she glanced at Frenhofer, and her eyes flashed; then as she saw how her lover had fallen again to gazing at the portrait which he had taken at first for a Giorgione—

"Ah!" she cried; "let us go up to the studio. He never gave me such a look."

The sound of her voice recalled Poussin from his dreams.

"Old man," he said, "do you see this blade? I will plunge it into your heart at the first cry from this young girl; I will set fire to your house, and no one shall leave it alive. Do you understand?"

Nicolas Poussin scowled; every word was a menace. Gillette took comfort from the young painter's bearing, and yet more from that gesture, and almost forgave him for sacrificing her to his art and his glorious future.

Porbus and Poussin stood at the door of the studio and looked at each other in silence. At first the painter of the Saint Mary of Egypt hazarded some exclamations: "Ah! she has taken off her clothes; he told her to come into the light —he is comparing the two!" but the sight of the deep distress in Poussin's face suddenly silenced him; and though old painters no longer feel these scruples, so petty in the presence of art, he admired them because they were so natural and gracious in the lover. The young man kept his hand on the hilt of his dagger, and his ear was almost glued to the door. The two men standing in the shadow might have been conspirators waiting for the hour when they might strike down a tyrant.

"Come in, come in," cried the old man. He was radiant with delight. "My work is perfect. I can show her now with pride. Never shall painter, brushes, colors, light, and canvas produce a rival for 'Catherine Lescault,' the beautiful courtezan!"

Porbus and Poussin, burning with eager curiosity, hurried into a vast studio. Everything was in disorder and covered with dust, but they saw a few pictures here and there upon the wall. They stopped first of all in admiration before the life-size figure of a woman partially draped.

"Oh! never mind that," said Frenhofer; "that is a rough daub that I made, a study, a pose, it is nothing. These are my failures," he went on, indicating the enchanting compositions upon the walls of the studio.

This scorn for such works of art struck Porbus and Poussin dumb with amazement. They looked round for the picture of which he had spoken, and could not discover it.

"Look here!" said the old man. His hair was disordered, his face aglow with a more than human exaltation, his eyes glittered, he breathed hard like a young lover frenzied by love.

"Aha!" he cried, "you did not expect to see such perfection! You are looking for a picture, and you see a woman before you. There is such depth in that canvas, the atmosphere is so true that you can not distinguish it from the air that surrounds us. Where is art? Art has vanished, it is invisible! It is the form of a living girl that you see before you. Have I not caught the very hues of life, the spirit of the living line that defines the figure? Is there not the effect produced there like that which all natural objects present in the atmosphere about them, or fishes in the water? Do you see how the figure stands out against the background? Does it not seem to you that you pass your hand along the back? But then for seven years I studied and watched how the daylight blends with the objects on which it falls. And the hair, the light pours over it like a flood, does it not? . . . Ah! she breathed, I am sure that she breathed! Her breast—ah, see! Who would not fall on his knees before her? Her pulses throb. She will rise to her feet. Wait!"

"Do you see anything?" Poussin asked of Porbus.

"No . . . do you?"

"I see nothing."

The two painters left the old man to his ecstasy, and tried to ascertain whether the light that fell full upon the canvas had in some way neutralized all the effect for them. They moved to the right and left of the picture; they came in front, bending down and standing upright by turns.

"Yes, yes, it is really canvas," said Frenhofer,

who mistook the nature of this minute investigation.

"Look! the canvas is on a stretcher, here is the easel; indeed, here are my colors, my brushes," and he took up a brush and held it out to them, all unsuspicious of their thought.

"The old *lansquenet* is laughing at us," said Poussin, coming once more toward the supposed picture. "I can see nothing there but confused masses of color and a multitude of fantastical lines that go to make a dead wall of paint."

"We are mistaken, look!" said Porbus.

In a corner of the canvas, as they came nearer, they distinguished a bare foot emerging from the chaos of color, half-tints and vague shadows that made up a dim, formless fog. Its living delicate beauty held them spellbound. This fragment that had escaped an incomprehensible, slow, and gradual destruction seemed to them like the Parian marble torso of some Venus emerging from the ashes of a ruined town.

"There is a woman beneath," exclaimed Porbus, calling Poussin's attention to the coats of paint with which the old artist had overlaid and concealed his work in the quest of perfection.

Both artists turned involuntarily to Frenhofer. They began to have some understanding, vague though it was, of the ecstasy in which he lived.

"He believes it in all good faith," said Porbus.

"Yes, my friend," said the old man, rousing himself from his dreams, "it needs faith, faith in

64

art, and you must live for long with your work to produce such a creation. What toil some of those shadows have cost me. Look! there is a faint shadow there upon the cheek beneath the eyes—if you saw that on a human face, it would seem to you that you could never render it with paint. Do you think that that effect has not cost unheard of toil?

"But not only so, dear Porbus. Look closely at my work, and you will understand more clearly what I was saying as to methods of modeling and outline. Look at the high lights on the bosom, and see how by touch on touch, thickly laid on, I have raised the surface so that it catches the light itself and blends it with the lustrous whiteness of the high lights, and how by an opposite process, by flattening the surface of the paint, and leaving no trace of the passage of the brush, I have succeeded in softening the contours of my figures and enveloping them in half-tints until the very idea of drawing, of the means by which the effect is produced, fades away, and the picture has the roundness and relief of nature. Come closer. You will see the manner of working better; at a little distance it can not be seen. There! Just there, it is, I think, very plainly to be seen," and with the tip of his brush he pointed out a patch of transparent color to the two painters.

Porbus, laying a hand on the old artist's shoulder, turned to Poussin with a "Do you know that in him we see a very great painter?"

"He is even more of a poet than a painter," Poussin answered gravely.

"There," Porbus continued, as he touched the canvas, "lies the utmost limit of our art on earth."

"Beyond that point it loses itself in the skies," said Poussin.

"What joys lie there on this piece of canvas!" exclaimed Porbus.

The old man, deep in his own musings, smiled at the woman he alone beheld, and did not hear.

"But sooner or later he will find out that there is nothing there!" cried Poussin.

"Nothing on my canvas!" said Frenhofer, looking in turn at either painter and at his picture.

"What have you done?" muttered Porbus, turning to Poussin.

The old man clutched the young painter's arm and said, "Do you see nothing? clodpate! Huguenot! varlet! cullion! What brought you here into my studio?—My good Porbus," he went on, as he turned to the painter, "are you also making a fool of me? Answer! I am your friend. Tell me, have I ruined my picture after all?"

Porbus hesitated and said nothing, but there was such intolerable anxiety in the old man's white face that he pointed to the easel.

"Look!" he said.

Frenhofer looked for a moment at his picture, and staggered back.

"Nothing! nothing! After ten years of work . . ." He sat down and wept.

"So I am a dotard, a madman, I have neither talent nor power! I am only a rich man, who works for his own pleasure, and makes no progress. I have done nothing after all!"

He looked through his tears at his picture. Suddenly he rose and stood proudly before the two painters.

"By the body and blood of Christ," he cried with flashing eyes, "you are jealous! You would have me think that my picture is a failure because you want to steal her from me! Ah! I see her, I see her," he cried "she is marvelously beautiful . . ."

At that moment Poussin heard the sound of weeping; Gillette was crouching forgotten in a corner. All at once the painter once more became the lover. "What is it, my angel?" he asked her.

"Kill me!" she sobbed. "I must be a vile thing if I love you still, for I despise you. . . . I admire you, and I hate you! I love you, and I feel that I hate you even now!"

While Gillette's words sounded in Poussin's ears, Frenhofer drew a green serge covering over his "Catherine" with the sober deliberation of a jeweler who locks his drawers when he suspects his visitors to be expert thieves. He gave the two painters a profoundly astute glance that expressed to the full his suspicions, and his contempt for them, saw them out of his studio with impetuous haste and in silence, until from the threshold of his house he bade them "Good-by, my young friends!"

That farewell struck a chill of dread into the two painters. Porbus, in anxiety, went again on the morrow to see Frenhofer, and learned that he had died in the night after burning his canvases.

Paris, *February, 1832.*

MY FRIEND THE MURDERER

BY A. CONAN DOYLE

MY FRIEND THE MURDERER

BY A. CONAN DOYLE

"NUMBER 43 is no better, doctor," said
the head-warder, in a slightly reproach-
ful accent, looking in round the corner
of my door.

"Confound 43!" I responded from behind the
pages of the *Australian Sketcher*.

"And 61 says his tubes are paining him.
Couldn't you do anything for him?"

He is a walking drug-shop," said I. "He has
the whole British pharmacopœa inside him. I
believe his tubes are as sound as yours are."

"Then there's 7 and 108, they are chronic,"
continued the warder, glancing down a blue slip
of paper. "And 28 knocked off work yesterday
—said lifting things gave him a stitch in the side.
I want you to have a look at him, if you don't
mind, doctor. There's 31, too—him that killed
John Adamson in the Corinthian brig—he's been
carrying on awful in the night, shrieking and
yelling, he has, and no stopping him either."

"All right, I'll have a look at him afterward," I
said, tossing my paper carelessly aside, and pour-
ing myself out a cup of coffee. "Nothing else to
report, I suppose, warder?"

The official protruded his head a little further

into the room. "Beg pardon, doctor," he said, in a confidential tone, "but I notice as 82 has a bit of a cold, and it would be a good excuse for you to visit him and have a chat, maybe."

The cup of coffee was arrested half-way to my lips as I stared in amazement at the man's serious face.

"An excuse?" I said. "An excuse? What the deuce are you talking about, McPherson? You see me trudging about all day at my practise, when I'm not looking after the prisoners, and coming back every night as tired as a dog, and you talk about finding an excuse for doing more work."

"You'd like it, doctor," said Warder McPherson, insinuating one of his shoulders into the room. "That man's story's worth listening to if you could get him to tell it, though he's not what you'd call free in his speech. Maybe you don't know who 82 is?"

"No, I don't, and I don't care either," I answered, in the conviction that some local ruffian was about to be foisted upon me as a celebrity.

"He's Maloney," said the warder, "him that turned Queen's evidence after the murders at Bluemansdyke."

"You don't say so?" I ejaculated, laying down my cup in astonishment. I had heard of this ghastly series of murders, and read an account of them in a London magazine long before setting foot in the colony. I remembered that the atrocities committed had thrown the Burke and Hare crimes completely into the shade, and that one of the most villainous of the gang had saved his own skin by betraying his companions. "Are you sure?" I asked.

"Oh, yes, it's him right enough. Just you draw him out a bit, and he'll astonish you. He's a man to know, is Maloney; that's to say, in moderation;" and the head grinned, bobbed, and disappeared, leaving me to finish my breakfast and ruminate over what I had heard.

The surgeonship of an Australian prison is not an enviable position. It may be endurable in Melbourne or Sydney, but the little town of Perth has few attractions to recommend it, and those few had been long exhausted. The climate was detestable, and the society far from congenial. Sheep and cattle were the staple support of the community; and their prices, breeding, and diseases the principal topic of conversation. Now as I, being an outsider, possessed neither the one nor the other, and was utterly callous to the new "dip" and the "rot" and other kindred topics, I found myself in a state of mental isolation, and was ready to hail anything which might relieve the monotony of my existence. Maloney, the murderer, had at least some distinctiveness and individuality in his character, and might act as a tonic to a mind sick of the commonplaces of existence. I determined that I should follow the warder's advice, and take the excuse for making his acquaintance. When, therefore, I went upon my usual matutinal round, I turned the lock of the door which bore the convict's number upon it, and walked into the cell.

The man was lying in a heap upon his rough bed as I entered, but, uncoiling his long limbs, he started up and stared at me with an insolent look of defiance on his face which augured badly for our interview. He had a pale, set face, with sandy hair and a steely-blue eye, with something feline in its expression. His frame was tall and muscular, though there was a curious bend in his shoulders, which almost amounted to a deformity. An ordinary observer meeting him in the street might have put him down as a well-developed man, fairly handsome, and of studious habits— even in the hideous uniform of the rottenest convict establishment he imparted a certain refinement to his carriage which marked him out among the inferior ruffians around him.

"I'm not on the sick-list," he said, gruffly. There was something in the hard, rasping voice which dispelled all softer illusions, and made me realize that I was face to face with the man of the Lena Valley and Bluemansdyke, the bloodiest bushranger that ever stuck up a farm or cut the throats of its occupants.

"I know you're not," I answered. "Warder McPherson told me you had a cold, though, and I thought I'd look in and see you."

"Blast Warder McPherson, and blast you,

too!" yelled the convict, in a paroxysm of rage. "Oh, that's right," he added in a quieter voice; "hurry away; report me to the governor, do! Get me another six months or so—that's your game."

"I'm not going to report you," I said.

"Eight square feet of ground," he went on, disregarding my protest, and evidently working himself into a fury again. "Eight square feet, and I can't have that without being talked to and stared at, and—oh, blast the whole crew of you!" and he raised his two clinched hands above his head and shook them in passionate invective.

"You've got a curious idea of hospitality," I remarked, determined not to lose my temper, and saying almost the first thing that came to my tongue.

To my surprise the words had an extraordinary effect upon him. He seemed completely staggered at my assuming the proposition for which he had been so fiercely contending—namely, that the room in which he stood was his own.

"I beg your pardon," he said; "I didn't mean to be rude. Won't you take a seat?" and he motioned toward a rough trestle, which formed the head-piece of his couch.

I sat down, rather astonished at the sudden change. I don't know that I liked Maloney better under this new aspect. The murderer had, it is true, disappeared for the nonce, but there was something in the smooth tones and obsequious manner which powerfully suggested the witness of the queen, who had stood up and sworn away the lives of his companions in crime.

"How's your chest?" I asked, putting on my professional air.

"Come, drop it, doctor—drop it!" he answered, showing a row of white teeth as he resumed his seat upon the side of the bed. "It wasn't anxiety after my precious health that brought you along here; that story won't wash at all. You came to have a look at Wolf Tone Maloney, forger, murderer, Sydney-slider, ranger, and government peach. That's about my figure, ain't it? There it is, plain and straight; there's nothing mean about me."

He paused as if he expected me to say something; but as I remained silent, he repeated once or twice, "There's nothing mean about me."

"And why shouldn't I?" he suddenly yelled, his eyes gleaming and his whole satanic nature reasserting itself. "We were bound to swing, one and all, and they were none the worse if I saved myself by turning against them. Every man for himself, say I, and the devil take the luckiest. You haven't a plug of tobacco, doctor, have you?"

He tore at the piece of "Barrett's" which I handed him, as ravenously as a wild beast. It seemed to have the effect of soothing his nerves, for he settled himself down in the bed and reassumed his former deprecating manner.

MY FRIEND THE MURDERER

"You wouldn't like it yourself, you know, doctor," he said: "it's enough to make any man a little queer in his temper. I'm in for six months this time for assault, and very sorry I shall be to go out again, I can tell you. My mind's at ease in here; but when I'm outside, what with the government and what with Tattooed Tom, of Hawkesbury, there's no chance of a quiet life."

"Who is he?" I asked.

"He's the brother of John Grimthorpe, the same that was condemned on my evidence; and an infernal scamp he was, too! Spawn of the devil, both of them! This tattooed one is a murderous ruffian, and he swore to have my blood after that trial. It's seven year ago, and he's following me yet; I know he is, though he lies low and keeps dark. He came up to me in Ballarat in '75; you can see on the back of my hand here where the bullet clipped me. He tried again in '76, at Port Philip, but I got the drop on him and wounded him badly. He knifed me in '79, though, in a bar at Adelaide, and that made our account about level. He's loafing round again now, and he'll let daylight into me—unless—unless by some extraordinary chance some one does as much for him." And Maloney gave a very ugly smile.

"I don't complain of *him* so much," he continued. "Looking at it in his way, no doubt it is a sort of family matter that can hardly be neglected. It's the government that fetches me.

When I think of what I've done for this country, and then of what this country has done for me, it makes me fairly wild—clean drives me off my head. There's no gratitude nor common decency left, doctor!"

He brooded over his wrongs for a few minutes, and then proceeded to lay them before me in detail.

"Here's nine men," he said; "they've been murdering and killing for a matter of three years, and maybe a life a week wouldn't more than average the work that they've done. The government catches them and the government tries them, but they can't convict; and why?—because the witnesses have all had their throats cut, and the whole job's been very neatly done. What happens then? Up comes a citizen called Wolf Tone Maloney; he says, 'The country needs me, and here I am.' And with that he gives his evidence, convicts the lot, and enables the beaks to hang them. That's what I did. There's nothing mean about me! And now what does the country do in return? Dogs me, sir, spies on me, watches me night and day, turns against the very man that worked so very hard for it. There's something mean about that, anyway. I didn't expect them to knight me, nor to make me colonial secretary; but, damn it! I did expect that they would let me alone!"

"Well," I remonstrated, "if you choose to break laws and assault people, you can't expect it to be looked over on account of former services."

"I don't refer to my present imprisonment, sir," said Maloney, with dignity. "It's the life I've been leading since that cursed trial that takes the soul out of me. Just you sit there on that trestle, and I'll tell you all about it, and then look me in the face and tell me that I've been treated fair by the police."

I shall endeavor to transcribe the experience of the convict in his own words, as far as I can remember them, preserving his curious perversions of right and wrong. I can answer for the truth of his facts, whatever may be said for his deductions from them. Months afterward, Inspector H. W. Hann, formerly governor of the jail at Dunedin, showed me entries in his ledger which corroborated every statement. Maloney reeled the story off in a dull, monotonous voice, with his head sunk upon his breast and his hands between his knees. The glitter of his serpentlike eyes was the only sign of the emotions which were stirred up by the recollection of the events which he narrated.

You've read of Bluemansdyke (he began, with some pride in his tone). We made it hot while it lasted; but they ran us to earth at last, and a trap called Braxton, with a damned Yankee, took the lot of us. That was in New Zealand, of course, and they took us down to Dunedin, and there they were convicted and hanged. One and all they put up their hands in the dock, and cursed me till your blood would have run cold to hear them—which was scurvy treatment, seeing that we had all been pals together; but they were a blackguard lot, and thought only of themselves. I think it is as well that they were hung.

They took me back to Dunedin Jail, and clapped me into the old cell. The only difference they made was, that I had no work to do and was well fed. I stood this for a week or two, until one day the governor was making his rounds, and I put the matter to him.

"How's this?" I said. "My conditions were a free pardon, and you're keeping me here against the law."

He gave a sort of a smile. "Should you like very much to get out?" he asked.

"So much," said I, "that unless you open that door I'll have an action against you for illegal detention."

He seemed a bit astonished by my resolution.

"You're very anxious to meet your death," he said.

"What d'ye mean?" I asked.

"Come here, and you'll know what I mean," he answered. And he led me down the passage to a window that overlooked the door of the prison. "Look at that!" said he.

I looked out, and there were a dozen or so rough-looking fellows standing outside the street, some of them smoking, some playing cards on the pavement. When they saw me they gave a yell and crowded round the door, shaking their fists and hooting.

"They wait for you, watch and watch about," said the governor. "They're the executive of the vigilance committee. However, since you are determined to go, I can't stop you."

"D'ye call this a civilized land," I cried, "and let a man be murdered in cold blood in open daylight?"

When I said this the governor and the warder and every fool in the place grinned, as if a man's life was a rare good joke.

"You've got the law on your side," says the governor; "so we won't detain you any longer. Show him out, warder."

He'd have done it, too, the black-hearted villain, if I hadn't begged and prayed and offered to pay for my board and lodging, which is more than any prisoner ever did before me. He let me stay on those conditions; and for three months I was caged up there with every larrikin in the township clamoring at the other side of the wall. That was pretty treatment for a man that had served his country!

At last, one morning up came the governor again.

"Well, Maloney," he said, "how long are you going to honor us with your society?"

I could have put a knife into his cursed body,

and would, too, if we had been alone in the bush; but I had to smile, and smooth him and flatter, for I feared that he might have me sent out.

"You're an infernal rascal," he said; those were his very words, to a man that had helped him all he knew how. "I don't want any rough justice here, though; and I think I see my way to getting you out of Dunedin."

"I'll never forget you, governor," said I; and, by God! never will."

"I don't want your thanks nor your gratitude," he answered; "it's not for your sake that I do it, but simply to keep order in the town. There's a steamer starts from the West Quay to Melbourne to-morrow, and we'll get you aboard it. She is advertised at five in the morning, so have yourself in readiness."

I packed up the few things I had, and was smuggled out by a back door, just before daybreak. I hurried down, took my ticket under the name of Isaac Smith, and got safely aboard the Melbourne boat. I remember hearing her screw grinding into the water as the warps were cast loose, and looking back at the lights of Dunedin as I leaned upon the bulwarks, with the pleasant thought that I was leaving them behind me forever. It seemed to me that a new world was before me, and that all my troubles had been cast off. I went down below and had some coffee, and came up again feeling better than I had done since the morning that I woke to find that cursed

Irishman that took me standing over me with a six-shooter.

Day had dawned by that time, and we were steaming along by the coast, well out of sight of Dunedin. I loafed about for a couple of hours, and when the sun got well up some of the other passengers came on deck and joined me. One of them, a little perky sort of fellow, took a good long look at me, and then came over and began talking.

"Mining, I suppose?" says he.

"Yes," I says.

"Made your pile?" he asks.

"Pretty fair," says I.

"I was at it myself," he says; "I worked at the Nelson fields for three months, and spent all I made in buying a salted claim which busted up the second day. I went at it again, though, and struck it rich; but when the gold wagon was going down to the settlements, it was stuck up by those cursed rangers, and not a red cent left."

"That was a bad job," I says.

"Broke me—ruined me clean. Never mind, I've seen them all hanged for it; that makes it easier to bear. There's only one left—the villain that gave the evidence. I'd die happy if I could come across him. There are two things I have to do if I meet him."

"What's that?" says I, carelessly.

"I've got to ask him where the money lies— they never had time to make away with it, and it's *cachéd* somewhere in the mountains—and then I've got to stretch his neck for him, and send his soul down to join the men that he betrayed."

It seemed to me that I knew something about that *caché,* and I felt like laughing; but he was watching me, and it struck me that he had a nasty, vindictive kind of mind.

"I'm going up on the bridge," I said, for he was not a man whose acquaintance I cared much about making.

He wouldn't hear of my leaving him, though. "We're both miners," he says, "and we're pals for the voyage. Come down to the bar. I'm not too poor to shout."

I couldn't refuse him well, and we went down together; and that was the beginning of the trouble. What harm was I doing any one on the ship? All I asked for was a quiet life, leaving others alone and getting left alone myself. No man could ask fairer than that. And now just you listen to what came of it.

We were passing the front of the ladies' cabin, on our way to the saloon, when out comes a servant lass—a freckled currency she-devil—with a baby in her arms. We were brushing past her, when she gave a scream like a railway whistle, and nearly dropped the kid. My nerves gave a sort of a jump when I heard that scream, but I turned and begged her pardon, letting on that I thought I might have trod on her foot. I knew the game was up, though, when I saw her white face, and her leaning against the door and pointing.

"It's him!" she cried; "it's him! I saw him in the court-house. Oh, don't let him hurt the baby!"

"Who is it?" asked the steward and half a dozen others in a breath.

"It's him—Maloney—Maloney, the murderer —oh, take him away—take him away!"

I don't rightly remember what happened just at that moment. The furniture and me seemed to get kind of mixed, and there was cursing, and smashing, and some one shouting for his gold, and a general stamping round. When I got steadied a bit, I found somebody's hand in my mouth. From what I gathered afterward, I concluded that it belonged to that same little man with the vicious way of talking. He got some of it out again, but that was because the others were choking me. A poor chap can get no fair play in this world when once he is down—still, I think he will remember me till the day of his death— longer, I hope.

They dragged me out on to the poop and held a damned court-martial—on *me,* mind you; *me,* that had thrown over my pals in order to serve them. What were they to do with me? Some said this, some said that; but it ended by the captain deciding to send me ashore. The ship stopped, they lowered a boat, and I was hoisted in, the whole gang of them hooting at me from

over the bulwarks. I saw the man I spoke of
tying up his hand, though, and I felt that things
might be worse.

I changed my opinion before we got to the
land. I had reckoned on the shore being deserted, and that I might make my way inland;
but the ship had stopped too near the Heads, and
a dozen beach-combers and such like had come
down to the water's edge and were staring at us,
wondering what the boat was after. When we
got to the edge of the surf the cockswain hailed
them, and after singing out who I was, he and his
men threw me into the water. You may well
look surprised—neck and crop into ten feet of
water, with sharks as thick as green parrots in the
bush, and I heard them laughing as I floundered
to the shore.

I soon saw it was a worse job than ever. As I
came scrambling out through the weeds, I was
collared by a big chap with a velveteen coat, and
half a dozen others got round me and held me
fast. Most of them looked simple fellows
enough, and I was not afraid of them; but there
was one in a cabbage-tree hat that had a very
nasty expression on his face, and the big man
seemed to be chummy with him.

They dragged me up the beach, and then they
let go their hold of me and stood round in a circle.

"Well, mate," says the man with the hat,
"we've been looking out for you some time in
these parts."

"And very good of you, too," I answers.

"None of your jaw," says he. "Come, boys, what shall it be—hanging, drowning, or shooting? Look sharp!"

This looked a bit too like business. "No, you don't!" I said. "I've got government protection, and it'll be murder."

"That's what they call it," answered the one in the velveteen coat, as cheery as a piping crow.

"And you're going to murder me for being a ranger?"

"Ranger be damned!" said the man. "We're going to hang you for peaching against your pals; and that's an end of the palaver."

They slung a rope round my neck and dragged me up to the edge of the bush. There were some big she-oaks and blue-gums, and they pitched on one of these for the wicked deed. They ran the rope over a branch, tied my hands, and told me to say my prayers. It seemed as if it was all up; but Providence interfered to save me. It sounds nice enough sitting here and telling about it, sir; but it was sick work to stand with nothing but the beach in front of you, and the long white line of surf, with the steamer in the distance, and a set of bloody-minded villains round you thirsting for your life.

I never thought I'd owe anything good to the police; but they saved me that time. A troop of them were riding from Hawkes Point Station to Dunedin, and hearing that something was up, they came down through the bush and interrupted the proceedings. I've heard some bands in my time, doctor, but I never heard music like the jingle of those traps' spurs and harness as they galloped out on to the open. They tried to hang me even then, but the police were too quick for them; and the man with the hat got one over the head with the flat of a sword. I was clapped on to a horse, and before evening I found myself in my old quarters in the city jail.

The governor wasn't to be done, though. He was determined to get rid of me, and I was equally anxious to see the last of him. He waited a week or so until the excitement had begun to die away, and then he smuggled me aboard a three-masted schooner bound to Sydney with tallow and hides.

We got far away to sea without a hitch, and things began to look a bit more rosy. I made sure that I had seen the last of the prison, anyway. The crew had a sort of an idea who I was, and if there'd been any rough weather, they'd have hove me overboard, like enough; for they were a rough, ignorant lot, and had a notion that I brought bad luck to the ship. We had a good passage, however, and I was landed safe and sound upon Sydney Quay.

Now just you listen to what happened next. You'd have thought they would have been sick of ill-using me and following me by this time— wouldn't you, now? Well, just you listen. It seems that a cursed steamer started from Dunedin to Sydney on the very day we left, and got in before us, bringing news that I was coming. Blessed if they hadn't called a meeting—a regular mass-meeting—at the docks to discuss about it, and I marched right into it when I landed. They didn't take long about arresting me, and I listened to all the speeches and resolutions. If I'd been a prince there couldn't have been more excitement. The end of all was that they agreed that it wasn't right that New Zealand should be allowed to foist her criminals upon her neighbors, and that I was to be sent back again by the next boat. So they posted me off again as if I was a damned parcel; and after another eight-hundred-mile journey I found myself back for the third time moving in the place that I started from.

By this time I had begun to think that I was going to spend the rest of my existence traveling about from one port to another. Every man's hand seemed turned against me, and there was no peace or quiet in any direction. I was about sick of it by the time I had come back; and if I could have taken to the bush I'd have done it, and chanced it with my old pals. They were too quick for me, though, and kept me under lock and key; but I managed, in spite of them, to negotiate that *caché* I told you of, and sewed the gold up in my belt. I spent another month in jail, and then they slipped me aboard a bark that was bound for England.

This time the crew never knew who I was, but the captain had a pretty good idea, though he didn't let on to me that he had any suspicions. I guessed from the first that the man was a villain. We had a fair passage, except a gale or two off the Cape; and I began to feel like a free man when I saw the blue loom of the old country, and the saucy little pilot-boat from Falmouth dancing toward us over the waves. We ran down the Channel, and before we reached Gravesend I had agreed with the pilot that he should take me ashore with him when he left. It was at this time that the captain showed me that I was right in thinking him a meddling, disagreeable man. I got my things packed, such as they were, and left him talking earnestly to the pilot, while I went below for my breakfast. When I came up again we were fairly into the mouth of the river, and the boat in which I was to have gone ashore had left us. The skipper said the pilot had forgotten me; but that was too thin, and I began to fear that all my old troubles were going to commence once more.

It was not long before my suspicions were confirmed. A boat darted out from the side of the river, and a tall cove with a long black beard came aboard. I heard him ask the mate whether they didn't need a mud-pilot to take them up in the reaches, but it seemed to me that he was a man who would know a deal more about handcuffs than he did about steering, so I kept away from him. He came across the deck, however, and made some remark to me, taking a good look at me the while. I don't like inquisitive people at any time, but an inquisitive stranger with glue about the roots of his beard is the worst of all to stand, especially under the circumstances. I began to feel that it was time for me to go.

I soon got a chance, and made good use of it. A big collier came athwart the bows of our steamer, and we had to slacken down to dead slow. There was a barge astern, and I slipped down by a rope and was into the barge before any one missed me. Of course I had to leave my luggage behind me, but I had the belt with the nuggets round my waist, and the chance of shaking the police off my track was worth more than a couple of boxes. It was clear to me now that the pilot had been a traitor, as well as the captain, and had set the detectives after me. I often wish I could drop across those two men again.

I hung about the barge all day as she drifted down the stream. There was one man in her, but she was a big, ugly craft, and his hands were too full for much looking about. Toward evening, when it got a bit dusky, I struck out for the shore, and found myself in a sort of marsh place, a good many miles to the east of London. I was soaking wet and half dead with hunger, but I trudged into the town, got a new rig-out at a slop-shop, and after having some supper, engaged a bed at the quietest lodgings I could find.

I woke pretty early—a habit you pick up in the bush—and lucky for me that I did so. The very first thing I saw when I took a look through a chink in the shutter was one of these infernal policemen standing right opposite and staring up at the windows. He hadn't epaulets nor a sword, like our traps, but for all that there was a sort of family likeness, and the same busybody expression. Whether they followed me all the time, or whether the woman that let me the bed didn't like the looks of me, is more than I have ever been able to find out. He came across as I was watching him, and noted down the address of the house in a book. I was afraid that he was going to ring at the bell, but I suppose his orders were simply to keep an eye on me, for after another good look at the windows he moved on down the street.

I saw that my only chance was to act at once. I threw on my clothes, opened the window softly, and, after making sure that there was nobody about, dropped out onto the ground and made off as hard as I could run. I traveled a matter of two or three miles, when my wind gave out; and as I saw a big building with people going in and out, I went in too, and found that it was a railway station. A train was just going off for Dover to meet the French boat, so I took a ticket and jumped into a third-class carriage.

There were a couple of other chaps in the carriage, innocent-looking young beggars, both of them. They began speaking about this and that, while I sat quiet in the corner and listened. Then they started on England and foreign countries, and such like. Look ye now, doctor, this is a fact. One of them begins jawing about the justice of England's laws. "It's all fair and above-board," says he; "there ain't any secret police, nor spying, like they have abroad," and a lot more of the same sort of wash. Rather rough on me, wasn't it, listening to the damned young fool, with the police following me about like my shadow?

I got to Paris right enough, and there I changed some of my gold, and for a few days I imagined I'd shaken them off, and began to think of settling down for a bit of rest. I needed it by that time, for I was looking more like a ghost than a man. You've never had the police after you, I suppose? Well, you needn't look offended, I didn't mean any harm. If ever you had you'd know that it wastes a man away like a sheep with the rot.

I went to the opera one night and took a box, for I was very flush. I was coming out between the acts when I met a fellow lounging along in the passage. The light fell on his face, and I saw that it was the mud-pilot that had boarded us in the Thames. His beard was gone, but I recognized the man at a glance, for I've a good memory for faces.

I tell you, doctor, I felt desperate for a moment. I could have knifed him if we had been alone, but he knew me well enough never to give me the chance. It was more than I could stand any longer, so I went right up to him and drew him aside, where we'd be free from all the loungers and theater-goers.

"How long are you going to keep it up?" I asked him.

He seemed a bit flustered for a moment, but then he saw there was no use beating about the bush, so he answered straight:

"Until you go back to Australia," he said.

"Don't you know," I said, "that I have served the government and got a free pardon?"

He grinned all over his ugly face when I said this.

"We know all about you, Maloney," he answered. "If you want a quiet life, just you go back where you came from. If you stay here, you're a marked man; and when you are found tripping it'll be a lifer for you, at the least. Free trade's a fine thing but the market's too full of men like you for us to need to import any."

It seemed to me that there was something in what he said, though he had a nasty way of putting it. For some days back I'd been feeling a sort of homesick. The ways of the people weren't my ways. They stared at me in the street; and if I dropped into a bar, they'd stop talking and edge away a bit, as if I was a wild beast. I'd sooner have had a pint of old Stringybark, too, than a bucketful of their rot-gut liquors. There was too much damned propriety. What was the use of having money if you couldn't dress as you liked, nor bust in properly? There was no sympathy for a man if he shot about a little when he was half-over. I've seen a man dropped at Nelson many a time with less row than they'd make over a broken window-pane. The thing was slow, and I was sick of it.

"You want me to go back?" I said.

"I've my order to stick fast to you until you do," he answered.

"Well," I said, "I don't care if I do. All I bargain is that you keep your mouth shut and don't let on who I am, so that I may have a fair start when I get there."

He agreed to this, and we went over to Southampton the very next day, where he saw me safely off once more. I took a passage round to Adelaide, where no one was likely to know me; and there I settled, right under the nose of the police. I'd been there ever since, leading a quiet life, but for little difficulties like the one I'm in for now, and for that devil, Tattooed Tom, of Hawkesbury. I don't know what made me tell you all this, doctor, unless it is that being lonely makes a man inclined to jaw when he gets a chance. Just you take warning from me, though. Never put yourself out to serve your country; for your country will do precious little for you. Just you let them look after their own affairs; and if they find difficulty in hanging a set of scoundrels, never mind chipping in, but let them alone to do as best they can. Maybe they'll remember how they treated me after I'm dead, and be sorry for neglecting me. I was rude to you when you came in, and swore a trifle promiscuous: but don't you mind me, it's only my way. You'll allow, though, that I have cause to be a bit touchy now and again when I think of all that's passed. You're not going, are you? Well, if you must, you must; but I hope you will look me up at odd times when you are going your rounds. Oh, I say, you've left the balance of that cake of tobacco behind you, haven't you? No; it's in your pocket—that's all right. Thank ye, doctor, you're a good sort, and as quick at a hint as any man I've met.

A couple of months after narrating his experiences, Wolf Tone Maloney finished his term, and was released. For a long time I neither saw him nor heard of him, and he had almost slipped from my memory, until I was reminded, in a somewhat tragic manner, of his existence. I had been attending a patient some distance off in the country, and was riding back, guiding my tired horse among the boulders which strewed the pathway, and endeavoring to see my way through the gathering darkness, when I came suddenly upon a little wayside inn. As I walked my horse up toward the door, intending to make sure of my bearings before proceeding further, I heard the sound of a violent altercation within the little bar.

There seemed to be a chorus of expostulation or remonstrance, above which two powerful voices rang out loud and angry. As I listened, there was a momentary hush, two pistol shots sounded almost simultaneously, and with a crash the door burst open and a pair of dark figures staggered out into the moonlight. They struggled for a moment in a deadly wrestle, and then went down together among the loose stones. I had sprung off my horse, and, with the help of half a dozen rough fellows from the bar, dragged them away from one another.

A glance was sufficient to convince me that one of them was dying fast. He was a thick-set burly fellow, with a determined cast of countenance. The blood was welling from a deep stab in his throat, and it was evident that an important artery had been divided. I turned away from him in despair, and walked over to where his antagonist was lying. He was shot through the lungs, but managed to raise himself up on his hand as I approached, and peered anxiously up into my face. To my surprise, I saw before me the haggard features and flaxen hair of my prison acquaintance, Maloney.

"Ah, doctor!" he said, recognizing me. "How is he? Will he die?"

He asked the question so earnestly that I imagined he had softened at the last moment, and feared to leave the world with another homicide upon his conscience. Truth, however, compelled me to shake my head mournfully, and to intimate that the wound would prove a mortal one.

Maloney gave a wild cry of triumph, which brought the blood welling out from between his lips. "Here, boys," he gasped to the little group around him. "There's money in my inside pocket. Damn the expense! Drinks round. There's nothing mean about me. I'd drink with you, but I'm going. Give the doc my share, for he's as good—" Here his head fell back with a thud, his eye glazed, and the soul of Wolf Tone Maloney, forger, convict, ranger, murderer, and government peach, drifted away into the Great Unknown.

I cannot conclude without borrowing the account of the fatal quarrel which appeared in the column of the *West Australian Sentinel*. The curious will find it in the issue of October 4, 1881:

"FATAL AFFRAY.—W. T. Maloney, a well-know citizen of New Montrose, and proprietor of the Yellow Boy gambling saloon, has met with his death under rather painful circumstances. Mr. Maloney was a man who had led a checkered existence, and whose past history is replete with interest. Some of our readers may recall the Lena Valley murders, in which he figured as the principal criminal. It is conjectured that during the seven months that he owned a bar in that region, from twenty to thirty travelers were hocussed and made away with. He succeeded, however, in evading the vigilance of the officers of the law, and allied himself with the bush-rangers of Bluemansdyke, whose heroic capture and subsequent execution are matters of history. Maloney extricated himself from the fate which awaited him by turning Queen's evidence. He afterward visited Europe, but returned to West Australia, where he has long played a prominent part in local matters. On Friday evening he encountered an old enemy, Thomas Grimthorpe, commonly known as Tattooed Tom, of Hawkesbury. Shots were exchanged, and both were badly wounded, only surviving a few minutes. Mr. Maloney had the reputation of being not only the most wholesale murderer that ever lived, but also of having a finish and attention to detail in matters of evidence which has been unapproached by any European criminal. *Sic transit gloria mundi!"*

THE DEAD ARE SILENT

BY ARTHUR SCHNITZLER

THE DEAD ARE SILENT

BY ARTHUR SCHNITZLER

HE could endure the quiet waiting in the carriage no longer; it was easier to get out and walk up and down. It was now dark; the few scattered lamps in the narrow side street quivered uneasily in the wind. The rain had stopped, the sidewalks were almost dry, but the rough-paved roadway was still moist, and little pools gleamed here and there.

"Strange, isn't it?" thought Franz. "Here we are scarcely a hundred paces from the Prater, and yet it might be a street in some little country town. Well, it's safe enough, at any rate. She won't meet any of the friends she dreads so much here."

He looked at his watch. "Only just seven, and so dark already! It is an early autumn this year . . . and then this confounded storm! . . ." He turned his coat-collar up about his neck and quickened his pacing. The glass in the street lamps rattled lightly.

"Half an hour more," he said to himself, "then I can go home. I could almost wish—that that half-hour were over." He stood for a moment on the corner, where he could command a view of both streets. "She'll surely come to-day," his thoughts ran on, while he struggled with his hat, which threatened to blow away. "It's Friday. . . . Faculty meeting at the University; she needn't hurry home." He heard the clanging of street-car gongs, and the hour chimed from a nearby church tower. The street became more animated. Hurrying figures passed him, clerks of neighboring shops; they hastened onward, fighting against the storm. No one noticed him; a couple of half-grown girls glanced up in idle curiosity as they went by. Suddenly he saw a familiar figure coming toward him. He hastened to meet her. . . . Could it be she? On foot?

She saw him, and quickened her pace.

"You are walking?" he asked.

"I dismissed the cab in front of the theatre. I think I've had that driver before."

A man passed them, turning to look at the lady. Her companion glared at him, and the other passed on hurriedly. The lady looked after him. "Who was it?" she asked, anxiously.

"Don't know him. We'll see no one we know here, don't worry. But come now, let's get into the cab."

"Is that your carriage?"

"Yes."

"An open one?"

"It was warm and pleasant when I engaged it an hour ago."

They walked to the carriage; the lady stepped in.

"Driver!" called the man.

"Why, where is he?" asked the lady.

Franz looked around. "Well, did you ever? I don't see him anywhere."

"Oh—" her tone was low and timid.

"Wait a moment, child, he must be around here somewhere."

The young man opened the door of a little saloon, and discovered his driver at a table with several others. The man rose hastily. "In a minute, sir," he explained, swallowing his glass of wine.

"What do you mean by this?"

"All right, sir. . . . Be there in a minute." His step was a little unsteady as he hastened to his horses. "Where'll you go, sir?"

"Prater—Summer-house."

Franz entered the carriage. His companion sat back in a corner, crouching fearsomely under the shadow of the cover.

He took both her hands in his. She sat silent. "Won't you say good evening to me?"

"Give me a moment to rest, dear. I'm still out of breath."

He leaned back in his corner. Neither spoke for some minutes. The carriage turned into the Prater Street, passed the Tegethoff Monument, and a few minutes later was rolling swiftly through the broad, dark Prater Avenue.

Emma turned suddenly and flung both arms around her lover's neck. He lifted the veil that still hung about her face, and kissed her.

"I have you again—at last!" she exclaimed.

"Do you know how long it is since we have seen each other?" he asked.

"Since Sunday."

"Yes, and that wasn't good for much."

"Why not? You were in our house."

"Yes—in your house. That's just it. This can't go on. I shall not enter your house again. . . . What's the matter?"

"A carriage passed us."

"Dear girl, the people who are driving in the Prater at such an hour, and in such weather, aren't noticing much what other people are doing."

"Yes—that's so. But some one might look in here, by chance."

"We couldn't be recognized. It's too dark."

"Yes—but can't we drive somewhere else?"

"Just as you like." He called to the driver, who did not seem to hear. Franz leaned forward and touched the man.

"Turn around again. What are you whipping your horses like that for? We're in no hurry, I tell you. Drive—let me see—yes—drive down the avenue that leads to the Reichs Bridge."

"The Reichsstrasse?"

"Yes. But don't hurry so, there's no need of it."

"All right, sir. But it's the wind that makes the horses so crazy."

Franz sat back again as the carriage turned in the other direction.

"Why didn't I see you yesterday?"

"How could I?" . . .

"You were invited to my sister's."

"Oh—yes."

"Why weren't you there?"

"Because I can't be with you—like that—with others around. No, I just can't." She shivered. "Where are we now?" she asked, after a moment.

They were passing under the railroad bridge at the entrance to the Reichsstrasse.

"On the way to the Danube," replied Franz. "We're driving toward the Reichs Bridge. We'll certainly not meet any of our friends here," he added, with a touch of mockery.

"The carriage jolts dreadfully."

"We're on cobblestones again."

"But he drives so crooked."

"Oh, you only think so."

He had begun to notice himself that the vehicle was swaying to and fro more than was necessary, even on the rough pavement. But he said nothing, not wishing to alarm her.

"There's a great deal I want to say to you today, Emma."

"You had better begin then; I must be home at nine o'clock."

"A few words may decide everything."

"Oh, goodness, what was that!" she screamed. The wheels had caught in a car-track, and the carriage turned partly over as the driver attempted to free it. Franz caught at the man's coat. "Stop that!" he cried. "Why, you're drunk, man!"

The driver halted his horses with some difficulty. "Oh, no—sir—"

"Let's get out here, Emma, and walk."

"Where are we?"

"Here's the bridge already. And the wind is not nearly as strong as it was. It will be nicer to walk a little. It's so hard to talk in the carriage."

Emma drew down her veil and followed him. "Don't you call this windy?" she exclaimed as she struggled against the gust that met her at the corner.

He took her arm, and called to the driver to follow them.

They walked on slowly. Neither spoke as they mounted the ascent of the bridge; and they halted where they could hear the flow of the water below them. Heavy darkness surrounded them. The broad stream stretched itself out in gray, indefinite outlines; red lights in the distance, floating above the water, awoke answering gleams from its surface. Trembling stripes of light reached down from the shore they had just left; on the other side of the bridge the river lost itself in the blackness of open fields. Thunder rumbled in the distance; they looked over to where the red lights soared. A train with lighted windows rolled between iron arches that seemed to spring up out of the night for an instant, to sink back into darkness again. The thunder grew fainter and more distant; silence fell again; only the wind moved, in sudden gusts.

Franz spoke at last, after a long silence. "We must go away."

"Of course," Emma answered, softly.

"We must go away," he continued, with more animation. "Go away altogether, I mean—"

"Oh, we can't!"

"Only because we are cowards, Emma."

"And my child?"

"He will let you have the boy, I know."

"But how shall we go?" Her voice was very low. "You mean—to run away—"

"Not at all. You have only to be honest with him; to tell him that you cannot live with him any longer; that you belong to me."

"Franz—are you mad?"

"I will spare you that trial, if you wish. I will tell him myself."

"No, Franz, you will do nothing of the kind."

He endeavored to read her face. But the darkness showed him only that her head was turned toward him.

He was silent a few moments more. Then he spoke quietly: "You need not fear; I shall not do it."

They walked toward the farther shore. "Don't you hear a noise?" she asked. "What is it?"

"Something is coming from the other side," he said.

A slow rumbling came out of the darkness. A little red light gleamed out at them. They could see that it hung from the axle of a clumsy country cart, but they could not see whether the cart was laden or not, and whether there were human beings on it. Two other carts followed the first. They could just see the outlines of a man in peasant garb on the last cart, and could see that he was lighting his pipe. The carts passed them slowly. Soon there was nothing to be heard but the low rolling of the wheels as their own carriage followed them. The bridge dropped gently to the farther shore. They saw the street disappear into blackness between rows of trees. Open fields lay before them to the right and to the left; they gazed out into gloom indistinguishable.

There was another long silence before Franz spoke again. "Then it is the last time—"

"What?—" Emma's tone was anxious.

"The last time we are to be together. Stay with him, if you will. I bid you farewell."

"Are you serious?"

"Absolutely."

"There, now you see, it is you who always spoil the few hours we have together?—not I."

"Yes, you're right," said Franz. "Let's drive back to town."

She held his arm closer. "No," she insisted, tenderly, "I don't want to go back. I won't be sent away from you."

She drew his head down to hers, and kissed him tenderly. "Where would we get to if we drove on down there?" she asked.

"That's the road to Prague, dear."

"We won't go quite that far," she smiled, "but I'd like to drive on a little, down there." She pointed into the darkness.

Franz called to the driver. There was no answer; the carriage rumbled on, slowly. Franz ran after it, and saw that the driver was fast asleep. Franz roused him roughly. "We want to drive on down that street. Do you hear me?"

"All right, sir."

Emma entered the carriage first, then Franz. The driver whipped his horses, and they galloped madly over the moist earth of the road-bed. The couple inside the cab held each other closely as they swayed with the motion of the vehicle.

"Isn't this quite nice?" whispered Emma, her lips on his.

In the moment of her words she seemed to feel the cab mounting into the air. She felt herself thrown over violently, reached for some hold, but grasped only the empty air. She seemed to be spinning madly like a top, her eyes closed, suddenly she found herself lying on the ground, a great silence about her, as if she were alone, far away from all the world. Then noises began to come into her consciousness again; hoofs beat the ground near her; a low moaning came from somewhere; but she could see nothing. Terror seized her; she screamed aloud. Her terror grew stronger, for she could not hear her own voice. Suddenly she knew what had happened; the carriage had hit some object, possibly a mile-stone; had upset, and she had been thrown out. Where is Franz? was her next thought. She called his name. And now she could hear her voice, not distinctly yet, but she could hear it. There was no answer to her call. She tried to get up. After some effort she rose to a sitting posture, and, reaching out, she felt something, a human body, on the ground beside her. She could now begin to see a little through the dimness. Franz lay beside her, motionless. She put out her hand and touched his face; something warm and wet covered it. Her heart seemed to stop beating—Blood?— Oh, what had happened? Franz was wounded and unconscious. Where was the coachman? She called him, but no answer came. She still sat there on the ground. She did not seem to be injured, although she ached all over. "What shall I do?" she thought; "what shall I do? How can it be that I am not injured? Franz!" she called again. A voice answered from somewhere near her.

"Where are you, lady? And where is the gentleman? Wait a minute, Miss—I'll light the lamps, so we can see. I don't know what's got into the beasts to-day. It ain't my fault, Miss, sure—they ran into a pile of stones."

Emma managed to stand up, although she was bruised all over. The fact that the coachman seemed quite uninjured reassured her somewhat. She heard the man opening the lamp and striking a match. She waited anxiously for the light. She did not dare to touch Franz again. "It's all so much worse when you can't see plainly," she thought. "His eyes may be open now—there won't be anything wrong. . . ."

A tiny ray of light came from one side. She saw the carriage, not completely upset, as she had thought, but leaning over toward the ground, as if one wheel were broken. The horses stood quietly. She saw the milestone, then a heap of loose stones, and beyond them a ditch. Then the light touched Franz's feet, crept up over his body to his face, and rested there. The coachman had set the lamp on the ground beside the head of the unconscious man. Emma dropped to her knees, and her heart seemed to stop beating as she looked into the face before her. It was ghastly white; the eyes were half open, only the white showing. A thin stream of blood trickled down from one temple and ran into his collar. The teeth were fastened into the under lip. "No—no—it isn't possible," Emma spoke, as if to herself.

The driver knelt also and examined the face of the man. Then he took the head in both his hands and raised it. "What are you doing?"

screamed Emma, hoarsely, shrinking back at the sight of the head that seemed to be rising of its own volition.

"Please, Miss—I'm afraid—I'm thinking— there's a great misfortune happened—"

"No—no—it's not true!" said Emma. "It can't be true!— You are not hurt? Nor am I—"

The man let the head he held fall back again into the lap of the trembling Emma. "If only some one would come—if the peasants had only passed fifteen minutes later."

"What shall we do?" asked Emma, her lips trembling.

"Why, you see, Miss, if the carriage was all right—but it's no good as it is—we've got to wait till some one comes—" he talked on, but Emma did not hear him. Her brain seemed to awake suddenly, and she knew what was to be done. "How far is it to the nearest house?" she asked.

"Not much further, Miss—there's Franz-Josefsland right there. We'd see the houses if it was lighter—it won't take five minutes to get there."

"Go there, then; I'll stay here— Go and fetch some one."

"I think I'd better stay here with you, Miss. Somebody must come; it's the main road."

"It'll be too late; we need a doctor at once."

The coachman looked down at the quiet face, then he looked at Emma, and shook his head.

"You can't tell," she cried.

"Yes, Miss—but there'll be no doctor in those houses."

"But there'll be somebody to send to the city—"

"Oh, yes, Miss—they'll be having a telephone there, anyway! We'll telephone to the Rescue Society."

"Yes, yes, that's it. Go at once, run—and bring some men back with you. Why do you wait? Go at once. Hurry!"

The man looked down again at the white face in her lap. "There'll be no use here for doctor or Rescue Society, Miss."

"Oh, go!—for God's sake go!"

"I'm going, Miss—but don't get afraid in the darkness here."

He hurried down the street. " 'Twasn't my fault," he murmured as he ran. "Such an idea! to drive down this road this time o' night."

Emma was left alone with the unconscious man in the gloomy street.

"What shall I do now?" she thought. "It can't be possible—it can't." The thought circled dizzily in her brain—"It can't be possible." Suddenly she seemed to hear a low breathing. She bent to the pale lips—no—not the faintest breath came from them. The blood had dried on temple and cheek. She gazed at the eyes, the half-closed eyes, and shuddered. Why couldn't she believe it? . . . It must be true—this was Death! A shiver ran through her—she felt but one thing— "This is a corpse. I am here alone with a corpse!

—a corpse that rests on my lap!" With trembling
hands she pushed the head away, until it rested
on the ground. Then a feeling of horrible alone-
ness came over her. Why had she sent the coachman away? What should she do here all alone
with this dead man in the darkness? If only some
one would come—but what was she to do then if
anybody did come? How long would she have to
wait here? She looked down at the corpse again.
"But I'm not alone with him," she thought, "the
light is there." And the light seemed to her to
become alive, something sweet and friendly, to
which she owed gratitude. There was more life
in this little flame than in all the wide night about
her. It seemed almost as if this light was a protection for her, a protection against the terrible
pale man who lay on the ground beside her. She
stared into the light until her eyes wavered and
the flame began to dance. Suddenly she felt herself awake—wide awake. She sprang to her feet.
Oh, this would not do! It would not do at all—
no one must find her here with him. She seemed
to be outside of herself, looking at herself standing there on the road, the corpse and the light
below her; she saw herself grow into strange,
enormous proportions, high up into the darkness.
"What am I waiting for?" she asked herself, and
her brain reeled. "What am I waiting for? The
people who might come? They don't need me.
They will come, and they will ask questions—and
I—why am I here? They will ask who I am—

what shall I answer? I will not answer them—I
will not say a word—they cannot compel me to
talk."

The sound of voices came from the distance.

"Already?" she thought, listening in terror.
The voices came from the bridge. It could not
be the men the driver was bringing with him.
But whoever it was would see the light—and they
must not see it, for then she would be discovered.
She overturned the lantern with her foot, and the
light went out. She stood in utter darkness. She
could see nothing—not even him. The pile of
stones shone dimly. The voices came nearer. She
trembled from head to foot; they must not find
her here. That was the only thing of real importance in all the wide world—that no one should
find her here. She would be lost if they knew that
this—this corpse—was her lover. She clasps her
hands convulsively, praying that the people, whoever they were, might pass by on the farther side
of the road, and not see her. She listens breath-
less. Yes, they are there, on the other side—
women, two women, or perhaps three. What are
they talking about? They have seen the carriage,
they speak of it—she can distinguish words. "A
carriage upset—" What else do they say? She
cannot understand—they walk on—they have
passed her— Ah—thanks—thanks to Heaven!—
And now? What now? Oh, why isn't she dead,
as he is? He is to be envied; there is no more
danger, no more fear for him. But so much—so

much for her to tremble for. She shivers at the thought of being found here, of being asked, "Who are you?" She will have to go to the police station, and all the world will know about it—her husband—her child. She cannot understand why she has stood there motionless so long. She need not stay here—she can do no good here—and she is only courting disaster for herself. She makes a step forward— Careful! the ditch is here—she crosses it—how wet it is—two paces more and she is in the middle of the street. She halts a moment, looks straight ahead, and can finally distinguish the gray line of the road leading onward into darkness. There—over there—lies the city. She cannot see it, but she knows the way. She turns once more. It does not seem so dark now. She can see the carriage and the horses quite distinctly—and, looking hard, she seems to see the outline of a human body on the ground. Her eyes open wide. Something seems to clutch at her and hold her here—it is he—she feels his power to keep her with him. With an effort she frees herself. Then she perceives that it was the soft mud of the road that held her. And she walks onward—faster—faster—her pace quickens to a run. Only to be away from here, to be back in the light—in the noise—among men. She runs along the street, raising her skirt high, that her steps may not be hindered. The wind is behind her, and seems to push her along. She does not know what it is she flees from. Is it the pale

man back there by the ditch? No, now she knows,
she flees the living, not the dead, the living, who
will soon be there, and who will look for her.
What will they think? Will they follow her?
But they cannot catch up with her now, she is so
far away, she is nearing the bridge, there is
danger. No one can know who she was, no one
can possibly imagine who the woman was who
drove down through the country road with the
dead man. The driver does not know her; he
would not recognize her if he should ever see her
again. They will not take the trouble to find out
who she is. Who cares? It was wise of her not to
stay—and it was not cowardly either. Franz
himself would say it was wise. She must go home;
she has a husband, a child; she would be lost if
any one should see her there with her dead lover.
There is the bridge; the street seems lighter—she
hears the water beneath her. She stands there,
where they stood together, arm in arm—when
was it? How many hours ago? It cannot be long
since then. And yet—perhaps she lay unconscious long, and it is midnight now, or near morning, and they have missed her at home. Oh, no—it
is not possible. She knows that she was not unconscious, she remembers everything clearly. She
runs across the bridge, shivering at the sound of
her own steps. Now she sees a figure coming
toward her; she slows her pace. It is a man in
uniform. She walks more slowly, she does not
want to attract attention. She feels the man's

eyes resting on her—suppose he stops her! Now he is quite near; it is a policeman. She walks calmly past him, and hears him stop behind her. With an effort she continues in the same slow pace. She hears the jingle of street-car bells— ah, it cannot be midnight yet. She walks more quickly—hurrying toward the city, the lights of which begin there by the railroad viaduct—the growing noise tells her how near she is. One lonely stretch of street, and then she is safe. Now she hears a shrill whistle coming rapidly nearer —a wagon flies swiftly past her. She stops and looks after it; it is the ambulance of the Rescue Society. She knows where it is going. "How quickly they have come," she thinks; "it is like magic." For a moment she feels that she must call to them, must go back with them. Shame, terrible, overwhelming shame, such as she has never known before, shakes her from head to foot— she knows how vile, how cowardly she is. Then, as the whistle and the rumble of wheels fade away in the distance, a mad joy takes hold of her. She is saved—saved! She hurries on; she meets more people, but she does not fear them—the worst is over. The noise of the city grows louder, the street is lighter, the skyline of the Prater street rises before her, and she knows that she can sink into a flood tide of humanity there and lose herself in it. When she comes to a street lamp she is quite calm enough now to take out her watch and look at it. It is ten minutes to nine. She

holds the watch to her ear—it is ticking merrily.
And she thinks: "Here I am, alive, unharmed—
and he—he—dead. It is Fate." She feels as if
all had been forgiven—as if she had never sinned.
And what if Fate had willed otherwise? If it
were she lying there in the ditch, and he who remained alive? He would not have run away—
but then he is a man. She is only a woman, she
has a husband, a child—it was her right—her
duty—to save herself. She knows that it was not
a sense of duty that impelled her to do it. But
what she has done was right—she had done right
instinctively—as all good people do. If she had
stayed she would have been discovered by this
time. The doctors would question her. And all
the papers would report it next morning; she
would have been ruined forever, and yet her ruin
could not bring him back to life. Yes, that was the
main point, her sacrifice would have been all in
vain. She crosses under the railway bridge and hurries on. There is the Tegethoff Column, where
so many streets meet. There are but few people
in the park on this stormy evening, but to her it
seems as if the life of the city was roaring about
her. It was so horribly still back there. She had
plenty of time now. She knows that her husband
will not be home before ten o'clock. She will have
time to change her clothes. And then it occurs
to her to look at her gown. She is horrified to
see how soiled it is. What shall she say to the
maid about it? And next morning the papers will

all bring the story of the accident, and they will tell of a woman who had been in the carriage, and who had run away. She trembled afresh. One single carelessness and she is lost, even now. But she has her latch-key with her; she can let herself in; no one will hear her come. She jumps into a cab and is about to give her address, then suddenly she remembers that this would not be wise. She gives any number that occurs to her.

As she drives through the Prater street she wishes that she might feel something—grief—horror—but she cannot. She has but one thought, one desire—to be at home, in safety. All else is indifferent to her. When she had decided to leave him alone, dead, by the roadside—in that moment everything seemed to have died within her, everything that would mourn and grieve for him. She has no feeling but that of fear for herself. She is not heartless—she knows that the day will come when her sorrow will be despair—it may kill her even. But she knows nothing now, except the desire to sit quietly at home, at the supper table with her husband and child. She looks out through the cab window. She is driving through the streets of the inner city. It is brilliantly light here, and many people hurry past. Suddenly all that she has experienced in the last few hours seems not to be true, it is like an evil dream; not something real, irreparable. She stops her cab in one of the side streets of the Ring, gets out, turns a corner quickly, and takes another carriage, giving her own address this time. She does not seem able to think of anything any more. "Where is he now?" She closes her eyes and sees him on the litter, in the ambulance. Suddenly she feels that he is here beside her. The cab sways, she feels the terror of being thrown out again, and she screams aloud. The cab halts before the door of her home. She dismounts hastily, hurries with light steps through the house door, unseen by the concierge, runs up the stairs, opens her apartment door very gently, and slips unseen into her own room. She undresses hastily, hiding the mud-stained clothes in her cupboard. To-morrow, when they are dry, she can clean them herself. She washes hands and face, and slips into a loose housegown.

The bell rings. She hears the maid open the door, she hears her husband's voice, and the rattle of his cane on the hat-stand. She feels she must be brave now or it will all have been in vain. She hurries to the dining-room, entering one door as her husband comes in at the other.

"Ah, you're home already?" he asks.

"Why, yes," she replies, "I have been home some time."

"They evidently didn't hear you come in."

She smiles without effort. But it fatigues her horribly to have to smile. He kisses her forehead.

The little boy is already at his place by the table. He has been waiting some time, and has fallen asleep, his head resting on an open book.

She sits down beside him; her husband takes his chair opposite, takes up a paper, and glances carelessly at it. Then he says: "The others are still talking away there."

"What about?" she asks.

And he begins to tell her about the meeting, at length. Emma pretends to listen, and nods now and then. But she does not hear what he is saying, she feels dazed, like one who has escaped terrible danger as by a miracle; she can feel only this: "I am safe; I am at home." And while her husband is talking she pulls her chair nearer the boy's and lifts his head to her shoulder. Fatigue inexpressible comes over her. She can no longer control herself; she feels that her eyes are closing, that she is dropping asleep.

Suddenly another possibility presents itself to her mind, a possibility that she had dismissed the moment she turned to leave the ditch where she had fallen. Suppose he were not dead! Suppose —oh, but it is impossible—his eyes—his lips—not a breath came from them! But there are trances that are like death, which deceive even practised eyes, and she knows nothing about such things. Suppose he is still alive—suppose he has regained consciousness and found himself alone by the roadside—suppose he calls her by her name? He might think she had been injured; he might tell the doctors that there was a woman with him, and that she must have been thrown to some distance. They will look for her. The coachman will come

back with the men he has brought, and will tell
them that she was there, unhurt—and Franz will
know the truth. Franz knows her so well—he
will know that she has run away—and a great
anger will come over him. He will tell them her
name in revenge. For he is mortally injured, and
it will hurt him cruelly that she has left him alone
in his last hour. He will say: "That is Mrs.
Emma ———. I am her lover. She is cowardly
and stupid, too, gentlemen, for she might have
known you would not ask her name; you would
be discreet; you would have let her go away un-
molested. Oh, she might at least have waited
until you came. But she is vile—utterly vile—
ah!—"

"What is the matter?" asks the Professor, very
gravely, rising from his chair.

"What? What?"

"Yes, what is the matter with you?"

"Nothing." She presses the boy closer to her
breast.

The Professor looks at her for a few minutes
steadily.

"Didn't you know that you had fallen asleep,
and—"

"Well?— And—"

"And then you screamed out in your sleep."

"Did I?"

"You screamed as if you were having a night-
mare. Were you dreaming?"

"I don't know—"

And she sees her face in a mirror opposite, a face tortured into a ghastly smile. She knows it is her own face, and it terrifies her. She sees that it is frozen; that this hideous smile is frozen on it, and will always be there, all her life. She tries to cry out. Two hands are laid on her shoulders, and between her own face and the mirrored one her husband's face pushes its way in; his eyes pierce into hers. She knows that unless she is strong for this last trial all is lost. And she feels that she is strong; she has regained control of her limbs, but the moment of strength is short. She raises her hands to his, which rest on her shoulders; she draws him down to her, and smiles naturally and tenderly into his eyes.

She feels his lips on her forehead, and she thinks: "It is all a dream—he will never tell—he will never take revenge like that—he is dead— really dead—and the dead are silent—"

"Why did you say that?" she hears her husband's voice suddenly.

She starts. "What did I say?" And it seems to her as if she had told everything, here at the table—aloud before every one—and again she asks, shuddering before his horrified eyes, "What did I say?"

"The dead are silent," her husband repeats very slowly.

"Yes," she answers.

And she reads in his eyes that she can no longer hide anything from him. They look long and silently at each other. "Put the boy to bed," he says at last. "You have something to tell me, have you not?"

"Yes—"

She knows now that within a few moments she will tell this man everything—this man, whom she has deceived for many years.

And while she goes slowly through the door, holding her boy, she feels her husband's eyes still resting on her, and a great peace comes over her, the assurance that now many things would be right again.

HOW THE REDOUBT WAS TAKEN

BY PROSPER MÉRIMÉE

HOW THE REDOUBT WAS TAKEN

BY PROSPER MÉRIMÉE

A FRIEND of mine, a soldier, who died in Greece of fever some years since, described to me one day his first engagement. His story so impressed me that I wrote it down from memory. It was as follows:

I joined my regiment on September 4th. It was evening. I found the colonel in the camp. He received me rather bruskly, but having read the general's introductory letter he changed his manner and addressed me courteously.

By him I was presented to my captain, who had just come in from reconnoitring. This captain, whose acquaintance I had scarcely time to make, was a tall, dark man, of harsh, repelling aspect. He had been a private soldier, and had won his cross and epaulettes upon the field of battle. His voice, which was hoarse and feeble, contrasted strangely with his gigantic stature. This voice of his he owed, as I was told, to a bullet which had passed completely through his body at the battle of Jena.

On learning that I had just come from college

at Fontainebleau, he remarked, with a wry face:
"My lieutenant died last night."

I understood what he implied, "It is for you to
take his place, and you are good for nothing."

A sharp retort was on my tongue, but I re-
strained it.

The moon was rising behind the redoubt of
Cheverino, which stood two cannon-shots from
our encampment. The moon was large and red,
as is common at her rising; but that night she
seemed to me of extraordinary size. For an instant the redoubt stood out coal-black against
the glittering disk. It resembled the cone of a
volcano at the moment of eruption.

An old soldier, at whose side I found myself,
observed the color of the moon.

"She is very red," he said. "It is a sign
that it will cost us dear to win this wonderful
redoubt."

I was always superstitious, and this piece of
augury, coming at that moment, troubled me. I
sought my couch, but could not sleep. I rose,
and walked about a while, watching the long line
of fires upon the heights beyond the village of
Cheverino.

When the sharp night air had thoroughly re-
freshed my blood I went back to the fire. I
rolled my mantle round me, and I shut my eyes,
trusting not to open them till daybreak. But
sleep refused to visit me. Insensibly my thoughts
grew doleful. I told myself that I had not a

friend among the hundred thousand men who filled that plain. If I were wounded, I should be placed in hospital, in the hands of ignorant and careless surgeons. I called to mind what I had heard of operations. My heart beat violently, and I mechanically arranged, as a kind of rude cuirass, my handkerchief and pocketbook upon my breast. Then, overpowered with weariness, my eyes closed drowsily, only to open the next instant with a start at some new thought of horror.

Fatigue, however, at last gained the day. When the drums beat at daybreak I was fast asleep. We were drawn up in ranks. The roll was called, then we stacked our arms, and everything announced that we should pass another uneventful day.

But about three o'clock an aide-de-camp arrived with orders. We were commanded to take arms.

Our sharpshooters marched into the plain. We followed slowly, and in twenty minutes we saw the outposts of the Russians falling back and entering the redoubt. We had a battery of artillery on our right, another on our left, but both some distance in advance of us. They opened a sharp fire upon the enemy, who returned it briskly, and the redoubt of Cheverino was soon concealed by volumes of thick smoke. Our regiment was almost covered from the Russians' fire by a piece of rising ground. Their bullets (which besides were rarely aimed at us, for they preferred to fire upon our cannoneers) whistled over us, or at worst knocked up a shower of earth and stones.

Just as the order to advance was given, the captain looked at me intently. I stroked my sprouting mustache with an air of unconcern; in truth, I was not frightened, and only dreaded lest I might be thought so. These passing bullets aided my heroic coolness, while my self-respect assured me that the danger was a real one, since I was veritably under fire. I was delighted at my self-possession, and already looked forward to the pleasure of describing in Parisian drawing-rooms the capture of the redoubt of Cheverino.

The colonel passed before our company. "Well," he said to me, "you are going to see warm work in your first action."

I gave a martial smile, and brushed my cuff, on which a bullet, which had struck the earth at thirty paces distant, had cast a little dust.

It appeared that the Russians had discovered that their bullets did no harm, for they replaced them by a fire of shells, which began to reach us in the hollows where we lay. One of these, in its explosion, knocked off my shako and killed a man beside me.

"I congratulate you," said the captain, as I picked up my shako. "You are safe now for the day."

HOW THE REDOUBT WAS TAKEN

I knew the military superstition which believes that the axiom *"non bis in idem"* is as applicable to the battlefield as to the courts of justice. I replaced my shako with a swagger.

"That's a rude way to make one raise one's hat," I said, as lightly as I could. And this wretched piece of wit was, in the circumstances, received as excellent.

"I compliment you," said the captain. "You will command a company to-night; for I shall not survive the day. Every time I have been wounded the officer below me has been touched by some spent ball; and," he added, in a lower tone, "all the names began with P."

I laughed skeptically; most people would have done the same; but most would also have been struck, as I was, by these prophetic words. But, conscript though I was, I felt that I could trust my thoughts to no one, and that it was my duty to seem always calm and bold.

At the end of half an hour the Russian fire had sensibly diminished. We left our cover to advance on the redoubt.

Our regiment was composed of three battalions. The second had to take the enemy in flank; the two others formed a storming party. I was in the third.

On issuing from behind the cover, we were received by several volleys, which did but little harm.

The whistling of the balls amazed me. But

after all," I thought, "a battle is less terrible than I expected."

We advanced at a smart run, our musketeers in front.

All at once the Russians uttered three hurrahs—three distinct hurrahs—and then stood silent, without firing.

"I don't like that silence," said the captain. "It bodes no good."

I began to think our people were too eager. I could not help comparing, mentally, their shouts and clamor with the striking silence of the enemy.

We quickly reached the foot of the redoubt. The palisades were broken and the earthworks shattered by our balls. With a roar of "Vive l'Empereur," our soldiers rushed across the ruins.

I raised my eyes. Never shall I forget the sight which met my view. The smoke had mostly lifted, and remained suspended, like a canopy, at twenty feet above the redoubt. Through a bluish mist could be perceived, behind the shattered parapet, the Russian Grenadiers, with rifles lifted, as motionless as statues. I can see them still—the left eye of every soldier glaring at us, the right hidden by his lifted gun. In an embrasure at a few feet distant, a man with a fuse stood by a cannon.

I shuddered. I believed that my last hour had come.

HOW THE REDOUBT WAS TAKEN

"Now for the dance to open," cried the captain. These were the last words I heard him speak.

There came from the redoubts a roll of drums. I saw the muzzles lowered. I shut my eyes; I heard a most appalling crash of sound, to which succeeded groans and cries. Then I looked up, amazed to find myself still living. The redoubt was once more wrapped in smoke. I was surrounded by the dead and wounded. The captain was extended at my feet; a ball had carried off his head, and I was covered with his blood. Of all the company, only six men, except myself, remained erect.

This carnage was succeeded by a kind of stupor. The next instant the colonel, with his hat on his sword's point, had scaled the parapet with a cry of "Vive l'Empereur." The survivors followed him. All that succeeded is to me a kind of dream. We rushed into the redoubt, I know not how, we fought hand to hand in the midst of smoke so thick that no man could perceive his enemy. I found my sabre dripping blood; I heard a shout of "Victory"; and, in the clearing smoke, I saw the earthworks piled with dead and dying. The cannons were covered with a heap of corpses. About two hundred men in the French uniform were standing, without order, loading their muskets or wiping their bayonets. Eleven Russian prisoners were with them.

The colonel was lying, bathed in blood, upon

a broken cannon. A group of soldiers crowded round him. I approached them.

"Who is the oldest captain?" he was asking of a sergeant.

The sergeant shrugged his shoulders most expressively.

"Who is the oldest lieutenant?"

"This gentleman, who came last night," replied the sergeant calmly.

The colonel smiled bitterly.

"Come, sir," he said to me, "you are now in chief command. Fortify the gorge of the redoubt at once with wagons, for the enemy is out in force. But General C—— is coming to support you."

"Colonel," I asked him, "are you badly wounded?"

"Pish, my dear fellow. The redoubt is taken."

THE SLANDERER

BY ANTON CHEKHOV

THE SLANDERER

BY ANTON CHEKHOV

SERGEY KAPITONICH AKHI-
NEYEV, the teacher of calligraphy, gave
his daughter Natalya in marriage to the
teacher of history and geography, Ivan Petro-
vich Loshadinikh. The wedding feast went on
swimmingly. They sang, played, and danced in
the parlor. Waiters, hired for the occasion from
the club, bustled about hither and thither like
madmen, in black frock coats and soiled white
neckties. A loud noise of voices smote the air.
From the outside people looked in at the windows—their social standing gave them no right
to enter.

Just at midnight the host, Akhineyev, made
his way to the kitchen to see whether everything
was ready for the supper. The kitchen was filled
with smoke from the floor to the ceiling; the
smoke reeked with the odors of geese, ducks, and
many other things. Victuals and beverages were
scattered about on two tables in artistic disorder.
Marfa, the cook, a stout, red-faced woman, was
busying herself near the loaded tables.

"Show me the sturgeon, dear," said Akhineyev,

Translated by Herman Bernstein. Copyright, 1901, by the Globe and
Commercial Advertiser.

rubbing his hands and licking his lips. "What a fine odor! I could just devour the whole kitchen! Well, let me see the sturgeon!"

Marfa walked up to one of the benches and carefully lifted a greasy newspaper. Beneath that paper, in a huge dish, lay a big fat sturgeon, amid capers, olives, and carrots. Akhineyev glanced at the sturgeon and heaved a sigh of relief. His face became radiant, his eyes rolled. He bent down, and, smacking his lips, gave vent to a sound like a creaking wheel. He stood a while, then snapped his fingers for pleasure, and smacked his lips once more.

"Bah! The sound of a hearty kiss. Whom have you been kissing there, Marfusha?" some one's voice was heard from the adjoining room, and soon the closely cropped head of Vankin, the assistant school instructor, appeared in the doorway. "Whom have you been kissing here? A-a-ah! Very good! Sergey Kapitonich! A fine old man indeed! With the female sex tête-à-tête!"

"I wasn't kissing at all," said Akhineyev, confused; "who told you, you fool? I only—smacked my lips on account of—in consideration of my pleasure—at the sight of the fish."

"Tell that to some one else, not to me!" exclaimed Vankin, whose face expanded into a broad smile as he disappeared behind the door. Akhineyev blushed.

"The devil knows what may be the outcome of

this!" he thought. "He'll go about tale-bearing now, the rascal. He'll disgrace me before the whole town, the brute!"

Akhineyev entered the parlor timidly and cast furtive glances to see what Vankin was doing. Vankin stood near the piano and, deftly bending down, whispered something to the inspector's sister-in-law, who was laughing.

"That's about me!" thought Akhineyev. "About me, the devil take him! She believes him, she's laughing. My God! No, that mustn't be left like that. No. I'll have to fix it so that no one shall believe him. I'll speak to all of them, and he'll remain a foolish gossip in the end."

Akhineyev scratched his head, and, still confused, walked up to Padekoi.

"I was in the kitchen a little while ago, arranging things there for the supper," he said to the Frenchman. "You like fish, I know, and I have a sturgeon just so big. About two yards. Ha, ha, ha! Yes, by the way, I have almost forgotten. There was a real anecdote about that sturgeon in the kitchen. I entered the kitchen a little while ago and wanted to examine the food. I glanced at the sturgeon and for pleasure, I smacked my lips—it was so piquant! And just at that moment the fool Vankin entered and says —ha, ha, ha—and says: 'A-a! A-a-ah! You have been kissing here?'—with Marfa; just think of it—with the cook! What a piece of invention,

that blockhead. The woman is ugly, she looks
like a monkey, and he says we were kissing.
What a queer fellow!"

"Who's a queer fellow?" asked Tarantulov, as
he approached them.

"I refer to Vankin. I went out into the kitchen—"

The story of Marfa and the sturgeon was repeated.

"That makes me laugh. What a queer fellow
he is. In my opinion it is more pleasant to kiss
the dog than to kiss Marfa," added Akhineyev,
and, turning around, he noticed Mzda.

"We have been speaking about Vankin," he
said to him. "What a queer fellow. He entered
the kitchen and noticed me standing beside
Marfa, and immediately he began to invent different stories. 'What?' he says, 'you have been
kissing each other!' He was drunk, so he must
have been dreaming. 'And I,' I said, 'I would
rather kiss a duck than kiss Marfa. And I have
a wife,' said I, 'you fool.' He made me appear
ridiculous."

"Who made you appear ridiculous?" inquired
the teacher of religion, addressing Akhineyev.

"Vankin. I was standing in the kitchen, you
know, and looking at the sturgeon—" And so
forth. In about half an hour all the guests knew
the story about Vankin and the sturgeon.

"Now let him tell," thought Akhineyev, rubbing his hands. "Let him do it. He'll start to

tell them, and they'll cut him short: 'Don't talk nonsense, you fool! We know all about it.'"

And Akhineyev felt so much appeased that, for joy, he drank four glasses of brandy over and above his fill. Having escorted his daughter to her room, he went to his own and soon slept the sleep of an innocent child, and on the following day he no longer remembered the story of the sturgeon. But, alas! Man proposes and God disposes. The evil tongue does its wicked work, and even Akhineyev's cunning did not do him any good. One week later, on a Wednesday, after the third lesson, when Akhineyev stood in the teachers' room and discussed the vicious inclinations of the pupil Visyekin, the director approached him, and, beckoning to him, called him aside.

"See here, Sergey Kapitonich," said the director. "Pardon me. It isn't my affair, yet I must make it clear to you, nevertheless. It is my duty— You see, rumors are on foot that you are on intimate terms with that woman—with your cook— It isn't my affair, but— You may be on intimate terms with her, you may kiss her— You may do whatever you like, but, please, don't do it so openly! I beg of you. Don't forget that you are a pedagogue."

Akhineyev stood as though frozen and petrified. Like one stung by a swarm of bees and scalded with boiling water, he went home. On his way it seemed to him as though the whole town stared at him as at one besmeared with tar— At home new troubles awaited him.

"Why don't you eat anything?" asked his wife at their dinner. "What are you thinking about? Are you thinking about Cupid, eh? You are longing for Marfushka. I know everything already, you Mahomet. Kind people have opened my eyes, you barbarian!"

And she slapped him on the cheek.

He rose from the table, and staggering, without cap or coat, directed his footsteps toward Vankin. The latter was at home.

"You rascal!" he said to Vankin. "Why have you covered me with mud before the whole world? Why have you slandered me?"

"How; what slander? What are you inventing?"

"And who told everybody that I was kissing Marfa? Not you, perhaps? Not you, you murderer?"

Vankin began to blink his eyes, and all the fibres of his face began to quiver. He lifted his eyes toward the image and ejaculated:

"May God punish me, may I lose my eyesight and die, if I said even a single word about you to any one! May I have neither house nor home!"

Vankin's sincerity admitted of no doubt. It was evident that it was not he who had gossiped.

"But who was it? Who?" Akhineyev asked himself, going over in his mind all his acquaintances, and striking his chest. "Who was it?"

THE NECKLACE

BY GUY DE MAUPASSANT

THE NECKLACE

BY GUY DE MAUPASSANT

SHE was one of those charming girls, born by a freak of destiny in a family of toilers. She had no fortune, no expectations, no means of satisfying her ambitions, except by a marriage with a rich and distinguished man, and, as she knew none, in order to escape from her surroundings, she married a clerk in the office of the Minister of Public Instruction.

She dressed simply, because she had no means of adornment; but she was as unhappy as though she had fallen from a high social position, for the women who have neither caste nor race use their beauty, grace, and charm as stepping-stones to those heights from which they are otherwise barred, their natural tact and instinctive elegance and quick perceptions being their only inheritance, and, skilfully used, make them the equal of their more fortunate sisters. She suffered incessantly when she glanced around her humble home, and felt the absence of all those delicacies and luxuries which are enjoyed only by the rich. In short, all the little nothings, that another woman of her caste would not have seen, tor-

Translated by Mathilde Weissenhorn. Copyright, 1898, by The Current Literature Publishing Company.

tured and wounded her. The sight of the old Breton peasant woman who performed her simple household duties awakened in her vain longings and troubled dreams.

She dreamed of beautiful halls, discreetly lighted by candles in great bronze candlesticks, whose rich carpets gave back no sounds and whose walls were covered with silks from the Orient, and of obsequious footmen half asleep in their large armchairs, ready to attend to your every want at a moment's notice; of large salons draped in ancient silks; of "étagers" covered with priceless bric-à-brac. She thought also of coquettish small salons, made expressly for the "five o'clock," when one receives only one's intimates or distinguished men of letters, from whom it is every woman's ambition to receive attentions.

When she was seated at the table (whose cloth had already done duty for three days) or opposite her husband—who evinced his entire satisfaction with the evening's repast by such exclamations as: "Oh, the good 'pot-au-feu'! I know nothing better!"—her imagination carried her away to stately banquet halls, whose walls were covered with rich tapestries, portraying scenes in which ancient personages and strange birds were pictured in the middle of a fairy-like forest. She pictured the glittering silver, strange dishes, exquisitely served on marvelous plate, and gallantries whispered and listened to with the sphinx-like smile with which a woman of the world knows so well how to conceal her emotions, all the while eating a rosy trout or dallying with a wing of a lark. She had no toilets, no jewels, and it was for these things that she longed, as the fleet Arabian longs for his native desert. What pleasure to have pleased, been envied, to be seductive and sought after!

She had a rich friend, a comrade from the convent, whom she no longer visited, because she suffered from seeing the things she could not have, and on returning wept whole days for grief, regret, despair, and distress.

One evening her husband came home radiant, holding in his hand a large envelope.

"See," said he, "here is something for you."

She nervously tore open the envelope, drew out a card, on which these words were printed:

"The Minister of Public Instruction and Madame Georges Ramponeau beg the honor of the company of Monsieur and Madame Loisel for the evening of Monday, January 18th."

Instead of being wild with delight, as he had expected, she threw the invitation on the table, with an exclamation of disgust, saying sullenly:

"What do you wish me to do with that?"

"But, my dear, I thought you would be so pleased. You never go out, and this is an event. I only obtained it after infinite trouble. Everybody wants one; they are much sought after, and they are not generally given to employees. You will see there all of the official world."

She looked at him with supreme disdain, and said impatiently:

"What would you like me to wear?" The secret was out. Manlike, he had not thought of that.

"But—the dress—that you wear to the theatre," stammered he. "You always look beautiful to me in that."

He stopped speaking, stupefied and dismayed on seeing his wife in tears. Two large tears trickled slowly down her cheeks.

"What is the matter? What is the matter?" asked he tenderly. By violent effort she conquered her grief and calmly said, while wiping her humid cheeks:

"Nothing; only I have no toilet, and, of course, can not go. Give the card to one of your comrades whose wife is fortunate enough to have something suitable for the occasion."

Despairingly he said:

"See, Mathilde, how much will a dress cost to wear to this ball; one which can also be used for other occasions—something very simple."

She reflected a few moments, figuring in her own mind the sum she could ask without danger of immediate refusal and frightening her economical husband. Finally she hesitatingly said:

"I do not know exactly; but it seems to me I might manage with about 400 francs."

THE NECKLACE

He paled a little, because he had been saving just that sum to buy a gun for the following summer, when he would go with some of his friends to the plains of Nanterre on Sundays to shoot larks. Stifling his regrets, however, he replied:

"Very well, I will give you 400 francs, but try to have a beautiful dress."

The day of the fête drew near; but Madame Loisel seemed sad, anxious, and uneasy. Her toilet was ready, what could it be? Her husband said to her one evening:

"What is the matter? You have been so queer for the last few days!"

She replied: "It worries me that I have not one jewel, not a precious stone to wear. What a miserable figure I shall be! I think I would rather not go at all!"

"You can wear natural flowers; it is all the rage at this season, and for ten francs you can have two or three magnificent roses."

But she was not convinced.

"No; there is nothing more humiliating than to be poorly dressed among so many rich women."

"But how silly you are! Go to your friend, Madame Forestier, and ask her to lend you her jewels. You are friendly enough with her to do that."

She gave a cry of joy.

"Yes; that is true—I had not thought of it."

The following day she went to her friend and explained her predicament. Madame Forestier went to a closet and took out a large casket, and, opening it, said:

"Choose, my dear; they are at your service."

She saw first bracelets, then a necklace of pearls, a Venetian cross, gold and precious stones of exquisite workmanship. She tried them on before the glass, unable to decide whether to wear them or not.

"Have you nothing else?" said she.

"Oh, yes; look them over, I don't know what might please you."

Suddenly she opened a black satin case, disclosing to view a superb rivière of diamonds, her heart beat furiously with the desire of possession.

She took them in her trembling hands and put them on over her simple high-neck gown, and stood lost in an ecstasy of admiration of herself. Then, fearfully, hesitatingly, dreading the agony of a refusal:

"Can you lend me only that?"

"Why, certainly; if it pleases you."

She fell on her friend's neck, embraced her tempestuously and then left hastily with her treasure.

The day of the ball arrived. Madame Loisel was a success. Among all the beautiful women she was the most beautiful, elegant, gracious, and smiling with joy. She attracted the attention of some of the most distinguished men present, and on all sides was heard:

"Who is she?"

All the attachés of the cabinet sought her dancing card eagerly, and even the Minister himself expressed his approval. She danced with pleasure, thinking of nothing but the triumph of her beauty and the glory of her success. Intoxicated by all the admiration, she seemed to float through a cloud of happiness, intensified by her complete victory and the tribute paid to her charms, so sweet to the hearts of women. She left about four o'clock in the morning; her husband had slept since midnight in a small room, deserted except by two or three gentlemen who also awaited their wives.

He threw over her shoulders the modest cloak which she had brought, whose shabbiness seemed to mock the elegance of the ball toilet. She felt the incongruity, and walked swiftly away in order not to be seen by those whose rich furs were more in accordance with the occasion.

"Wait," said her husband, "you will take cold; I will call a carriage."

But she heeded him not, and rapidly descended the staircase. When they reached the street, there was no carriage in sight, and they were obliged to look for one, calling to the drivers who passed by, but in vain. Shiveringly they walked toward the Seine and finally found on the quay one of those nocturnal coupés one finds only in Paris after dark, hovering about the great city like grim birds of prey, who conceal their misery during the day. It carried them to their door (Rue de Martyrs), and they slowly and sadly entered their small apartments. It was ended for her, and he only remembered that he would have to be at his desk at ten o'clock.

She took off her cloak in front of the glass in order to admire herself once more in all her bravery, but, suddenly, she cried out: "The diamonds are gone!" Her husband, almost half asleep, started at the cry and asked:

"What is the matter?"

She turned toward him with a frightened air.

"I—I have lost Madame Forestier's necklace!"

He rose dismayed.

"What—how! But it is not possible!" And they immediately began to search in the folds of the dress, the cloak, in the pockets—everywhere, and found nothing.

"Are you sure that you had it when you left the ball?"

"Yes; I felt it while still in the vestibule at the Minister's."

"But if you had lost it in the street we should have heard it drop. It ought to be in the carriage."

"Yes; it is possible. Did you take the number?"

"No; and you have not looked at it, either?"

"No."

They looked at each other fearfully; finally Loisel dressed himself.

"I shall go over the whole ground that we traveled on foot, to see whether I can not find it."

He went out. She sat still in her brilliant ball toilet; no desire to sleep, no power to think, all swallowed up in the fear of the calamity which had fallen upon them.

Her husband came in at seven o'clock. He had found nothing. He had been to the Prefecture of the Police, to the papers offering a reward, to all small cab companies, anywhere, in short, where he could have the shadow of hope of recovery.

She waited all day in the same state of fear in the face of this frightful disaster.

Loisel returned in the evening pallid and haggard. No news as yet.

"You must write to your friend that you have broken the clasp of the necklace and are having it repaired. That will give us time to look around."

.   .   .   .

At the end of the week they had lost all hope, and Loisel, to whom it seemed this care and trouble had added five years to his age, said:

"We must try and replace the jewels."

The following day they went to the jeweler whose name was stamped inside the case. He consulted his books: "I did not sell that necklace, madame, I only furnished the case."

Then they went from jeweler to jeweler, racking their memories to find the same, both of them sick with grief and agony. At last, in a small shop in the Palais Royal, they found one which seemed to them like the one they had lost. With beating hearts they asked the price.

Forty thousand francs; but they could have it for 36,000 francs.

They asked the jeweler not to dispose of it for three days, and he also promised to take it back at 34,000 francs if the first one was found before the end of February.

Loisel had inherited 18,000 francs from his father. He borrowed the rest.

He borrowed a thousand francs from one, five hundred from another, five louis here, five louis there—he gave notes, made ruinous engagements, had recourse to the usurers, ran the whole gamut of money-lenders. He compromised his whole existence risking his signature, without knowing that it would be honored, terrified by the agony of the future, by the black misery which enveloped him, by the prospect of all the physical privations and moral tortures. He went for the new necklace and deposited on the counter his 36,000 francs.

When Madame Loisel returned the necklace to Madame Forestier, she coldly said:

"You should have returned it sooner, as I might have needed it."

She did not open the case, the one thing

Madame Loisel had dreaded. What if she had discovered the change—what would she have thought? Would she not be taken for a thief?

.   .   .   .

From that time on Madame Loisel knew what life meant to the very poor in all its phases. She took her part heroically. This frightful debt must be paid. Her share of privations was bravely borne. They discharged their one domestic, changed their location, and rented smaller apartments near the roof.

She knew now what meant the duties of the household, the heavy work of the kitchen. Her pretty hands soon lost all semblance of the care of bygone days. She washed the soiled linen and dried it in her room. She went every morning to the street with the refuse of the kitchen, carrying the water, stopping at each flight of stairs to take breath—wearing the dress of the women of the people; she went each day to the grocer, the fruiterer, the butcher, carrying her basket on her arm, bargaining, defending cent by cent her miserable money.

They were obliged each month to pay some notes and renew others in order to gain time. Her husband worked in the evening balancing the books of merchants, and often was busy all night, copying at five cents a page.

And this life then endured for ten years.

At the end of this time they had paid all the tax of the usurers and compound interest.

Madame Loisel seemed an old woman now. She had become strong and hardy as the women of the provinces, and with tousled head, short skirts, red hands, she was foremost among the loud-voiced women of the neighborhood, who passed their time gossiping at their doorsteps.

But sometimes when her husband was at his office she seated herself at the window and thought of that evening in the past and that ball, where she had been so beautiful and so admired.

What would have happened if she had not lost the necklace? Who knows? Life is a singular and changeable thing, full of vicissitudes. How little it takes to save or wreck us!

. . . .

One Sunday as she was walking in the Champs Elysées to divert herself from the cares and duties of the week she suddenly perceived a lady, with a little child, coming toward her. It was Madame Forestier, still young, beautiful and charming. Madame Loisel stopped short, too agitated to move. Should she speak to her? Yes, certainly. And now that the necklace was paid for she would tell her everything. Why not?

She walked up to her and said: "Good day, Jeanne."

Madame Forestier did not recognize her and seemed astonished at being spoken to so familiarly by this woman of the people.

"But—madame—I do not—I think you are mistaken."

"No; I am Mathilde Loisel."

"Oh!—my poor Mathilde, how you are changed!"

"Yes; I have had lots of trouble and misery since I last saw you—and all for you."

"For me! And how was that?"

"Do you remember the necklace of diamonds you lent me, to wear to the Minister's ball?"

"Yes; well?"

"Well, I lost it."

"Lost it! How could you, since you returned it to me?"

"I returned you one just like it, and for ten years we have been paying for it. You know, it was not easy for us, who had nothing—but it is finished, and I am very happy."

"You say that you bought a necklace of diamonds to replace mine," said Madame Forestier.

"Yes; and you never found it out! They were so much alike," and she smiled proudly.

Touched to the heart, Madame Forestier took the poor, rough hands in hers, drawing her tenderly toward her, her voice filled with tears:

"Oh, my poor Mathilde! But mine were false. They were not worth more than 500 francs at most."

PUTOIS

BY ANATOLE FRANCE

PUTOIS

BY ANATOLE FRANCE

I

THIS garden of our childhood, said Monsieur Bergeret, this garden that one could pace off in twenty steps, was for us a whole world, full of smiles and surprises.

"Lucien, do you recall Putois?" asked Zoe, smiling as usual, the lips pressed, bending over her work.

"Do I recall Putois! Of all the faces I saw as a child that of Putois remains the clearest in my remembrance. All the features of his face and his character are fixed in my mind. He had a pointed cranium . . ."

"A low forehead," added Mademoiselle Zoe.

And the brother and sister recited alternately, in a monotonous voice, with an odd gravity, the points in a sort of description:

"A low forehead."

"Squinting eyes."

"A shifty glance."

"Crow's-feet at the temples."

"The cheek-bones sharp, red and shining."

Translated by William Patten. Copyright, 1907, by P. F. Collier & Son.

"His ears had no rims to them."

"The features were devoid of all expression."

"His hands, which were never still, alone expressed his meaning."

"Thin, somewhat bent, feeble in appearance . . ."

"In reality he was unusually strong."

"He easily bent a five-franc piece between the first finger and the thumb . . ."

"Which was enormous."

"His voice was drawling . . ."

"And his speech mild."

Suddenly Monsieur Bergeret exclaimed: "Zoe! we have forgotten 'Yellow hair and sparse beard.' Let us begin all over again."

Pauline, who had listened with astonishment to this strange recital, asked her father and aunt how they had been able to learn by heart this bit of prose, and why they recited it as if it were a litany.

Monsieur Bergeret gravely answered:

"Pauline, what you have heard is a text, I may say a liturgy, used by the Bergeret family. It should be handed down to you so that it may not perish with your aunt and me. Your grandfather, my daughter, your grandfather, Eloi Bergeret, who was not amused with trifles, thought highly of this bit, principally because of its origin. He called it 'The Anatomy of Putois.' And he used to say that he preferred, in certain respects, the anatomy of Putois to the anatomy

of Quaresmeprenant. 'If the description by
Xenomanes,' he said, 'is more learned and richer
in unusual and choice expressions, the description
of Putois greatly surpasses it in clarity and sim-
plicity of style.' He held this opinion because
Doctor Ledouble, of Tours, had not yet explained chapters thirty, thirty-one, and thirty-
two of the fourth book of Rabelais."

"I do not understand at all," said Pauline.

"That is because you did not know Putois, my
daughter. You must understand that Putois was
the most familiar figure in my childhood and in
that of your Aunt Zoe. In the house of your
grandfather Bergeret we constantly spoke of
Putois. Each believed that he had seen him."

Pauline asked:

"Who was this Putois?"

Instead of replying, Monsieur Bergeret commenced to laugh, and Mademoiselle Bergeret also
laughed, her lips pressed tight together. Pauline
looked from one to the other. She thought it
strange that her aunt should laugh so heartily,
and more strange that she should laugh with and
in sympathy with her brother. It was indeed singular, as the brother and sister were quite different in character.

"Papa, tell me what was Putois? Since you
wish me to know, tell me."

"Putois, my daughter, was a gardener. The
son of honest market-gardeners, he set up for
himself as nurseryman at Saint-Omer. But he

did not satisfy his customers and got in a bad way. Having given up business, he went out by the day. Those who employed him could not always congratulate themselves."

At this, Mademoiselle Bergeret, laughing, rejoined:

"Do you recall, Lucien, when our father could not find his ink, his pens, his sealing-wax, his scissors, he said: 'I suspect Putois has been here'?"

"Ah!" said Monsieur Bergeret, "Putois had not a good reputation."

"Is that all?" asked Pauline.

"No, my daughter, it is not all. Putois was remarkable in this, that while we knew him and were familiar with him, nevertheless—"

"—He did not exist," said Zoe.

Monsieur Bergeret looked at his sister with an air of reproach.

"What a speech, Zoe! and why break the charm like that? Do you dare say it, Zoe? Zoe, can you prove it? To maintain that Putois did not exist, that Putois never was, have you sufficiently considered the conditions of existence and the modes of being? Putois existed, my sister. But it is true that his was a peculiar existence."

"I understand less and less," said Pauline, discouraged.

"The truth will be clear to you presently, my daughter. Know then that Putois was born fully grown. I was still a child and your aunt was a little girl. We lived in a little house, in a suburb

of Saint-Omer. Our parents led a peaceful, retired life, until they were discovered by an old
lady named Madame Cornouiller, who lived at
the manor of Montplaisir, twelve miles from
town, and proved to be a great-aunt of my
mother's. By right of relationship she insisted
that our father and mother come to dine every
Sunday at Montplaisir, where they were exces-
sively bored. She said that it was the proper
thing to have a family dinner on Sunday and that
only people of common origin failed to observe
this ancient custom. My father was bored to the
point of tears at Montplaisir. His desperation
was painful to contemplate. But Madame Cornouiller did not notice it. She saw nothing. My
mother was braver. She suffered as much as my
father, and perhaps more, but she smiled."

"Women are made to suffer," said Zoe.

"Zoe, every living thing is destined to suffer.
In vain our parents refused these fatal invita-
tions. Madame Cornouiller came to take them
each Sunday afternoon. They had to go to
Montplaisir; it was an obligation from which
there was absolutely no escape. It was an estab-
lished order that only a revolt could break. My
father finally revolted and swore not to accept
another invitation from Madame Cornouiller,
leaving it to my mother to find decent pretexts
and varied reasons for these refusals, for which
she was the least capable. Our mother did not
know how to pretend."

"Say, Lucien, that she did not like to. She could tell a fib as well as any one."

"It is true that when she had good reasons she gave them rather than invent poor ones. Do you recall, my sister, that one day she said at table: 'Fortunately, Zoe has the whooping-cough; we shall not have to go to Montplaisir for some time'?"

"That was true!" said Zoe.

"You got over it, Zoe. And one day Madame Cornouiller said to my mother: 'Dearest, I count on your coming with your husband to dine Sunday at Montplaisir.' Our mother, expressly bidden by her husband to give Madame Cornouiller a good reason for declining, invented, in this extremity, a reason that was not the truth. 'I am extremely sorry, dear Madame, but that will be impossible for us. Sunday I expect the gardener.'

"On hearing this, Madame Cornouiller looked through the glass door of the salon at the little wild garden, where the prickwood and the lilies looked as though they had never known the pruning-knife and were likely never to know it. 'You expect the gardener! What for?'

" 'To work in the garden.'

And my mother, having involuntarily turned her eyes on this little square of weeds and plants run wild, that she had called a garden, recognized with dismay the improbability of her excuse.

" 'This man,' said Madame Cornouiller, 'could just as well work in your garden Monday or

170

Tuesday. Moreover, that will be much better.
One should not work on Sunday.'

" 'He works all the week.'

"I have often noticed that the most absurd and
ridiculous reasons are the least disputed: they
disconcert the adversary. Madame Cornouiller
insisted, less than one might expect of a person
so little disposed to give up. Rising from her
armchair, she asked:

" 'What do you call your gardener, dearest?'

" 'Putois,' answered my mother without hesitation.

"Putois was named. From that time he existed. Madame Cornouiller took herself off,
murmuring: 'Putois! It seems to me that I know
that name. Putois! Putois! I must know him.
But I do not recollect him. Where does he
live?'

" 'He works by the day. When one wants him
one leaves word with this one or that one.'

" 'Ah! I thought so, a loafer and a vagabond—
a good-for-nothing. Don't trust him, dearest.'

"From that time Putois had a character."

II

Messieurs Goubin and Jean Marteau having
arrived, Monsieur Bergeret put them in touch
with the conversation.

"We were speaking of him whom my mother
caused to be born gardener at Saint-Omer and

whom she christened. He existed from that time on."

"Dear master, will you kindly repeat that?" said Monsieur Goubin, wiping the glass of his monocle.

"Willingly," replied Monsieur Bergeret. "There was no gardener. The gardener did not exist. My mother said: 'I am waiting for the gardener.' At once the gardener was. He lived."

"Dear master," said Monsieur Goubin, "how could he live since he did not exist?"

"He had a sort of existence," replied Monsieur Bergeret.

"You mean an imaginary existence," Monsieur Goubin replied, disdainfully.

"Is it nothing then, but an imaginary existence?" exclaimed the master. "And have not mythical beings the power to influence men? Consider mythology, Monsieur Goubin, and you will perceive that they are not real beings but imaginary beings that exercise the most profound and lasting influence on the mind. Everywhere and always, beings who have no more reality than Putois have inspired nations with hatred and love, terror and hope, have advised crimes, received offerings, made laws and customs. Monsieur Goubin, think of the eternal mythology. Putois is a mythical personage, the most obscure, I grant you, and of the lowest order. The coarse satyr, who in olden times sat at the table with our peasants in the North, was

considered worthy of appearing in a picture by
Jordaens and a fable by La Fontaine. The hairy
son of Sycorax appeared in the noble world of
Shakespeare. Putois, less fortunate, will be always neglected by artists and poets. He lacks
bigness and the unusual style and character. He
was conceived by minds too reasonable, among
people who knew how to read and write, and who
had not that delightful imagination in which
fables take root. I think, Messieurs, that I have
said enough to show you the real nature of
Putois."

"I understand it," said Monsieur Goubin. And
Monsieur Bergeret continued his discourse.

"Putois was. I can affirm it. He was. Consider it, gentlemen, and you will admit that a
state of being by no means implies substance,
and means only the bonds attributed to the subject, expresses only a relation."

"Undoubtedly," said Jean Marteau; "but a being without attributes is a being less than nothing. I do not remember who at one time said, 'I
am that I am.' Pardon my lapse of memory. One
cannot remember everything. But the unknown
who spoke in that fashion was very imprudent.
In letting it be understood by this thoughtless
observation that he was deprived of attributes
and denied all relations, he proclaimed that he
did not exist and thoughtlessly suppressed himself. I wager that no one has heard of him since."
—"You have lost," answered Monsieur Bergeret.

"He corrected the bad effect of these egotistical expressions by employing quantities of adjectives, and he is often spoken of, most often without judgment."—"I do not understand," said Monsieur Goubin.—"It is not necessary to understand," replied Jean Marteau. And he begged Monsieur Bergeret to speak of Putois.—"It is very kind of you to ask me," said the master.— "Putois was born in the second half of the nineteenth century, at Saint-Omer. He would have been better off if he had been born some centuries before in the forest of Arden or in the forest of Brocéliande. He would then have been a remarkably clever evil spirit."—"A cup of tea, Monsieur Goubin," said Pauline.—"Was Putois, then, an evil spirit?" said Jean Marteau.—"He was evil," replied Monsieur Bergeret; "he was, in a way, but not absolutely. It was true of him as with those devils that are called wicked, but in whom one discovers good qualities when one associates with them. And I am disposed to think that injustice has been done Putois. Madame Cornouiller, who, warned against him, had at once suspected him of being a loafer, a drunkard, and a robber, reflected that since my mother, who was not rich, employed him, it was because he was satisfied with little, and asked herself if she would not do well to have him work instead of her gardener, who had a better reputation, but expected more. The time had come for trimming the yews. She thought that if Madame Eloi

PUTOIS

Bergeret, who was poor, did not pay Putois much, she herself, who was rich, would give him still less, for it is customary for the rich to pay less than the poor. And she already saw her yews trimmed in straight hedges, in balls and in pyramids, without her having to pay much. 'I will keep an eye open,' she said, 'to see that Putois does not loaf or rob me. I risk nothing, and it will be all profit. These vagabonds sometimes do better work than honest laborers.' She resolved to make a trial, and said to my mother: 'Dearest, send me Putois. I will set him to work at Montplaisir.' My mother would have done so willingly. But really it was impossible. Madame Cornouiller waited for Putois at Montplaisir, and waited in vain. She followed up her ideas and did not abandon her plans. When she saw my mother again, she complained of not having any news of Putois. 'Dearest, didn't you tell him that I was expecting him?'—'Yes! but he is strange, odd.'—'Oh, I know that kind. I know your Putois by heart. But there is no workman so crazy as to refuse to come to work at Montplaisir. My house is known, I think. Putois must obey my orders, and quickly, dearest. It will be sufficient to tell me where he lives; I will go and find him myself.' My mother answered that she did not know where Putois lived, that no one knew his house, that he was without hearth or home. 'I have not seen him again, Madame. I believe he is hiding.' What better could she say?

Madame Cornouiller heard her distrustfully; she suspected her of misleading, of removing Putois from inquiry, for fear of losing him or making him ask more. And she thought her too selfish. Many judgments accepted by the world that history has sanctioned are as well founded as that." —"That is true," said Pauline.—"What is true?" asked Zoe, half asleep.—"That the judgments of history are often false. I remember, papa, that you said one day: 'Madame Roland was very ingenuous to appeal to the impartiality of posterity, and not perceive that, if her contemporaries were ill-natured monkeys, their posterity would be also composed of ill-natured monkeys.' "—"Pauline," said Mademoiselle Zoe severely, "what connection is there between the story of Putois and this that you are telling us?" —"A very great one, my aunt."—"I do not grasp it."—Monsieur Bergeret, who was not opposed to digressions, answered his daughter: "If all injustices were finally redressed in the world, one would never have imagined another for these adjustments. How do you expect posterity to pass righteous judgment on the dead? How question them in the shades to which they have taken flight? As soon as we are able to be just to them we forget them. But can one ever be just? And what is justice? Madame Cornouiller, at least, was finally obliged to recognize that my mother had not deceived her and that Putois was not to be found. However, she did not give up trying to find him. She asked all her relatives, friends, neighbors, servants, and tradesmen if they knew Putois. Only two or three answered that they had never heard of him. For the most part they believed they had seen him. 'I have heard that name,' said the cook, 'but I cannot recall his face.'—'Putois! I must know him,' said the street-sweeper, scratching his ear. 'But I cannot tell you who it is.' The most precise description came from Monsieur Blaise, receiver of taxes, who said that he had employed Putois to cut wood in his yard, from the 19th to the 23d of October, the year of the comet. One morning, Madame Cornouiller, out of breath, dropped into my father's office. 'I have seen Putois. Ah! I have seen him.'—'You believe it?'—'I am sure. He was passing close by Monsieur Tenchant's wall. Then he turned into the Rue des Abbesses, walking quickly. I lost him.'—'Was it really he?' —'Without a doubt. A man of fifty, thin, bent, the air of a vagabond, a dirty blouse.'—'It is true,' said my father, 'that this description could apply to Putois.'—'You see! Besides, I called him. I cried: "Putois!" and he turned around.'— 'That is the method,' said my father, 'that they employ to assure themselves of the identity of evil-doers that they are hunting for.'—'I told you that it was he! I know how to find him, your Putois. Very well! He has a bad face. You had been very careless, you and your wife, to employ him. I understand physiognomy, and though I only saw his back, I could swear that he is a robber, and perhaps an assassin. The rims of his ears are flat, and that is a sign that never fails.'—'Ah! you noticed that the rims of his ears were flat?'—'Nothing escapes me. My dear Monsieur Bergeret, if you do not wish to be assassinated with your wife and your children, do not let Putois come into your house again. Take my advice: have all your locks changed.'—Well, a few days afterward, it happened that Madame Cornouiller had three melons stolen from her vegetable garden. The robber not having been found, she suspected Putois. The gendarmes were called to Montplaisir, and their report confirmed the suspicions of Madame Cornouiller. Bands of marauders were ravaging the gardens of the countryside. But this time the robbery seemed to have been committed by one man, and with singular dexterity. No trace of anything broken, no footprints in the damp earth. The robber could be no one but Putois. That was the opinion of the corporal, who knew all about Putois, and had tried hard to put his hand on that bird. The 'Journal of Saint-Omer' devoted an article to the three melons of Madame Cornouiller, and published a portrait of Putois from descriptions furnished by the town. 'He has,' said the paper, 'a low forehead, squinting eyes, a shifty glance, crow's-feet, sharp cheek-bones, red and shining. No rims to the ears. Thin, somewhat bent, feeble in appearance, in reality he is unusually strong.

He easily bends a five-franc piece between the first finger and the thumb.' There were good reasons for attributing to him a long series of robberies committed with surprising dexterity. The whole town was talking of Putois. One day it was learned that he had been arrested and locked up in prison. But it was soon recognized that the man that had been taken for him was an almanac seller named Rigobert. As no charge could be brought against him, he was discharged after fourteen months of detention on suspicion. And Putois remained undiscoverable. Madame Cornouiller was the victim of another robbery, more audacious than the first. Three small silver spoons were taken from her sideboard. She recognized in this the hand of Putois, had a chain put on the door of her bedroom, and was unable to sleep." ...

About ten o'clock in the evening, Pauline having gone to her room, Mademoiselle Bergeret said to her brother: "Do not forget to relate how Putois betrayed Madame Cornouiller's cook."— "I was thinking of it, my sister," answered Monsieur Bergeret. "To omit it would be to lose the best of the story. But everything must be done in order. Putois was carefully searched for by the police, who could not find him. When it was known that he could not be found, each one considered it his duty to find him; the shrewd ones succeeded. And as there were many shrewd ones at Saint-Omer and in the suburbs, Putois was seen simultaneously in the streets, in the fields, and in the woods. Another trait was thus added to his character. He was accorded the gift of ubiquity, the attribute of many popular heroes. A being capable of leaping long distances in a moment, and suddenly showing himself at the place where he was least expected, was honestly frightening. Putois was the terror of Saint-Omer. Madame Cornouiller, convinced that Putois had stolen from her three melons and three little spoons, lived in a state of fear, barricaded at Montplaisir. Bolts, bars, and locks did not reassure her. Putois was for her a frightfully subtle being who could pass through doors. Trouble with her servants redoubled her fear. Her cook having been betrayed, the time came when she could no longer hide her misfortune. But she obstinately refused to name her betrayer."—"Her name was Gudule," said Mademoiselle Zoe.—"Her name was Gudule, and she believed that she was protected from danger by a long, forked beard that she wore on her chin. The sudden appearance of a beard protected the innocence of that holy daughter of the king that Prague venerates. A beard, no longer youthful, did not suffice to protect the virtue of Gudule. Madame Cornouiller urged Gudule to tell her the man. Gudule burst into tears, but kept silent. Prayers and menaces had no effect. Madame Cornouiller made a long and circumstantial inquiry. She adroitly questioned her neighbors and tradespeople, the gardener, the street-sweeper, the gendarmes; nothing put her on the track of the culprit. She tried again to obtain from Gudule a complete confession. 'In your own interest, Gudule, tell me who it is.' Gudule remained mute. All at once a ray of light flashed through the mind of Madame Cornouiller: 'It is Putois!' The cook cried, but did not answer. 'It is Putois! Why did I not guess it sooner? It is Putois! Miserable! miserable! miserable!' and Madame Cornouiller remained convinced that it was Putois. Everybody at Saint-Omer, from the judge to the lamplighter's dog, knew Gudule and her basket. At the news that Putois had betrayed Gudule, the town was filled with surprise, wonder, and merriment.... With this reputation in the town and its environs he remained attached to our house by a thousand subtle ties. He passed before our door, and it was believed that he sometimes climbed the wall of our garden. He was never seen face to face. At any moment we would recognize his shadow, his voice, his footsteps. More than once we thought we saw his back in the twilight, at the corner of a road. To my sister and me he gradually changed in character. He remained mischievous and malevolent, but he became childlike and very ingenuous. He became less real and, I dare say, more poetical. He entered in the artless cycle of childish traditions. He became more like Croquemitaine,[1]

[1] The national "bugaboo" or "bogy man."

like Père Fouettard, or the sand man who closes the children's eyes when evening comes. It was not that imp that tangled the colts' tails at night in the stable. Less rustic and less charming, but equally and frankly roguish, he made ink mustaches on my sister's dolls. In our bed, before going to sleep, we listened; he cried on the roofs with the cats, he howled with the dogs, he filled the mill hopper with groans, and imitated the songs of belated drunkards in the streets. What made Putois ever-present and familiar to us, what interested us in him, was that the remembrance of him was associated with all the objects about us. Zoe's dolls, my school books, in which he had many times rumpled and besmeared the pages; the garden wall, over which we had seen his red eyes gleam in the shadow; the blue porcelain jar that he cracked one winter's night, unless it was the frost; the trees, the streets, the benches—everything recalled Putois, the children's Putois, a local and mythical being. He did not equal in grace and poetry the dullest satyr, the stoutest fawn of Sicily or Thessaly. But he was still a demigod. He had quite a different character for our father; he was symbolical and philosophical. Our father had great compassion for men. He did not think them altogether rational; their mistakes, when they were not cruel, amused him and made him smile. The belief in Putois interested him as an epitome and a summary of all human beliefs. As he was ironical

and a joker, he spoke of Putois as if he were a
real being. He spoke with so much insistence
sometimes, and detailed the circumstances with
such exactness, that my mother was quite surprised and said to him in her open-hearted way:
'One would say that you spoke seriously, my
friend: you know well, however . . .' He replied
gravely: 'All Saint-Omer believes in the existence
of Putois. Would I be a good citizen if I deny
him? One should look twice before setting aside
an article of common faith.' Only a perfectly
honest soul has such scruples. At heart my father
was a Gassendiste.[2] He keyed his own particular sentiment with the public sentiment, believing, like the countryside, in the existence of Putois, but not admitting his direct responsibility
for the theft of the melons and the betrayal of
the cook. Finally, he professed faith in the existence of a Putois, to be a good citizen; and he
eliminated Putois in his explanations of the
events that took place in the town. By doing so
in this instance, as in all others, he was an honorable and a sensible man.

"As for our mother, she reproached herself
somewhat for the birth of Putois, and not without reason. Because, after all, Putois was the
child of our mother's invention, as Caliban was
the poet's invention. Without doubt the faults
were not equal, and my mother was more innocent than Shakespeare. However, she was fright-

[2] A follower of Gassendi (d. 1655), an exponent of Epicurus

ened and confused to see her little falsehood grow inordinately, and her slight imposture achieve such a prodigious success, that, without stopping, extended all over town and threatened to extend over the world. One day she even turned pale, believing that she would see her falsehood rise up before her. That day, a servant she had, new to the house and the town, came to say to her that a man wished to see her. He wished to speak to Madame. 'What man is it?' —'A man in a blouse. He looks like a laborer.'— 'Did he give his name?'—'Yes, Madame.'— 'Well! what is his name?'—'Putois.'—'He told you that was his name?'—'Putois, yes, Madame.' —'He is here?'—'Yes, Madame. He is waiting in the kitchen.'—'You saw him?'—'Yes, Madame.'—'What does he want?'—'He did not say. He will only tell Madame.'—'Go ask him.'

"When the servant returned to the kitchen Putois was gone. This meeting of the new servant with Putois was never cleared up. But from that day I think my mother commenced to believe that Putois might well exist and that she had not told a falsehood after all."

THE COURTING OF T'NOW HEAD'S BELL

BY JAMES MATTHEW BARRIE

THE COURTING OF T'NOW-
HEAD'S BELL

BY JAMES MATTHEW BARRIE

FOR two years it had been notorious in the
square that Sam'l Dickie was thinking
of courting T'nowhead's Bell, and that if
little Sanders Elshioner (which is the Thrums
pronunciation of Alexander Alexander) went in
for her, he might prove a formidable rival. Sam'l
was a weaver in the Tenements, and Sanders a
coal-carter whose trade-mark was a bell on his
horse's neck that told when coals were coming.
Being something of a public man, Sanders had
not, perhaps, so high a social position as Sam'l,
but he had succeeded his father on the coal-cart,
while the weaver had already tried several trades.
It had always been against Sam'l, too, that once
when the kirk was vacant he had advised the selection of the third minister who preached for it,
on the ground that it came expensive to pay a
large number of candidates. The scandal of the
thing was hushed up, out of respect for his father,
who was a God-fearing man, but Sam'l was
known by it in Lang Tammas's circle. The coal-
carter was called Little Sanders, to distinguish
him from his father, who was not much more than
half his size. He had grown up with the name,

and its inapplicability now came home to nobody.
Sam'l's mother had been more far-seeing than
Sanders'. Her man had been called Sammy all
his life, because it was the name he got as a boy,
so when their eldest son was born she spoke of
him as Sam'l while still in his cradle. The neighbors imitated her, and thus the young man had a
better start in life than had been granted to
Sammy, his father.

It was Saturday evening — the night in the
week when Auld Licht young men fell in love.
Sam'l Dickie, wearing a blue Glengarry bonnet
with a red ball on the top, came to the door of a
one-story house in the Tenements, and stood there
wriggling, for he was in a suit of tweed for the
first time that week, and did not feel at one with
them. When his feeling of being a stranger to
himself wore off, he looked up and down the
road, which straggles between houses and gardens, and then, picking his way over the puddles,
crossed to his father's hen-house and sat down on
it. He was now on his way to the square.

Eppie Fargus was sitting on an adjoining dike,
knitting stockings, and Sam'l looked at her for a
time.

"Is't yersel', Eppie?" he said at last.

"It's a' that," said Eppie.

"Hoo's a' wi' ye?" asked Sam'l.

"We're juist aff an' on," replied Eppie, cautiously.

There was not much more to say, but as Sam'l

sidled off the hen-house, he murmured politely: "Ay, ay." In another minute he would have been fairly started, but Eppie resumed the conversation.

"Sam'l," she said, with a twinkle in her eye, "ye can tell Lisbeth Fargus I'll likely be drappin' in on her aboot Munday or Teisday."

Lisbeth was sister to Eppie, and wife of Tammas McQuhatty, better known as T'nowhead, which was the name of his farm. She was thus Bell's mistress.

Sam'l leaned against the hen-house, as if all his desire to depart had gone.

"Hoo'd 'ye kin I'll be at the T'nowhead the nicht?" he asked, grinning in anticipation.

"Ou, I'se warrant ye'll be after Bell," said Eppie.

"A'm no sae sure o' that," said Sam'l, trying to leer. He was enjoying himself now.

"A'm no sure o' that," he repeated, for Eppie seemed lost in stitches.

"Sam'l?"

"Ay."

"Ye'll be speirin' her sune noo, I dinna doot?"

This took Sam'l, who had only been courting Bell for a year or two, a little aback.

"Hoo d'ye mean, Eppie?" he asked.

"Maybe ye'll do't the nicht?"

"Na, there's nae hurry," said Sam'l.

"Weel, we're a' coontin' on't, Sam'l."

"Gae wa wi' ye."

"What for no?"

"Gae wa wi' ye," said Sam'l again.

"Bell's gei an' fond o' ye, Sam'l."

"Ay," said Sam'l.

"But am dootin' ye're a fellbilly wi' the lasses."

"Ay, oh, I d'na kin, moderate, moderate," said Sam'l, in high delight.

"I saw ye," said Eppie, speaking with a wire in her mouth, "gaen on terr'ble wi' Mysy Haggart at the pump last Saturday."

"We was juist amoosin' oorsels," said Sam'l.

"It'll be nae amoosement to Mysy," said Eppie, "gin ye brak her heart."

"Losh, Eppie," said Sam'l, "I didna think o' that."

"Ye maun kin weel, Sam'l, 'at there's mony a lass wid jump at ye."

"Ou, weel," said Sam'l, implying that a man must take these things as they come.

"For ye're a dainty child to look at, Sam'l."

"Do ye think so, Eppie? Ay, ay; oh, I d'na kin A'm anything by the ordinar."

"Ye mayna be," said Eppie, "but lasses doesna do to be ower partikler."

Sam'l resented this, and prepared to depart again.

"Ye'll no tell Bell that?" he asked, anxiously.

"Tell her what?"

"Aboot me an' Mysy."

'We'll see hoo ye behave yerself, Sam'l."

"No 'at I care, Eppie; ye can tell her gin ye like. I widna think twice o' tellin' her mysel'."

"The Lord forgie ye for leein', Sam'l," said Eppie, as he disappeared down Tammy Tosh's close. Here he came upon Henders Webster.

"Ye're late, Sam'l," said Henders.

"What for?"

"Ou, I was thinkin' ye wid be gaen the length o' T'nowhead the nicht, an' I saw Sanders Elshioner makkin's wy there an oor syne."

"Did ye?" cried Sam'l, adding craftily; "but it's naething to me."

"Tod, lad," said Henders; "gin ye dinna buckle to, Sanders'll be carryin' her off!"

Sam'l flung back his head and passed on.

"Sam'l!" cried Henders after him.

"Ay," said Sam'l, wheeling round.

"Gie Bell a kiss frae me."

The full force of this joke struck neither all at once. Sam'l began to smile at it as he turned down the school-wynd, and it came upon Henders while he was in his garden feeding his ferret. Then he slapped his legs gleefully, and explained the conceit to Will'um Byars, who went into the house and thought it over.

There were twelve or twenty little groups of men in the square, which was lighted by a flare of oil suspended over a cadger's cart. Now and again a staid young woman passed through the square with a basket on her arm, and if she had lingered long enough to give them time, some of the idlers would have addressed her. As it was, they gazed after her, and then grinned to each other.

"Ay, Sam'l," said two or three young men, as Sam'l joined them beneath the town clock.

"Ay, Davit," replied Sam'l.

This group was composed of some of the sharpest wits in Thrums, and it was not to be expected that they would let this opportunity pass. Perhaps when Sam'l joined them he knew what was in store for him.

"Was ye lookin' for T'nowhead's Bell?" asked one.

"Or mebbe ye was wantin' the minister?" suggested another, the same who had walked out twice with Christy Duff and not married her after all.

Sam'l could not think of a good reply at the moment, so he laughed good-naturedly.

"Ondoobtedly she's a snod bit crittur," said Davit, archly.

"An' michty clever wi' her fingers," added Jamie Deuchars.

"Man, I've thocht o' makkin' up to Bell myself," said Pete Ogle. "Wid there be ony chance, think ye, Sam'l?"

"I'm thinkin' she widna hae ye for her first, Pete," replied Sam'l, in one of those happy flashes that come to some men, "but there's nae sayin' but what she micht tak ye to finish up wi'."

The unexpectedness of this sally startled every

one. Sam'l did not set up for a wit, though, like Davit, it was notorious that he could say a cutting thing once in a way.

"Did ye ever see Bell reddin up?" asked Pete, recovering from his overthrow. He was a man who bore no malice.

"It's a sicht," said Sam'l, solemnly.

"Hoo will that be?" asked Jamie Deuchars.

"It's weel worth yer while," said Pete, "to ging atower to the T'nowhead an' see. Ye'll mind the closed-in beds i' the kitchen? Ay, weel, they're a fell spoilt crew, T'nowhead's litlins, an' no that aisy to manage. Th' ither lasses Lisbeth's hae'n had a michty trouble wi' them. When they war i' the middle o' their reddin up the bairns wid come tumlin' about the floor. but, sal, I assure ye, Bell didna fash lang wi' them. Did she, Sam'l?"

"She did not," said Sam'l, dropping into a fine mode of speech to add emphasis to his remark.

"I'll tell ye what she did," said Pete to the others. "She juist lifted up the litlins, twa at a time, an' flung them into the coffin-beds. Syne she snibbit the doors on them, an' keepit them there till the floor was dry."

"Ay, man, did she so?" said Davit, admiringly.

"I've seen her do't myself," said Sam'l.

"There's no a lassie maks better bannocks this side o' Fetter Lums," continued Pete.

"Her mither tocht her that," said Sam'l; "she was a gran' han' at the bakin', Kitty Ogilvy."

"I've heard say," remarked Jamie, putting it

193

this way so as not to tie himself down to anything,
" 'at Bell's scones is equal to Mag Lunan's."

"So they are," said Sam'l, almost fiercely.

"I kin she's a neat han' at singein' a hen," said
Pete.

"An' wi't a'," said Davit, "she's a snod, canty
bit stocky in her Sabbath claes."

"If onything, thick in the waist," suggested
Jamie.

"I dinna see that," said Sam'l.

"I d'na care for her hair either," continued
Jamie, who was very nice in his tastes; "something mair yallowchy wid be an improvement."

"A'body kins," growled Sam'l, " 'at black hair's
the bonniest."

The others chuckled.

"Puir Sam'l!" Pete said.

Sam'l, not being certain whether this should be
received with a smile or a frown, opened his
mouth wide as a kind of compromise. This was
position one with him for thinking things over.

Few Auld Lichts, as I have said, went the
length of choosing a helpmate for themselves.
One day a young man's friends would see him
mending the washing-tub of a maiden's mother.
They kept the joke until Saturday night, and
then he learned from them what he had been after.
It dazed him for a time, but in a year or so he
grew accustomed to the idea, and they were then
married. With a little help, he fell in love just
like other people.

T'NOWHEAD'S BELL

Sam'l was going the way of others, but he found it difficult to come to the point. He only went courting once a week, and he could never take up the running at the place where he left off the Saturday before. Thus he had not, so far, made great headway. His method of making up to Bell had been to drop in at T'nowhead on Saturday nights and talk with the farmer about the rinderpest.

The farm kitchen was Bell's testimonial. Its chairs, tables, and stools were scoured by her to the whiteness of Rob Angus's saw-mill boards, and the muslin blind on the window was starched like a child's pinafore. Bell was brave, too, as well as energetic. Once Thrums had been over-run with thieves. It is now thought that there may have been only one; but he had the wicked cleverness of a gang. Such was his repute, that there were weavers who spoke of locking their doors when they went from home. He was not very skilful, however, being generally caught, and when they said they knew he was a robber he gave them their things back and went away. If they had given him time there is no doubt that he would have gone off with his plunder. One night he went to T'nowhead, and Bell, who slept in the kitchen, was wakened by the noise. She knew who it would be, so she rose and dressed herself, and went to look for him with a candle. The thief had not known what to do when he got in, and as it was very lonely, he was glad to see

Bell. She told him he ought to be ashamed of himself, and would not let him out by the door until he had taken off his boots, so as not to soil the carpet.

On this Saturday evening Sam'l stood his ground in the square, until by and by he found himself alone. There were other groups there still, but his circle had melted away. They went separately, and no one said good-night. Each took himself off slowly, backing out of the group until he was fairly started.

Sam'l looked about him, and then, seeing that the others had gone, walked round the town-house into the darkness of the brae that leads down and then up to the farm of T'nowhead.

To get into the good graces of Lisbeth Fargus you had to know her ways and humor them. Sam'l, who was a student of women, knew this, and so, instead of pushing the door open and walking in, he went through the rather ridiculous ceremony of knocking. Sanders Elshioner was also aware of this weakness of Lisbeth, but, though he often made up his mind to knock, the absurdity of the thing prevented his doing so when he reached the door. T'nowhead himself had never got used to his wife's refined notions, and when any one knocked he always started to his feet, thinking there must be something wrong.

Lisbeth came to the door, her expansive figure blocking the way in.

"Sam'l," she said.

"Lisbeth," said Sam'l.

He shook hands with the farmer's wife, knowing that she liked it, but only said: "Ay, Bell," to his sweetheart, "Ay, T'nowhead," to McQuhatty, and "It's yersel', Sanders," to his rival.

They were all sitting round the fire, T'nowhead, with his feet on the ribs, wondering why he felt so warm, and Bell darned a stocking, while Lisbeth kept an eye on a goblet full of potatoes.

"Sit in to the fire, Sam'l," said the farmer, not, however, making way for him.

"Na, na," said Sam'l, "I'm to bide nae time." Then he sat in to the fire. His face was turned away from Bell, and when she spoke he answered her without looking round. Sam'l felt a little anxious. Sanders Elshioner, who had one leg shorter than the other, but looked well when sitting, seemed suspiciously at home. He asked Bell questions out of his own head, which was beyond Sam'l, and once he said something to her in such a low voice that the others could not catch it. T'nowhead asked curiously what it was, and Sanders explained that he had only said: "Ay, Bell, the morn's the Sabbath." There was nothing startling in this, but Sam'l did not like it. He began to wonder if he was too late, and had he seen his opportunity, would have told Bell of a nasty rumor that Sanders intended to go over to the Free Church if they would make him kirk-officer.

Sam'l had the good-will of T'nowhead's wife,

who liked a polite man. Sanders did his best, but from want of practise he constantly made mistakes. To-night, for instance, he wore his hat in the house, because he did not like to put up his hand and take it off. T'nowhead had not taken his off either, but that was because he meant to go out by and by and lock the byre door. It was impossible to say which of her lovers Bell preferred. The proper course with an Auld Licht lassie was to prefer the man who proposed to her.

"Ye'll bide a wee, an' hae something to eat?" Lisbeth asked Sam'l, with her eyes on the goblet.

"No, I thank ye," said Sam'l, with true gentility.

"Ye'll better?"

"I dinna think it."

"Hoots, ay; what's to hender ye?"

"Weel, since ye're sae pressin', I'll bide."

No one asked Sanders to stay. Bell could not, for she was but the servant, and T'nowhead knew that the kick his wife had given him meant that he was not to do so either. Sanders whistled to show that he was not uncomfortable.

"Ay, then, I'll be stappin' ower the brae," he said at last.

He did not go, however. There was sufficient pride in him to get him off his chair, but only slowly, for he had to get accustomed to the notion of going. At intervals of two or three minutes he remarked that he must now be going. In the same circumstances Sam'l would have acted similarly. For a Thrums man it is one of the hardest things in life to get away from anywhere.

At last Lisbeth saw that something must be done. The potatoes were burning, and T'nowhead had an invitation on his tongue.

"Yes, I'll hae to be movin'," said Sanders, hopelessly, for the fifth time.

"Guid-nicht to ye, then, Sanders," said Lisbeth. "Gie the door a fling-to ahent ye."

Sanders, with a mighty effort, pulled himself together. He looked boldly at Bell, and then took off his hat carefully. Sam'l saw with misgivings that there was something in it which was not a handkerchief. It was a paper bag glittering with gold braid, and contained such an assortment of sweets as lads bought for their lasses on the Muckle Friday.

"Hae, Bell," said Sanders, handing the bag to Bell in an off-hand way, as if it were but a trifle. Nevertheless, he was a little excited, for he went off without saying good-night.

No one spoke. Bell's face was crimson. T'nowhead fidgeted on his chair, and Lisbeth looked at Sam'l. The weaver was strangely calm and collected, though he would have liked to know whether this was a proposal.

"Sit in by to the table, Sam'l," said Lisbeth, trying to look as if things were as they had been before.

She put a saucerful of butter, salt, and pepper near the fire to melt, for melted butter is the shoeing-horn that helps over a meal of potatoes. Sam'l, however, saw what the hour required, and, jumping up, he seized his bonnet.

"Hing the tatties higher up the joist, Lisbeth," he said, with dignity; "I'se be back in ten meenits."

He hurried out of the house, leaving the others looking at each other.

"What do ye think?" asked Lisbeth.

"I d'na kin," faltered Bell.

"Thae tatties is lang o' comin' to the boil," said T'nowhead.

In some circles a lover who behaved like Sam'l would have been suspected of intent upon his rival's life, but neither Bell nor Lisbeth did the weaver that injustice. In a case of this kind it does not much matter what T'nowhead thought.

The ten minutes had barely passed when Sam'l was back in the farm kitchen. He was too flurried to knock this time, and, indeed, Lisbeth did not expect it of him.

"Bell, hae!" he cried, handing his sweetheart a tinsel bag twice the size of Sanders's gift.

"Losh preserve's!" exclaimed Lisbeth; "I'se warrant there's a shillin's worth."

"There's a' that, Lisbeth—an' mair," said Sam'l, firmly.

"I thank ye, Sam'l," said Bell, feeling an unwonted elation as she gazed at the two paper bags in her lap.

"Ye're ower extravegint, Sam'l," Lisbeth said.

"Not at all," said Sam'l; "not at all. But I wouldna advise ye to eat thae ither anes, Bell—they're second quality."

Bell drew back a step from Sam'l.

"How do ye kin?" asked the farmer, shortly; for he liked Sanders.

"I speired i' the shop," said Sam'l.

The goblet was placed on a broken plate on the table, with the saucer beside it, and Sam'l, like the others, helped himself. What he did was to take potatoes from the pot with his fingers, peel off their coats, and then dip them into the butter. Lisbeth would have liked to provide knives and forks, but she knew that beyond a certain point T'nowhead was master in his own house. As for Sam'l, he felt victory in his hands, and began to think that he had gone too far.

In the meantime, Sanders, little witting that Sam'l had trumped his trick, was sauntering along the kirk-wynd with his hat on the side of his head. Fortunately he did not meet the minister.

The courting of T'nowhead's Bell reached its crisis one Sabbath about a month after the events above recorded. The minister was in great force that day, but it is no part of mine to tell how he bore himself. I was there, and am not likely to forget the scene. It was a fateful Sabbath for T'nowhead's Bell and her swains, and destined to be remembered for the painful scandal which they perpetrated in their passion.

Bell was not in the kirk. There being an infant of six months in the house, it was a question of either Lisbeth or the lassie's staying at home with him, and though Lisbeth was unselfish in a general way, she could not resist the delight of going to church. She had nine children besides the baby, and being but a woman, it was the pride of her life to march them into the T'nowhead pew, so well watched that they dared not misbehave, and so tightly packed that they could not fall. The congregation looked at that pew, the mother enviously, when they sang the lines:

> " Jerusalem like a city is
> Compactly built together."

The first half of the service had been gone through on this particular Sunday without anything remarkable happening. It was at the end of the psalm which preceded the sermon that Sanders Elshioner, who sat near the door, lowered his head until it was no higher than the pews, and in that attitude, looking almost like a four-footed animal, slipped out of the church. In their eagerness to be at the sermon, many of the congregation did not notice him, and those who did put the matter by in their minds for future investigation. Sam'l, however, could not take it so coolly. From his seat in the gallery he saw Sanders disappear, and his mind misgave him.

With the true lover's instinct, he understood it
all. Sanders had been struck by the fine turn-
out in the T'nowhead pew. Bell was alone at the
farm. What an opportunity to work one's way
up to a proposal. T'nowhead was so overrun
with children that such a chance seldom occurred,
except on a Sabbath. Sanders, doubtless, was off
to propose, and he, Sam'l, was left behind.

The suspense was terrible. Sam'l and Sanders
had both known all along that Bell would take
the first of the two who asked her. Even those
who thought her proud admitted that she was
modest. Bitterly the weaver repented having
waited so long. Now it was too late. In ten
minutes Sanders would be at T'nowhead; in an
hour all would be over. Sam'l rose to his feet in
a daze. His mother pulled him down by the coat-
tail, and his father shook him, thinking he was
walking in his sleep. He tottered past them,
however, hurried up the aisle, which was so narrow that Dan'l Ross could only reach his seat by
walking sidewise, and was gone before the minister could do more than stop in the middle of a
whirl and gape in horror after him.

A number of the congregation felt that day
the advantage of sitting in the laft. What was a
mystery to those downstairs was revealed to them.
From the gallery windows they had a fine open
view to the south, and as Sam'l took the common,
which was a short cut, though a steep ascent, to
T'nowhead, he was never out of their line of

vision. Sanders was not to be seen, but they guessed rightly the reason why. Thinking he had ample time, he had gone round by the main road to save his boots—perhaps a little scared by what was coming. Sam'l's design was to forestall him by taking the shorter path over the burn and up the commonty.

It was a race for a wife, and several onlookers in the gallery braved the minister's displeasure to see who won. Those who favored Sam'l's suit exultingly saw him leap the stream, while the friends of Sanders fixed their eyes on the top of the common where it ran into the road. Sanders must come into sight there, and the one who reached this point first would get Bell.

As Auld Lichts do not walk abroad on the Sabbath, Sanders would probably not be delayed. The chances were in his favor. Had it been any other day in the week, Sam'l might have run. So some of the congregation in the gallery were thinking, when suddenly they saw him bend low and then take to his heels. He had caught sight of Sanders's head bobbing over the hedge that separated the road from the common, and feared that Sanders might see him. The congregation who could crane their necks sufficiently saw a black object, which they guessed to be the carter's hat, crawling along the hedge-top. For a moment it was motionless, and then it shot ahead. The rivals had seen each other. It was now a hot race. Sam'l, dissembling no longer, clattered up the common, becoming smaller and smaller to the onlookers as he neared the top. More than one person in the gallery almost rose to their feet in their excitement. Sam'l had it. No. Sanders was in front. Then the two figures disappeared from view. They seemed to run into each other at the top of the brae, and no one could say who was first. The congregation looked at one another. Some of them perspired. But the minister held on his course.

Sam'l had just been in time to cut Sanders out. It was the weaver's saying that Sanders saw this when his rival turned the corner; for Sam'l was sadly blown. Sanders took in the situation and gave in at once. The last hundred yards of the distance he covered at his leisure, and when he arrived at his destination he did not go in. It was a fine afternoon for the time of year, and he went round to have a look at the pig, about which T'nowhead was a little sinfully puffed up.

"Ay," said Sanders, digging his fingers critically into the grunting animal; "quite so."

"Grumph!" said the pig, getting reluctantly to his feet.

"Ou, ay; yes," said Sanders, thoughtfully.

Then he sat down on the edge of the sty, and looked long and silently at an empty bucket. But whether his thoughts were of T'nowhead's Bell, whom he had lost forever, or of the food the farmer fed his pig on, is not known.

"Lord preserve's! Are ye no at the kirk?"

cried Bell, nearly dropping the baby as Sam'l broke into the room.

"Bell!" cried Sam'l.

Then T'nowhead's Bell knew that her hour had come.

"Sam'l," she faltered.

"Will ye hae's, Bell?" demanded Sam'l, glaring at her sheepishly.

"Ay," answered Bell.

Sam'l fell into a chair.

"Bring's a drink o' water, Bell," he said.

But Bell thought the occasion required milk, and there was none in the kitchen. She went out to the byre, still with the baby in her arms, and saw Sanders Elshioner sitting gloomily on the pig-sty.

"Weel, Bell?" said Sanders.

"I thocht ye'd been at the kirk, Sanders," said Bell.

Then there was a silence between them.

"Has Sam'l speired ye, Bell?" asked Sanders stolidly.

"Ay," said Bell again, and this time there was a tear in her eye. Sanders was little better than an "orro man," and Sam'l was a weaver, and yet —but it was too late now. Sanders gave the pig a vicious poke with a stick, and when it had ceased to grunt, Bell was back in the kitchen. She had forgotten about the milk, however, and Sam'l only got water after all.

In after days, when the story of Bell's wooing

was told, there were some who held that the circumstances would have almost justified the lassie
in giving Sam'l the go-by. But these perhaps
forgot that her other lover was in the same predicament as the accepted one—that, of the two,
indeed, he was the more to blame, for he set off to
T'nowhead on the Sabbath of his own accord,
while Sam'l only ran after him. And then there
is no one to say for certain whether Bell heard of
her suitor's delinquencies until Lisbeth's return
from the kirk. Sam'l could never remember
whether he told her, and Bell was not sure
whether, if he did, she took it in. Sanders was
greatly in demand for weeks after to tell what he
knew of the affair, but though he was twice asked
to tea to the manse among the trees, and subjected thereafter to ministerial cross-examina-
tions, this is all he told. He remained at the pig-
sty until Sam'l left the farm, when he joined him
at the top of the brae, and they went home together.

"It's yersel', Sanders," said Sam'l.

"It is so, Sam'l," said Sanders.

"Very cauld," said Sam'l.

"Blawy," assented Sanders.

After a pause:

"Sam'l," said Sanders.

"Ay."

"I'm hearin' yer to be mairit."

"Ay."

"Weel, Sam'l, she's a snod bit lassie."

"Thank ye," said Sam'l.

"I had ance a kin' o' notion o' Bell mysel'," continued Sanders.

"Ye nad?"

"Yes, Sam'l; but I thocht better o't."

"Hoo d'ye mean?" asked Sam'l, a little anxiously.

"Weel, Sam'l, mairitch is a terrible responsibeelity."

"It is so," said Sam'l, wincing.

"An' no the thing to tak up withoot conseederation."

'But it's a blessed and honorable state, Sanders; ye've heard the minister on't."

"They say," continued the relentless Sanders, " 'at the minister doesna get on sa weel wi' the wife himsel'."

"So they do," cried Sam'l, with a sinking at the heart.

"I've been telt," Sanders went on, " 'at gin you can get the upper han' o' the wife for a while at first, there's the mair chance o' a harmonious exeestence."

"Bell's no the lassie," said Sam'l, appealingly, "to thwart her man."

Sanders smiled.

"D'ye think she is, Sanders?"

"Weel, Sam'l, I d'na want to fluster ye, but she's been ower lang wi' Lisbeth Fargus no to ha' learnt her ways. An' a'body kins what a life T'nowhead has wi' her."

"Guid sake, Sanders, hoo did ye no speak o' this afoore?"

"I thocht ye kent o't, Sam'l."

They had now reached the square, and the U. P. kirk was coming out. The Auld Licht kirk would be half an hour yet.

"But, Sanders," said Sam'l, brightening up, "ye was on yer way to speir her yersel'."

"I was, Sam'l," said Sanders, "and I canna but be thankfu' ye was ower quick for's."

"Gin't hadna been you," said Sam'l, "I wid never hae thocht o't."

"I'm sayin' naething agin Bell," pursued the other, "but, man Sam'l, a body should be mair deleeberate in a thing o' the kind."

"It was michty hurried," said Sam'l, wofully.

"It's a serious thing to speir a lassie," said Sanders.

"It's an awfu' thing," said Sam'l.

"But we'll hope for the best," added Sanders, in a hopeless voice.

They were close to the Tenements now, and Sam'l looked as if he were on his way to be hanged.

"Sam'l?"

"Ay, Sanders."

"Did ye—did ye kiss her, Sam'l?"

"Na."

"Hoo?"

"There's was vara little time, Sanders."

"Half an' 'oor," said Sanders.

"Was there? Man, Sanders, to tell ye the truth, I never thocht o't."

Then the soul of Elshioner was filled with contempt for Sam'l Dickie.

The scandal blew over. At first it was expected that the minister would interfere to prevent the union, but beyond intimating from the pulpit that the souls of Sabbath-breakers were beyond praying for, and then praying for Sam'l and Sanders at great length, with a word thrown in for Bell, he let things take their course. Some said it was because he was always frightened lest his young men should intermarry with other denominations, but Sanders explained it differently to Sam'l.

"I hav'na a word to say agin the minister," he said; "they're gran' prayers, but, Sam'l, he's a mairit man himsel'."

"He's a' the better for that, Sanders, isna he?"

"Do ye no see," asked Sanders, compassionately, " 'at he's tryin' to mak the best o't?"

"Oh, Sanders, man!" said Sam'l.

"Cheer up, Sam'l," said Sanders; "it'll sune be ower."

Their having been rival suitors had not interfered with their friendship. On the contrary, while they had hitherto been mere acquaintances they became inseparables as the wedding-day drew near. It was noticed that they had much to say to each other, and that when they could not get a room to themselves they wandered about together in the churchyard.

When Sam'l had anything to tell Bell, he sent Sanders to tell it, and Sanders did as he was bid. There was nothing that he would not have done for Sam'l.

The more obliging Sanders was, however, the sadder Sam'l grew. He never laughed now on Saturdays, and sometimes his loom was silent half the day. Sam'l felt that Sanders's was the kindness of a friend for a dying man.

It was to be a penny wedding, and Lisbeth Fargus said it was delicacy that made Sam'l superintend the fitting-up of the barn by deputy. Once he came to see it in person, but he looked so ill that Sanders had to see him home. This was on the Thursday afternoon, and the wedding was fixed for Friday.

"Sanders, Sanders!" said Sam'l, in a voice strangely unlike his own, "it'll a' be ower by this time the morn."

"It will," said Sanders.

"If I had only kent her langer," continued Sam'l.

"It wid hae been safer," said Sanders.

"Did ye see the yellow floor in Bell's bonnet?" asked the accepted swain.

"Ay," said Sanders, reluctantly.

"I'm dootin'—I'm sair dootin' she's but a flichty, licht-hearted critter, after a'."

"I had aye my suspeecions o't," said Sanders.

"Ye hae kent her langer than me," said Sam'l.

"Yes," said Sanders; "but there's nae gettin' at the heart o' women. Man Sam'l, they're desperate cunnin'."

"I'm dootin't; I'm sair dootin't."

"It'll be a warnin' to ye, Sam'l, no to be in sic a hurry i' the futur," said Sanders.

Sam'l groaned.

"Ye'll be gaein' up to the manse to arrange wi' the minister the morn's mornin'," continued Sanders, in a subdued voice.

Sam'l looked wistfully at his friend.

"I canna do't, Sanders," he said, "I canna do't."

"Ye maun," said Sanders.

"It's aisy to speak," retorted Sam'l, bitterly.

"We have a' oor troubles, Sam'l," said Sanders, soothingly, "an' every man maun bear his ain burdens. Johnny Davie's wife's dead, an' he's no repinin'."

"Ay," said Sam'l; "but a death's no mairitch. We hae haen deaths in our family too."

"It may a' be for the best," added Sanders, "an' there wid be a michty talk i' the hale countryside gin ye didna ging to the minister like a man."

"I maun hae langer to think o't," said Sam'l.

"Bell's mairitch is the morn," said Sanders, decisively.

Sam'l glanced up with a wild look in his eyes.

"Sanders!" he cried.

"Sam'l?"

"Ye hae been a guid friend to me, Sanders, in this sair affliction."

"Nothing ava," said Sanders; "doun't mention't."

"But, Sanders, ye canna deny but what your rinnin oot o' the kirk that awfu' day was at the bottom o't a'."

"It was so," said Sanders, bravely.

"An' ye used to be fond o' Bell, Sanders."

"I dinna deny't."

"Sanders, laddie," said Sam'l, bending forward and speaking in a wheedling voice. "I aye thocht it was you she likeit."

"I had some sic idea mysel'," said Sanders.

"Sanders, I canna think to pairt two fowk sae weel suited to ane anither as you an' Bell."

"Canna ye, Sam'l?"

"She wid mak ye a guid wife, Sanders. I hae studied her weel, and she's a thrifty, douce, clever lassie. Sanders, there's no the like o' her. Mony a time, Sanders, I hae said to mysel', 'There a lass ony man micht be prood to tak. A'body says the same, Sanders. There's nae risk ava, man; nane to speak o'. Tak her, laddie, tak her, Sanders; it's a grand chance, Sanders. She's yours for the speirin'. I'll gie her up, Sanders."

"Will ye, though?" said Sanders.

"What d'ye think?" asked Sam'l.

"If ye wid rayther," said Sanders, politely.

"There's my han' on't," said Sam'l. "Bless ye, Sanders; ye've been a true frien' to me."

Then they shook hands for the first time in their lives; and soon afterward Sanders struck up the brae to T'nowhead.

Next morning Sanders Elshioner, who had been very busy the night before, put on his Sabbath clothes and strolled up to the manse.

"But—but where is Sam'l?" asked the minister. "I must see himself."

"It's a new arrangement," said Sanders.

"What do you mean, Sanders?"

"Bell's to marry me," explained Sanders.

"But—but what does Sam'l say?"

"He's willin'," said Sanders.

"And Bell?"

"She's willin', too. She prefers it."

"It is unusual," said the minister.

"It's a' richt," said Sanders.

"Well, you know best," said the minister.

"You see, the house was taen, at ony rate," continued Sanders. "An' I'll juist ging in til't instead o' Sam'l."

"Quite so."

"An' I cudna think to disappoint the lassie."

"Your sentiments do you credit, Sanders," said the minister, "but I hope you do not enter upon the blessed state of matrimony without full consideration of its responsibilities. It is a serious business, marriage."

"It's a' that," said Sanders; "but I'm willin' to stan' the risk."

So, as soon as it could be done, Sanders Elshioner took to wife T'nowhead's Bell, and I remember seeing Sam'l Dickie trying to dance at the penny wedding.

Years afterward it was said in Thrums that Sam'l had treated Bell badly, but he was never sure about it himself.

"It was a near thing—a michty near thing," he admitted in the square.

"They say," some other weaver would remark, " 'at it was you Bell liked best."

"I d'na kin," Sam'l would reply, "but there's nae doot the lassie was fell fond o' me. Ou, a mere passin' fancy's ye micht say."

THE ROLL-CALL OF THE REEF

BY A. T. QUILLER-COUCH ("Q.")

THE ROLL-CALL OF THE REEF

BY A. T. QUILLER-COUCH ("Q.")

"YES, sir," said my host, the quarryman, reaching down the relics from their hook in the wall over the chimneypiece; "they've hung here all my time, and most of my father's. The women won't touch 'em; they're afraid of the story. So here they'll dangle, and gather dust and smoke, till another tenant comes and tosses 'em out o' doors for rubbish. Whew! 'tis coarse weather, surely."

He went to the door, opened it, and stood studying the gale that beat upon his cottage-front, straight from the Manacle Reef. The rain drove past him into the kitchen, aslant like threads of gold silk in the shine of the wreck-wood fire. Meanwhile, by the same firelight, I examined the relics on my knee. The metal of each was tarnished out of knowledge. But the trumpet was evidently an old cavalry trumpet, and the threads of its party-colored sling, though fretted and dusty, still hung together. Around the side-drum, beneath its cracked brown varnish, I could hardly trace a royal coat-of-arms and a legend running, "Per Mare Per Terram"—the motto of the marines. Its parchment, though black and scented with wood-smoke, was limp and mildewed; and I began to tighten up the straps—under which the drumsticks had been loosely thrust—with the idle purpose of trying if some music might be got out of the old drum yet.

But as I turned it on my knee, I found the drum attached to the trumpet-sling by a curious barrel-shaped padlock, and paused to examine this. The body of the lock was composed of half a dozen brass rings, set accurately edge to edge; and, rubbing the brass with my thumb, I saw that each of the six had a series of letters engraved around it.

I knew the trick of it, I thought. Here was one of those word padlocks, once so common; only to be opened by getting the rings to spell a certain word, which the dealer confides to you.

My host shut and barred the door, and came back to the hearth.

" 'Twas just such a wind—east by south—that brought in what you've got between your hands. Back in the year 'nine, it was; my father has told me the tale a score o' times. You're twisting round the rings, I see. But you'll never guess the word. Parson Kendall, he made the word, and he locked down a couple o' ghosts in their graves with it; and when his time came he went to his own grave and took the word with him."

"Whose ghosts, Matthew?"

"You want the story, I see, sir. My father could tell it better than I can. He was a young man in the year 'nine, unmarried at the time, and living in this very cottage, just as I be. That's how he came to get mixed up with the tale."

He took a chair, lighted a short pipe, and went on, with his eyes fixed on the dancing violet flames:

"Yes, he'd ha' been about thirty year old in January, eighteen 'nine. The storm got up in the night o' the twenty-first o' that month. My father was dressed and out long before daylight; he never was one to bide in bed, let be that the gale by this time was pretty near lifting the thatch over his head. Besides which, he'd fenced a small 'taty-patch that winter, down by Lowland Point, and he wanted to see if it stood the night's work. He took the path across Gunner's Meadow—where they buried most of the bodies afterward. The wind was right in his teeth at the time, and once on the way (he's told me this often) a great strip of oarweed came flying through the darkness and fetched him a slap on the cheek like a cold hand. But he made shift pretty well till he got to Lowland, and then had to drop upon hands and knees and crawl, digging his fingers every now and then into the shingle to hold on, for he declared to me that the stones, some of them as big as a man's head, kept rolling and driving past till it seemed the whole foreshore was moving westward under him. The fence was gone, of course; not a stick left to show where it stood; so that, when first he came to the place, he thought he must have missed his bearings. My father, sir, was a very religious man; and if he reckoned the end of the world was at hand—there in the great wind and night, among the moving stones—you may believe he was certain of it when he heard a gun fired, and, with the same, saw a flame shoot up out of the darkness to windward, making a sudden fierce light in all the place about. All he could find to think or say was, 'The Second Coming! The Second Coming! The Bridegroom cometh, and the wicked He will toss like a ball into a large country'; and being already upon his knees, he just bowed his head and 'bided, saying this over and over.

"But by'm by, between two squalls, he made bold to lift his head and look, and then by the light—a bluish color 'twas—he saw all the coast clear away to Manacle Point, and off the Manacles in the thick of the weather, a sloop-of-war with topgallants housed, driving stern foremost toward the reef. It was she, of course, that was burning the flare. My father could see the white streak and the ports of her quite plain as she rose to it, a little outside the breakers, and he guessed easy enough that her captain had just managed to wear ship and was trying to force her nose to the sea with the help of her small bower anchor and the scrap or two of canvas that hadn't yet been blown out of her. But while he looked, she fell off, giving her broadside to it foot by foot, and drifting back on the breakers around Carn Du and the Varses. The rocks lie so thick thereabout that 'twas a toss up which she struck first; at any rate, my father could'nt tell at the time, for just then the flare died down and went out.

"Well, sir, he turned then in the dark and started back for Coverack to cry the dismal tidings—though well knowing ship and crew to be past any hope, and as he turned the wind lifted him and tossed him forward 'like a ball,' as he'd been saying, and homeward along the foreshore. As you know, 'tis ugly work, even by daylight, picking your way among the stones there, and my father was prettily knocked about at first in the dark. But by this 'twas nearer seven than six o'clock, and the day spreading. By the time he reached North Corner, a man could see to read print; hows'ever, he looked neither out to sea nor toward Coverack, but headed straight for the first cottage—the same that stands above North Corner to-day. A man named Billy Ede lived there then, and when my father burst into the kitchen bawling, 'Wreck! wreck!' he saw Billy Ede's wife, Ann, standing there in her clogs with a shawl over her head, and her clothes wringing wet.

"'Save the chap!' says Billy Ede's wife, Ann.

'What d'ee mean by crying stale fish at that rate?'

" 'But 'tis a wreck, I tell 'ee.'

" 'Ive a-zeed 'n, too; and so has every one with an eye in his head.'

"And with that she pointed straight over my father's shoulder, and he turned; and there, close under Dolor Point, at the end of Coverack town, he saw another wreck washing, and the point black with people, like emmets, running to and fro in the morning light. While he stood staring at her, he heard a trumpet sounded on board, the notes coming in little jerks, like a bird rising against the wind; but faintly, of course, because of the distance and the gale blowing—though this had dropped a little.

" 'She's a transport,' said Billy Ede's wife, Ann, 'and full of horse-soldiers, fine long men. When she struck they must ha' pitched the horses over first to lighten the ship, for a score of dead horses had washed in afore I left, half an hour back. An' three or four soldiers, too—fine long corpses in white breeches and jackets of blue and gold. I held the lantern to one. Such a straight young man!'

"My father asked her about the trumpeting.

" 'That's the queerest bit of all. She was burnin' a light when me an' my man joined the crowd down there. All her masts had gone; whether they carried away, or were cut away to ease her, I don't rightly know. Her keelson was broke under her and her bottom sagged and stove, and she had just settled down like a sitting hen— just the leastest list to starboard; but a man could stand there easy. They had rigged up ropes across her, from bulwark to bulwark, an' besides these the men were mustered, holding on like grim death whenever the sea made a clean breach over them, an' standing up like heroes as soon as it passed. The captain an' the officers were clinging to the rail of the quarterdeck, all in their golden uniforms, waiting for the end as if 'twas King George they expected. There was no way to help, for she lay right beyond cast of line, though our folk tried it fifty times. And beside them clung a trumpeter, a whacking big man, an' between the heavy seas he would lift his trumpet with one hand, and blow a call; and every time he blew the men gave a cheer. There [she says]—hark 'ee now—there he goes agen! But you won't hear no cheering any more, for few are left to cheer, and their voices weak. Bitter cold the wind is, and I reckon it numbs their grip o' the ropes, for they were dropping off fast with every sea when my man sent me home to get his breakfast. Another wreck, you say? Well, there's no hope for the tender dears, if 'tis the Manacles. You'd better run down and help yonder; though 'tis little help any man can give. Not one came in alive while I was there. The tide's flowing, an' she won't hold together another hour, they say.'

"Well, sure enough, the end was coming fast when my father got down to the point. Six men had been cast up alive, or just breathing—a seaman and five troopers. The seaman was the only one that had breath to speak; and while they were carrying him into the town, the word went round that the ship's name was the 'Despatch,' transport, homeward-bound from Corunna, with a detachment of the Seventh Hussars, that had been fighting out there with Sir John Moore. The seas had rolled her further over by this time, and given her decks a pretty sharp slope; but a dozen men still held on, seven by the ropes near the ship's waist, a couple near the break of the poop, and three on the quarterdeck. Of these three my father made out one to be the skipper; close by him clung an officer in full regimentals —his name, they heard after, was Captain Duncanfield; and last came the tall trumpeter; and if you'll believe me, the fellow was making shift there, at the very last, to blow 'God Save the King.' What's more, he got to 'Send us victorious,' before an extra big sea came bursting across and washed them off the deck—every man but one of the pair beneath the poop—and he dropped his hold before the next wave; being stunned, I reckon. The others went out of sight at once, but the trumpeter—being, as I said, a powerful man as well as a tough swimmer—rose like a duck, rode out a couple of breakers, and came in on the crest of the third. The folks looked to see him broke like an egg at their very feet; but when the smother cleared, there he was, lying face downward on a ledge below them; and one of the men that happened to have a rope round him—I forgot the fellow's name, if I ever heard it—jumped down and grabbed him by the ankle as he began to slip back. Before the next big sea, the pair were hauled high enough to be out of harm, and another heave brought them up to grass. Quick work, but master trumpeter wasn't quite dead; nothing worse than a cracked head and three staved ribs. In twenty minutes or so they had him in bed, with the doctor to tend him.

"Now was the time—nothing being left alive upon the transport—for my father to tell of the sloop he'd seen driving upon the Manacles. And when he got a hearing, though the most were set upon salvage, and believed a wreck in the hand, so to say, to be worth half a dozen they couldn't see, a good few volunteered to start off with him and have a look. They crossed Lowland Point; no ship to be seen on the Manacles nor anywhere upon the sea. One or two was for calling my father a liar. 'Wait till we come to Dean Point,' said he. Sure enough, on the far side of Dean Pont they found the sloop's mainmast washing about with half a dozen men lashed to it, men in red jackets, every mother's son drowned and staring; and a little further on, just under the Dean, three or four bodies cast up on the shore, one of them a small drummer-boy, side-drum and all; and near by part of a ship's gig, with 'H.M.S. Primrose' cut on the stern-board. From this point on the shore was littered thick with wreckage and dead bodies—the most of them marines in uniform—and in Godrevy Cove, in particular, a heap of furniture from the captain's cabin, and among it a water-tight box, not much damaged, and full of papers, by which, when it came to be examined, next day, the wreck was easily made out to be the 'Primrose,' of eighteen guns, outward bound from Portsmouth, with a fleet of transports for the Spanish war—thirty sail, I've heard, but I've never heard what became of them. Being handled by merchant skippers, no doubt they rode out the gale, and reached the Tagus safe and sound. Not but what the captain of the 'Primrose'—Mein was his name—did quite right to try and club-haul his vessel when he found himself under the land; only he never ought to have got there, if he took proper soundings. But it's easy talking.

"The 'Primrose,' sir, was a handsome vessel— for her size one of the handsomest in the King's service—and newly fitted out at Plymouth Dock. So the boys had brave pickings from her in the way of brass-work, ship's instruments, and the like, let alone some barrels of stores not much spoiled. They loaded themselves with as much as they could carry, and started for home, meaning to make a second journey before the preventive men got wind of their doings, and came to spoil the fun. 'Hullo!' says my father, and dropped his gear, 'I do believe there's a leg moving?' and running fore, he stooped over the small drummer-boy that I told you about. The poor little chap was lying there, with his face a mass of bruises, and his eyes closed; but he had shifted one leg an inch or two, and was still breathing. So my father pulled out a knife, and cut him free from his drum—that was lashed on to him with a double turn of Manila rope—and took him up and carried him along here to this very room that we're sitting in. He lost a good deal by this; for when he went back to fetch the bundle he'd dropped, the preventive men had got hold of it, and were thick as thieves along the foreshore; so that 'twas only by paying one or two to look the other way that he picked up anything worth carrying off: which you'll allow to be hard, seeing that he was the first man to give news of the wreck.

"Well, the inquiry was held, of course, and my father gave evidence, and for the rest they had to trust to the sloop's papers, for not a soul was saved besides the drummer-boy, and he was raving in a fever, brought on by the cold and the fright. And the seaman and the five troopers gave evidence about the loss of the 'Despatch.' The tall trumpeter, too, whose ribs were healing, came forward and kissed the book; but somehow his head had been hurt in coming ashore, and he

talked foolish-like, and 'twas easy seen he would
never be a proper man again. The others were
taken up to Plymouth, and so went their ways;
but the trumpeter stayed on in Coverack; and
King George, finding he was fit for nothing, sent
him down a trifle of a pension after a while—
enough to keep him in board and lodging, with a
bit of tobacco over.

"Now the first time that this man—William
Tallifer he called himself—met with the drummer-boy, was about a fortnight after the little
chap had bettered enough to be allowed a short
walk out of doors, which he took, if you please,
in full regimentals. There never was a soldier
so proud of his dress. His own suit had shrunk
a brave bit with the salt water; but into ordinary
frock an' corduroys he declared he would not get,
not if he had to go naked the rest of his life; so
my father—being a good-natured man, and
handy with the needle—turned to and repaired
damages with a piece or two of scarlet cloth cut
from the jacket of one of the drowned Marines.
Well, the poor little chap chanced to be standing,
in this rig out, down by the gate of Gunner's
Meadow, where they had buried two score and
over of his comrades. The morning was a fine
one, early in March month; and along came the
cracked trumpeter, likewise taking a stroll.

" 'Hullo!' says he; 'good mornin'! And what
might you be doin' here?'

" 'I was a-wishin',' says the boy, 'I had a pair

o' drumsticks. Our lads were buried yonder
without so much as a drum tapped or a musket
fired; and that's not Christian burial for British
soldiers.'

" 'Phut!' says the trumpeter, and spat on the
ground; 'a parcel of Marines!'

"The boy eyed him a second or so, and answered up: 'If I'd a tav of turf handy, I'd bung
it at your mouth, you greasy cavalryman, and
learn you to speak respectful of your betters.
The Marines are the handiest body o' men in the
service.'

"The trumpeter looked down on him from the
height of six-foot two, and asked: 'Did they die
well?'

" 'They died very well. There was a lot of
running to and fro at first, and some of the men
began to cry, and a few to strip off their clothes.
But when the ship fell off for the last time, Captain Mein turned and said something to Major
Griffiths, the commanding officer on board, and
the Major called out to me to beat to quarters.
It might have been for a wedding, he sang it out
so cheerful. We'd had word already that 'twas
to be parade order; and the men fell in as trim
and decent as if they were going to church. One
or two even tried to shave at the last moment.
The Major wore his medals. One of the sea-
men, seeing I had work to keep the drum steady
—the sling being a bit loose for me, and the wind
what you remember—lashed it tight with a piece

of rope; and that saved my life afterward, a drum being as good as a cork until it's stove. I kept beating away until every man was on deck; and then the Major formed them up and told them to die like British soldiers, and the chaplain was in the middle of a prayer when she struck. In ten minutes she was gone. That was how they died, cavalryman.'

" 'And that was very well done, drummer of the Marines. What's your name?'

" 'John Christian.'

" 'Mine's William George Tallifer, trumpeter, of the Seventh Light Dragoons—the Queen's Own. I played "God Save the King" while our men were drowning. Captain Duncanfield told me to sound a call or two, to put them in heart; but that matter of "God Save the King" was a notion of my own. I won't say anything to hurt the feelings of a Marine, even if he's not much over five-foot tall; but the Queen's Own Hussars is a tearin' fine regiment. As between horse and foot, 'tis a question o' which gets a chance. All the way from Sahagun to Corunna 'twas we that took and gave the knocks—at Mayorga and Rueda, and Bennyventy.'—The reason, sir, I can speak the names so pat, is that my father learnt 'em by heart afterward from the trumpeter, who was always talking about Mayorga and Rueda and Bennyventy.'—We made the rear-guard, under General Paget; and drove the French every time; and all the infantry

did was to sit about in wine-shops till we whipped
'em out, an' steal an' straggle an' play the tom-
fool in general. And when it came to a stand-up
fight at Corunna, 'twas we that had to stay sea-
sick aboard the transports, an' watch the infantry
in the thick o' the caper. Very well they behaved, too—specially the Fourth Regiment, an'
the Forty-Second Highlanders, an' the Dirty
Half-Hundred. Oh, ay; they're decent regiments, all three. But the Queen's Own Hussars
is a tearin' fine regiment. So you played on your
drum when the ship was goin' down? Drummer
John Christian, I'll have to get you a new pair
of sticks.'

"The very next day the trumpeter marched
into Helston, and got a carpenter there to turn
him a pair of box-wood drumsticks for the boy.
And this was the beginning of one of the most
curious friendships you ever heard tell of. Nothing delighted the pair more than to borrow a boat
off my father and pull out to the rocks where the
'Primrose' and the 'Despatch' had struck and
sunk; and on still days 'twas pretty to hear them
out there off the Manacles, the drummer playing
his tattoo—for they always took their music with
them—and the trumpeter practising calls, and
making his trumpet speak like an angel. But if
the weather turned roughish, they'd be walking
together and talking; leastwise the youngster
listened while the other discoursed about Sir
John's campaign in Spain and Portugal, telling

how each little skirmish befell; and of Sir John
himself, and General Baird, and General Paget,
and Colonel Vivian, his own commanding officer,
and what kind of men they were; and of the last
bloody stand-up at Corunna, and so forth, as if
neither could have enough.

"But all this had to come to an end in the late
summer, for the boy, John Christian, being now
well and strong again, must go up to Plymouth to
report himself. 'Twas his own wish (for I believe King George had forgotten all about him),
but his friend wouldn't hold him back. As for
the trumpeter, my father had made an arrangement to take him on as lodger, as soon as the boy
left; and on the morning fixed for the start, he
was up at the door here by five o'clock, with his
trumpet slung by his side, and all the rest of his
belongings in a small valise. A Monday morning it was, and after breakfast he had fixed to
walk with the boy some way on the road toward
Helston, where the coach started. My father
left them at breakfast together, and went out to
meat the pig, and do a few odd morning jobs of
that sort. When he came back, the boy was still
at table, and the trumpeter sat with the rings in
his hands, hitched together just as they be at
this moment.

" 'Look at this,' he says to my father, showing
him the lock. 'I picked it up off a starving brass-
worker in Lisbon, and it is not one of your common locks that one word of six letters will open

at any time. There's janius in this lock; for
you've only to make the rings spell any six-letter
word you please and snap down the lock upon
that, and never a soul can open it—not the maker,
even—until somebody comes along that knows
the word you snapped it on. Now Johnny here's
goin', and he leaves his drum behind him; for,
though he can make pretty music on it, the parchment sags in wet weather, by reason of the sea-
water getting at it; an' if he carries it to Plymouth, they'll only condemn it and give him
another. And, as for me, I shan't have the heart
to put lip to the trumpet any more when
Johnny's gone. So we've chosen a word together, and locked 'em together upon that; and,
by your leave, I'll hang 'em here together on the
hook over your fireplace. Maybe Johnny'll come
back; maybe not. Maybe, if he comes, I'll be
dead an' gone, and he'll take 'em apart an' try
their music for old sake's sake. But if he never
comes, nobody can separate 'em; for nobody besides knows the word. And if you marry and
have sons, you can tell 'em that here are tied
together the souls of Johnny Christian, drummer
of the Marines, and William George Tallifer,
once trumpeter of the Queen's Own Hussars.
Amen.'

"With that he hung the two instruments 'pon
the hook there; and the boy stood up and thanked
my father and shook hands; and the pair went
out of the door, toward Helston.

"Somewhere on the road they took leave of one another; but nobody saw the parting, nor heard what was said between them. About three in the afternoon the trumpeter came walking back over the hill; and by the time my father came home from the fishing, the cottage was tidied up, and the tea ready, and the whole place shining like a new pin. From that time for five years he lodged here with my father, looking after the house and tilling the garden. And all the while he was steadily failing; the hurt in his head spreading, in a manner, to his limbs. My father watched the feebleness growing on him, but said nothing. And from first to last neither spake a word about the drummer, John Christian; nor did any letter reach them, nor word of his doings.

"The rest of the tale you're free to believe, sir, or not, as you please. It stands upon my father's words, and he always declared he was ready to kiss the Book upon it, before judge and jury. He said, too, that he never had the wit to make up such a yarn; and he defied any one to explain about the lock, in particular, by any other tale. But you shall judge for yourself.

"My father said that about three o'clock in the morning, April fourteenth, of the year 'fourteen, he and William Tallifer were sitting here, just as you and I, sir, are sitting now. My father had put on his clothes a few minutes before, and was mending his spiller by the light of the horn lantern, meaning to set off before daylight to haul the trammel. The trumpeter hadn't been to bed at all. Toward the last he mostly spent his nights (and his days, too) dozing in the elbow-chair where you sit at this minute. He was dozing then (my father said) with his chin dropped forward on his chest, when a knock sounded upon the door, and the door opened, and in walked an upright young man in scarlet regimentals.

"He had grown a brave bit, and his face the color of wood-ashes; but it was the drummer, John Christian. Only his uniform was different from the one he used to wear, and the figures '38' shone in brass upon his collar.

"The drummer walked past my father as if he never saw him, and stood by the elbow-chair and said:

" 'Trumpeter, trumpeter, are you one with me?'

"And the trumpeter just lifted the lids of his eyes, and answered: 'How should I not be one with you, drummer Johnny—Johnny boy? If you come, I count; if you march, I mark time; until the discharge comes.'

" 'The discharge has come to-night,' said the drummer; and the word is Corunna no longer.' And stepping to the chimney-place, he unhooked the drum and trumpet, and began to twist the brass rings of the lock, spelling the word aloud, so—'C-O-R-U-N-A.' When he had fixed the last letter, the padlock opened in his hand.

" 'Did you know, trumpeter, that, when I came to Plymouth, they put me into a line regiment?'

" 'The 38th is a good regiment,' answered the old Hussar, still in his dull voice; 'I went back with them from Sahagun to Corunna. At Corunna they stood in General Fraser's division, on the right. They behaved well.

" 'But I'd fain see the Marines again,' says the drummer, handing him the trumpet; 'and you, you shall call once more for the Queen's Own. Matthew,' he says, suddenly, turning on my father—and when he turned, my father saw for the first time that his scarlet jacket had a round hole by the breast-bone, and that the blood was welling there—'Matthew, we shall want your boat.'

"Then my father rose on his legs like a man in a dream, while they two slung on, the one his drum, and t'other his trumpet. He took the lantern and went quaking before them down to the shore, and they breathed heavily behind him; and they stepped into his boat, and my father pushed off.

" 'Row you first for Dolor Point,' says the drummer. So my father rowed them past the white houses of Coverack to Dolor Point, and there, at a word, lay on his oars. And the trumpeter, William Tallifer, put his trumpet to his mouth and sounded the reveille. The music of it was like rivers running.

" 'They will follow,' said the drummer. Matthew, pull you now for the Manacles.'

"So my father pulled for the Manacles, and came to an easy close outside Carn Du. And the drummer took his sticks and beat a tattoo, there by the edge of the reef; and the music of it was like a rolling chariot.

" 'That will do,' says he, breaking off; 'they will follow. Pull now for the shore under Gunner's Meadow.'

"Then my father pulled for the shore and ran his boat in under Gunner's Meadow. And they stepped out, all three, and walked up to the meadow. By the gate the drummer halted, and began his tattoo again, looking out toward the darkness over the sea.

"And while the drum beat, and my father held his breath, there came up out of the sea and the darkness a troop of many men, horse and foot, and formed up among the graves; and others rose out of the graves and formed up—drowned Marines with bleached faces, and pale Hussars, riding their horses, all lean and shadowy. There was no clatter of hoofs or accoutrements, my father said, but a soft sound all the while like the beating of a bird's wing; and a black shadow lay like a pool about the feet of all. The drummer stood upon a little knoll just inside the gate, and beside him the tall trumpeter, with hand on hip, watching them gather; and behind them both my father, clinging to the gate. When no more came, the drummer stopped playing, and said, 'Call the roll.'

"Then the trumpeter stepped toward the end man of the rank and called, 'Troop Sergeant-Major Thomas Irons,' and the man answered in a thin voice, 'Here.'

" 'Troop Sergeant-Major Thomas Irons, how is it with you?'

"The man answered, 'How should it be with me? When I was young, I betrayed a girl; and when I was grown, I betrayed a friend, and for these I must pay. But I died as a man ought. God save the King!'

"The trumpeter called to the next man, 'Trooper Henry Buckingham,' and the next man answered, 'Here.'

" 'Trooper Henry Buckingham, how is it with you?'

" 'How should it be with me? I was a drunkard, and I stole, and in Lugo, in a wine-shop, I killed a man. But I died as a man should. God save the King!'

"So the trumpeter went down the line; and when he had finished, the drummer took it up, hailing the dead Marines in their order. Each man answered to his name, and each man ended with 'God save the King!' When all were hailed, the drummer stepped back to his mound, and called:

" 'It is well. You are content, and we are content to join you. Wait, now, a little while.'

"With this he turned and ordered my father to pick up the lantern, and lead the way back. As my father picked it up, he heard the ranks of the dead men cheer and call, 'God save the King!' all together, and saw them waver and fade back into the dark, like a breath fading off a pane.

"But when they came back here to the kitchen, and my father set the lantern down, it seemed they'd both forgot about him. For the drummer turned in the lantern-light—and my father could see the blood still welling out of the hole in his breast—and took the trumpet-sling from around the other's neck, and locked drum and trumpet together again, choosing the letters on the lock very carefully. While he did this, he said:

" 'The word is no more Corunna, but Bayonne. As you left out an "n" in Corunna, so must I leave out an "n" in Bayonne.' And before snapping the padlock, he spelt out the word slowly— 'B-A-Y-O-N-E.' After that, he used no more speech; but turned and hung the two instruments back on the hook; and then took the trumpeter by the arm; and the pair walked out into the darkness, glancing neither to right nor left.

"My father was on the point of following, when he heard a sort of sigh behind him; and there, sitting in the elbow-chair, was the very trumpeter he had just seen walk out by the door!

If my father's heart jumped before, you may believe it jumped quicker now. But after a bit, he went up to the man asleep in the chair and put a hand upon him. It was the trumpeter in flesh and blood that he touched; but though the flesh was warm, the trumpeter was dead.

"Well, sir, they buried him three days after; and at first my father was minded to say nothing about his dream (as he thought it). But the day after the funeral, he met Parson Kendall coming from Helston market; and the parson called out: 'Have 'ee heard the news the coach brought down this mornin'?' 'What news?' says my father. 'Why, that peace is agreed upon.' 'None too soon,' says my father. 'Not soon enough for our poor lads at Bayonne,' the parson answered. 'Bayonne!' cries my father, with a jump. 'Why, yes;' and the parson told him all about a great sally the French had made on the night of April 13th. 'Do you happen to know if the 38th Regiment was engaged?' my father asked. 'Come, now,' said Parson Kendall, 'I didn't know you was so well up in the campaign. But, as it happens, I do know that the 38th was engaged, for 'twas they that held a cottage and stopped the French advance.'

"Still my father held his tongue; and when, a week later, he walked in Helston and bought a 'Mercury' off the Sherborne rider, and got the landlord of the 'Angel' to spell out the list of killed and wounded, sure enough, there among the killed was Drummer John Christian, of the 38th Foot.

"After this there was nothing for a religious man but to make a clean breast. So my father went up to Parson Kendall, and told the whole story. The parson listened, and put a question or two, and then asked:

" 'Have you tried to open the lock since that night?'

" 'I haven't dared to touch it,' says my father.

" 'Then come along and try.' When the parson came to the cottage here, he took the things off the hook and tried the lock. 'Did he say "Bayonne?" The word has seven letters.'

" 'Not if you spell it with one "n" as he did,' says my father.

"The parson spelt it out,—'B-A-Y-O-N-E.' 'Whew!' says he, for the lock had fallen open in his hand.

"He stood considering it a moment, and then he says: 'I tell you what. I shouldn't blab this all round the parish, if I was you. You won't get no credit for truth-telling, and a miracle's wasted on a set of fools. But if you like, I'll shut down the lock again upon a holy word that no one but me shall know, and neither drummer nor trumpeter, dead or alive, shall frighten the secret out of me.'

" 'I wish to heaven you would, parson,' said my father.

"The parson chose the holy word there and then, and shut the lock back upon it, and hung the drum and trumpet back in their place. He is gone long since, taking the word with him. And till the lock is broken by force nobody will ever separate those two."

THE RENDEZVOUS

BY IVAN TURGENEV

THE RENDEZVOUS

BY IVAN TURGENEV

I WAS sitting in a birch grove in autumn, near the middle of September. It had been drizzling ever since morning; occasionally the sun shone warmly—the weather was changeable. Now the sky was overcast with watery white clouds, now it suddenly cleared up for an instant, and then the bright, soft azure, like a beautiful eye, appeared from beyond the dispersed clouds. I was sitting looking about me and listening. The leaves were slightly rustling over my head; and by their very rustle one could tell what season of the year it was. It was not the gay, laughing palpitation of spring; not a soft whispering, nor the lingering chatter of summer, nor the timid and cold lisping of late autumn, but a barely audible, drowsy prattle. A faint breeze was whisking over the tree-tops. The interior of the grove, moist from the rain, was forever changing, as the sun shone or hid beyond the clouds; now the grove was all illuminated as if everything in it had burst into a smile; the trunks of the birch trees suddenly assumed the soft reflection of white silk; the small leaves which lay scattered on the ground all at once became variegated and flashed up like red gold; and the pretty stalks of the tall, branchy ferns, already tinted in their autumn hue, resembling the color of overripe grapes, appeared here and there tangling and crossing one another. Now again everything suddenly turned blue; the bright colors died out instantaneously, the birch trees stood all white, lustreless, like snow which had not yet been touched by the coldly playing rays of the winter sun—and stealthily, slyly, a drizzling rain began to sprinkle and whisper over the forest. The leaves on the birches were almost all green yet, though they had turned somewhat pale; only here and there stood a solitary young little birch, all red or all golden, and one should have seen how brightly these birches flushed in the sun when its rays suddenly appeared gliding and flashing through the dense net of the thin branches which had just been washed around by the sparkling rain. Not a single bird was heard; all had found shelter, and were silent; only rarely the mocking voice of the bluebird sang out like a little steel bell. Before stopping in this birch forest I passed with my dog through a poplar grove. I confess I am not very fond of the poplar tree with its pale lilac-colored trunk and its grayish-green, metallic leaves, which it lifts high and spreads in the air like a trembling fan—I do not like the constant shaking of its round, untidy leaves, which are so awkwardly attached to long stems. The poplar is pretty only on certain sum-

mer evenings when, rising high amid the low
shrubbery, it stands against the red rays of the
setting sun, shining and trembling, bathed from
root to top in uniform yellowish purple—or
when, on a clear windy day, it rocks noisily, lisping against the blue sky, and each leaf seems as
if eager to tear itself away, to fly and hurry off
into the distance. But in general I do not like
this tree, and, therefore, not stopping to rest in
the poplar grove, I made my way to the birch
forest, and seated myself under a tree whose
branches started near the ground, and thus could
protect me from the rain. Having admired the
surrounding view, I fell asleep—I slept that
tranquil, sweet sleep which is familiar to hunters
only.

I can not say how long I slept, but when I
opened my eyes the entire interior of the forest
was filled with sunshine, and everywhere the
bright blue sky was flashing through the cheer-
fully droning leaves; the clouds disappeared,
driven asunder by the wind which had begun to
play; the weather was clear now, and one felt
in the air that peculiar, dry freshness which, fill-
ing the heart with a certain vigorous sensation,
almost always predicts a quiet, clear night after
a rainy day. I was about to rise and try my luck
at hunting again, when my eyes suddenly fell on
a motionless human figure. I gazed at it fixedly;
it was a young peasant girl. She was sitting
some twenty feet away from me, her head bowed

pensively and her hands dropped on her knees;
in one hand, which was half open, lay a heavy
bunch of field flowers, and every time she
breathed the flowers were softly gliding over her
checkered skirt. A clear white shirt, buttoned
at the neck and the wrists, fell in short, soft folds
about her waist; large yellow beads were hanging
down from her neck on her bosom in two rows.
She was not at all bad-looking. Her heavy fair
hair, of a beautiful ash color, parted in two neatly
combed half-circles from under a narrow, dark-
red head-band, which was pulled down almost to
her ivory-white forehead; the rest of her face was
slightly tanned with the golden sunburn peculiar to a tender skin. I could not see her eyes—
she did not lift them; but I saw her thin, high
eyebrows, her long lashes; these were moist, and
on her cheek gleamed a dried-up teardrop, which
had stopped near her somewhat pale lips. Her
entire small head was very charming; even her
somewhat thick and round nose did not spoil it.
I liked especially the expression of her face; it
was so simple and gentle, so sad and so full of
childish perplexity before her own sadness. She
was apparently waiting for some one. Something cracked faintly in the forest. Immediately
she raised her head and looked around; her eyes
flashed quickly before me in the transparent
shade—they were large, bright, and shy like a
deer's. She listened for a few seconds, not moving her wide-open eyes from the spot whence the

faint sound had come; she heaved a sigh, turned her head slowly, bent down still lower and began to examine the flowers. Her eyelids turned red, her lips quivered bitterly and a new teardrop rolled down from under her heavy eyelashes, stopping and sparkling on her cheek. Thus quite a long while passed; the poor girl did not stir— only occasionally she moved her hands and listened—listened all the time. Something cracked once more in the forest—she started. This time the noise did not stop, it was becoming more distinct, it was nearing—at last firm footsteps were heard. She straightened herself, and it seemed as if she lost her courage, for her eyes began to quiver. The figure of a man appeared through the jungle. She looked fixedly, suddenly flushed, and, smiling joyously and happily, seemed about to rise, but she immediately cast down her head again, turned pale, confused— only then she lifted her quivering, almost prayerful, eyes to the man as he paused beside her.

I looked at him from my hiding-place with curiosity. I confess he did not produce a pleasant impression upon me. He was, by all appearances, a spoiled valet of some rich young man. His clothes betokened a claim to taste and smart carelessness. He wore a short top-coat of bronze color, which evidently belonged to his master, and which was buttoned up to the very top; he had on a pink necktie with lilac-colored edges; and his black velvet cap, trimmed with gold stripes, was pulled over his very eyebrows. The round collar of his white shirt propped his ears up and cut his cheeks mercilessly, and the starched cuffs covered his hands up to his red, crooked fingers, which were ornamented with silver and gold rings, set with forget-me-nots of turquoise. His red, fresh, impudent face belonged to those countenances which, as far as I have observed, are almost always repulsive to men, but, unfortunately, are often admired by women. Apparently trying to give an expression of contempt and of weariness to his rough features, he was forever closing his small, milky-gray eyes, knitting his brows, lowering the corners of his lips, yawning forcedly, and, with careless, although not too clever, ease, now adjusting his reddish, smartly twisted temple-curls, now fingering the yellow hair which bristled upon his thick upper lip—in a word, he was making an insufferable display of himself. He started to do this as soon as he noticed the young peasant girl who was awaiting him. He advanced to her slowly, with large strides, then stood for a while, twitched his shoulders, thrust both hands into the pockets of his coat, and, casting a quick and indifferent glance at the poor girl, sank down on the ground.

"Well?" he began, continuing to look aside, shaking his foot and yawning. "Have you waited long?"

The girl could not answer him at once.

"Long, Victor Alexandrich," she said at last, in a scarcely audible voice.

"Ah!" He removed his cap, majestically passed his hand over his thick, curly hair whose roots started almost at his eyebrows, and, looking around with dignity, covered his precious head again cautiously. "And I almost forgot all about it. Besides, you see, it's raining." He yawned again. "I have a lot of work to do; you can't look after everything, and he is yet scolding. We are leaving to-morrow—"

"To-morrow?" uttered the girl, and fixed a frightened look upon him.

"To-morrow— Come, come, come, please," he replied quickly, vexed, noticing that she quivered, and bowed her head in silence. "Please, Akulina, don't cry. You know I can't bear it" (and he twitched his flat nose). "If you don't stop, I'll leave you right away. What nonsense—to whimper!"

"Well, I shan't, I shan't," said Akulina hastily, swallowing the tears with an effort. "So you're going away to-morrow?" she added, after a brief silence. "When will it please God to have me meet you again, Victor Alexandrich?"

"We'll meet, we'll meet again. If it isn't next year, it'll be later. My master, it seems, wants to enter the service in St. Petersburg," he went on, pronouncing the words carelessly and somewhat indistinctly. "And it may be that we'll go abroad."

"You will forget me, Victor Alexandrich," said Akulina sadly.

"No—why should I? I'll not forget you, only you had rather be sensible; don't make a fool of yourself; obey your father— And I'll not forget you— Oh, no; oh, no." And he stretched himself calmly and yawned again.

"Do not forget me, Victor Alexandrich," she resumed in a beseeching voice. "I have loved you so much, it seems—all, it seems, for you— You tell me to obey father, Victor Alexandrich— How am I to obey my father—?"

"How's that?" He pronounced these words as if from the stomach, lying on his back and holding his hands under his head.

"Why, Victor Alexandrich—you know it yourself—"

She fell silent. Victor fingered his steel watch-chain.

"Akulina, you are not a foolish girl," he said at last, "therefore don't talk nonsense. It's for your own good, do you understand me? Of course, you are not foolish, you're not altogether a peasant, so to say, and your mother wasn't always a peasant either. Still, you are without education—therefore you must obey when you are told to."

"But it's terrible, Victor Alexandrich."

"Oh, what nonsense, my dear—what is she afraid of! What is that you have there," he added, moving closer to her, "flowers?"

"Flowers," replied Akulina sadly. "I have picked some field tansies," she went on, with some animation. "They're good for the calves. And here I have some marigolds—for scrofula. Here, look, what a pretty flower! I haven't seen such a pretty flower in all my life. Here are forget-me-nots, and—and these I have picked for you," she added, taking from under the tansies a small bunch of cornflowers, tied around with a thin blade of grass; "do you want them?"

Victor held out his hand lazily, took the flowers, smelt them carelessly, and began to turn them around in his fingers, looking up with thoughtful importance. Akulina gazed at him. There was so much tender devotion, reverent obedience, and love in her pensive eyes. She at once feared him, and yet she dared not cry, and inwardly she bade him farewell, and admired him for the last time; and he lay there, stretched out like a sultan, and endured her admiration with magnanimous patience and condescension. I confess I was filled with indignation as I looked at his red face, which betrayed satisfied selfishness through his feigned contempt and indifference. Akulina was so beautiful at this moment. All her soul opened before him trustingly and passionately—it reached out to him, caressed him, and he— He dropped the cornflowers on the grass, took out from the side-pocket of his coat a round glass in a bronze frame and began to force it into his eye; but no matter how hard he tried to hold it with his knitted brow, his raised cheek, and even with his nose, the glass dropped out and fell into his hands.

"What's this?" asked Akulina at last, with surprise.

"A lorgnette," he replied importantly.

"What is it for?"

"To see better."

"Let me see it."

Victor frowned, but gave her the glass.

"Look out; don't break it."

"Don't be afraid, I'll not break it." She lifted it timidly to her eye.

"I can't see anything," she said naively.

"Shut your eye," he retorted in the tone of a dissatisfied teacher. She closed the eye before which she held the glass.

"Not that eye, not that one, you fool! The other one!" exclaimed Victor, and, not allowing her to correct her mistake, he took the lorgnette away from her.

Akulina blushed, laughed slightly, and turned away.

"It seems it's not for us."

"Of course not!"

The poor girl maintained silence, and heaved a deep sigh.

"Oh, Victor Alexandrich, how will I get along without you?" she said suddenly.

Victor wiped the lorgnette and put it back into his pocket.

"Yes, yes," he said at last. "At first it will really be hard for you." He tapped her on the shoulder condescendingly; she quietly took his hand from her shoulder and kissed it. "Well, yes, yes, you are indeed a good girl," he went on, with a self-satisfied smile; "but it can't be helped! Consider it yourself! My master and I can't stay here, can we? Winter is near, and to pass the winter in the country is simply nasty—you know it yourself. It's a different thing in St. Petersburg! There are such wonders over there that you could not imagine even in your dreams, you silly— What houses, what streets, and society, education—it's something wonderful!—" Akulina listened to him with close attention, slightly opening her lips like a child. "However," he added, wriggling on the ground, "why do I say all this to you? You can't understand it anyway!"

"Why not, Victor Alexandrich? I understood, I understood everything."

"Just think of her!"

Akulina cast down her eyes.

"You did not speak to me like this before, Victor Alexandrich," she said, without lifting her eyes.

"Before?— Before! Just think of her!— Before!" he remarked, indignantly.

Both grew silent.

"However, it's time for me to go," said Victor, and leaned on his elbow, about to rise.

"Wait a little," said Akulina in an imploring voice.

"What for? I have already said to you, Good-by!"

"Wait," repeated Akulina.

Victor again stretched himself on the ground and began to whistle. Akulina kept looking at him steadfastly. I could see that she was growing agitated by degrees—her lips twitched, her pale cheeks were reddening.

"Victor Alexandrich," she said at last in a broken voice, "it's a sin for you, it's a sin, Victor Alexandrich, by God!"

"What's a sin?" he asked, knitting his brows. He raised his head and turned to her.

"It's a sin, Victor Alexandrich. If you would only say a good word to me before leaving—if you would only say one word to me, miserable little orphan that I am—"

"But what shall I say to you?"

"I don't know. You know better than I do, Victor Alexandrich. Here you are going away —if you would only say one word— What have I done to deserve this?"

"How strange you are! What can I say?"

"If only one word—"

"There she's firing away one and the same thing," he muttered with vexation, and got up.

"Don't be angry, Victor Alexandrich," she added hastily, unable to repress her tears.

"I'm not angry—only you are foolish— What

do you want? I can't marry you! I can't, can I? Well, then, what do you want? What?" He stared at her, as if awaiting an answer, and opened his fingers wide.

"I want nothing—nothing," she replied, stammering, not daring to outstretch her trembling hands to him, "but simply so, at least one word, at parting—"

And the tears began to stream from her eyes.

"Well, there you are, she's started crying," said Victor indifferently, pulling the cap over his eyes.

"I don't want anything," she went on, sobbing and covering her face with her hands; "but how will I feel now at home, how will I feel? And what will become of me, what will become of me, wretched one that I am? They'll marry the poor little orphan off to a man she does not like. My poor little head!"

"Keep on singing, keep on singing," muttered Victor in a low voice, stirring restlessly.

"If you only said one word, just one: 'Akulina —I—.'"

Sudden heartrending sobs interrupted her. She fell with her face upon the grass and cried bitterly, bitterly— All her body shook convulsively, the back of her neck seemed to rise— The long-suppressed sorrow at last burst forth in a stream of tears. Victor stood a while near her, then he shrugged his shoulders, turned around and walked off with long strides.

A few moments went by. She grew silent, lifted her head, looked around and clasped her hands; she was about to run after him, but her feet failed her—she fell down on her knees. I could not endure it any longer and rushed over to her; but before she had time to look at me, she suddenly seemed to have regained her strength—and with a faint cry she rose and disappeared behind the trees, leaving the scattered flowers on the ground.

I stood a while, picked up the bunch of cornflowers, and walked out of the grove to the field. The sun was low in the pale, clear sky; its rays seemed to have faded and turned cold; they did not shine now, they spread in an even, almost watery, light. There was only a half-hour left until evening, and twilight was setting in. A violent wind was blowing fast toward me across the yellow, dried-up stubble-field; the small withered leaves were carried quickly past me across the road; the side of the grove which stood like a wall by the field trembled and flashed clearly, but not brightly; everywhere on the reddish grass, on the blades, and the straw, innumerable autumn cobwebs flashed and trembled. I stopped. I began to feel sad; it seemed a dismal fear of approaching winter was stealing through the gay, though fresh, smile of fading nature. High above me, a cautious raven flew by, heavily and sharply cutting the air with his wings; then he turned his head, looked at me sidewise, and, croaking abruptly, disappeared beyond the forest; a large flock of pigeons rushed past me from a barn, and, suddenly whirling about in a column, they came down and stationed themselves bustlingly upon the field—a sign of spring autumn! Somebody rode by beyond the bare hillock, making much noise with an empty wagon.

I returned home, but the image of poor Akulina did not leave my mind for a long time, and the cornflowers, long withered, are in my possession to this day.

A BAL MASQUÉ

BY ALEXANDRE DAVY DE LA PAILLETERIE DUMAS

A BAL MASQUÉ

BY ALEXANDRE DAVY DE LA PAILLETERIE DUMAS

I SAID that I was in to no one; one of my friends forced admission.

My servant announced Mr. Anthony R——. Behind Joseph's livery I saw the corner of a black redingote[1]; it is probable that the wearer of the redingote, from his side, saw a flap of my dressing gown; impossible to conceal myself.

"Very well! Let him enter," I said out loud. "Let him go to the devil," I said to myself.

While working it is only the woman you love who can disturb you with impunity, for she is always at bottom interested in what you are doing.

I went up to him, therefore, with the half-bored face of an author interrupted in one of those moments of sorest self-mistrust, while I found him so pale and haggard that the first words I addressed to him were these:

"What is the matter? What has happened to you?"

[1] Redingote is a French corruption of the English word "riding coat" and means generally a long, plain double-breasted street coat.

Translated by R. W. Howes, 3d. Copyright, 1907, by P. F. Collier & Son.

"Oh! Let me take breath," said he. "I'm going to tell you all about it, besides, it's a dream perhaps, or perhaps I am mad."

He threw himself into an armchair, and let his head drop between his hands.

I looked at him in astonishment; his hair was dripping with rain; his shoes, his knees, and the bottom of his trousers were covered with mud. I went to the window; I saw at the door his servant and his cabriolet; I could make nothing out of it all.

He saw my surprise.

"I have been to the cemetery of Père-Lachaise," said he.

"At ten o'clock in the morning?"

"I was there at seven—cursed bal masqué!"

I could not imagine what a bal masqué and Père-Lachaise had to do with one another. I resigned myself, and turning my back to the mantelpiece began to roll a cigarette for him between my fingers with the phlegm and the patience of a Spaniard.

While he was coming to the point I hinted to Anthony that I, for my part, was commonly very susceptible to attentions of that kind.

He made me a sign of thanks, but pushed my hand away.

Finally I bent over to light the cigarette for myself: Anthony stopped me.

"Alexandre," he said to me, "Listen, I beg of you."

A BAL MASQUÉ

"But you have been here already a quarter of an hour and have not told me anything."

"Oh! it is a most strange adventure."

I got up, placed my cigarette on the mantel-piece and crossed my arms like a man resigned; only I began to believe, as he did, that he was fast becoming mad.

"You remember the ball at the Opéra, where I met you?" he said to me after a moment's silence.

"The last one where there were at least two hundred people?"

"The very same. I left you with the intention of abandoning myself to one of those varieties of which they spoke to me as being a curiosity even in the midst of our curious times; you wished to dissuade me from going; a fatality drove me on. Oh! you, why did you not see it all, you who have the knack of observation? Why were not Hoffman or Callot there to paint the picture as the fantastic, burlesque thing kept unrolling itself beneath my eyes? Unsatisfied and in melancholy mood I walked away, about to quit the Opéra; I came to a hall that was over-flowing and in high spirits: corridors, boxes, parterre. Everything was obstructed. I made a tour of the room; twenty masks called me by name and told me theirs. These were all leaders —aristocrats and merchants—in the undignified disguise of pierrots, of postilions, of merry-andrews, or of fishwives. They were all young people of family, of culture, of talent; and there, forgetful of family, talent, breeding, they were resurrecting in the midst of our sedate and serious times a soirée of the Regency. They had told me about it, and yet I could not have believed it!— I mounted a few steps and leaning against a pillar, half hidden by it, I fixed my eyes on that sea of human beings surging beneath me. Their dominoes, of all colors, their motley costumes, their grotesque disguises formed a spectacle resembling nothing human. The music began to play. Oh, it was then these gargoyle creatures stirred themselves to the sound of that orchestra whose harmony reached me only in the midst of cries, of laughs, of hootings; they hung on to each other by their hands, by their arms, by their necks; a long coil formed itself, beginning with a circular motion, the dancers, men and women, stamping with their feet, made the dust break forth with a noise, the atoms of which were rendered visible by the wan light of the lustres; turning at ever-increasing speed with bizarre postures, with unseemly gestures, with cries full of abandonment; turning always faster and still faster, swaying and swinging like drunken men, yelling like lost women, with more delirium than delight, with more passion than pleasure; resembling a coil of the damned doing infernal penance under the scourge of demons! All this passed beneath my eyes, at my feet. I felt the wind of their whirling past; as they rushed by each one

whom I knew flung a word at me that made me
blush. All this noise, all this humming, all this
confusion, all this music went on in my brain as
well as in the room! I soon came to the point
of no longer knowing whether that which I had
before my eyes was a dream or reality; I came
to the point of asking myself whether it was not
I who was mad and they who were sane; I was
seized with a weird temptation to throw myself
into the midst of this pandemonium, like Faust
through the Witches' Sabbath, and I felt that I
too, would then have cries, postures, laughs like
theirs. Oh! from that to madness there is but
one step. I was appalled; I flung myself out of
the room, followed even to the street door by
shrieks that were like those cries of passion
that come out of the caverns of the fallow
deer.

"I stopped a moment under the portico to
collect myself; I did not wish to venture into the
street; with such confusion still in my soul I
might not be able to find my way; I might, perhaps, be thrown under the wheels of some carriage I had not seen coming. I was as a drunken
man might be who begins to recover sufficient
reason in his clouded brain to recognize his condition, and who, feeling the will return but not
the power, with fixed eyes and staring, leans
motionless against some street post or some tree
on the public promenade.

"At that moment a carriage stopped before

the door, a woman alighted or rather shot herself from the doorway.

"She entered beneath the peristyle, turning her head from right to left like one who had lost her way; she was dressed in a black domino, had her face covered by a velvet mask. She presented herself at the door.

" 'Your ticket,' said the door-keeper.

" 'My ticket?' she replied. 'I have none.'

" 'Then get one at the box-office.'

"The domino came back under the peristyle, fumbled nervously about in all her pockets.

" 'No money!' she cried. 'Ah! this ring—a ticket of admission for this ring,' she said.

" 'Impossible,' replied the woman who was distributing the cards; 'we do not make bargains of that kind.'

"And she pushed away the brilliant, which fell to the ground and rolled to my side.

"The domino remained still without moving, forgetting the ring, sunk in thought.

"I picked up the ring and handed it to her.

"Through her mask I saw her eyes fixed on mine.

" 'You must help me to get in,' she said to me; 'You must, for pity's sake.'

" 'But I am going out, madame,' I said to her.

" 'Then give me six francs for this ring, and you will render me a service for which I shall bless you my life long.'

"I replaced the ring on her finger; I went to

the box-office, I took two tickets. We reentered together.

"As we arrived within the corridor I felt that she was tottering. Then with her second hand she made a kind of ring around my arm.

" 'Are you in pain?' I asked her.

" 'No, no, it is nothing,' she replied, 'a dizziness, that is all—'

"She hurried me into the hall.

"We reentered into that giddy Charenton.[2]

"Three times we made the tour, breaking our way with great difficulty through the waves of masks that were hurling themselves one upon the other; she trembling at every unseemly word that came to her ear; I blushing to be seen giving my arm to a woman who would thus put herself in the way of such words; then we returned to the end of the hall.

"She fell upon a sofa. I remained standing in front of her, my hand leaning on the back of her seat.

" 'Oh! this must seem to you very bizarre,' she said, 'but not more so than to me, I swear to you. I have not the slightest idea of all this' (she looked at the ball), 'for even in my dreams I could not imagine such things. But they wrote me, you see, that he would be here with a woman, and what sort of a woman should it be who could come to a place like this?'

---

[2] Charenton Saint Maurice, the lunatic asylum near Paris, commonly designated as Charenton.

"I made a gesture of surprise; she understood.

" 'But *I* am here, you wish to ask, do you not? Oh! but for me that is another thing: I, I am looking for him; I, I am his wife. As for these people, it is madness and dissipation that drives them hither. But I, I, it is jealousy infernal! I have been everywhere looking for him; I have been all night in a cemetery; I have been at Grève[3] on the day of an execution; and yet, I swear to you, as a young girl I have never once gone into the street without my mother; as a wife I have never taken one step out of doors without being followed by a lackey; and yet here I am, the same as all these women who are so familiar with the way; here I am giving my arm to a man whom I do not know, blushing under my mask at the opinion he ought to have of me! I know all this!—Have you ever been jealous, monsieur?'

" 'Unhappily,' I replied to her.

" 'Then you will forgive me, for you understand. You know that voice that cries out to you "Do!" as in the ear of a madame; you have felt that arm that pushes one into shame and crime, like the arm of fate. You know that at such a moment one is capable of everything, if one can only get vengeance.'

"I was about to reply; all at once she rose, her eyes fastened on two dominoes that were passing in front of us at that moment.

[3] The name of a public square in Paris where executions formerly took place.

" 'Silence!' she said.

"And she hurried me on following in their footsteps. I was thrown into the middle of an intrigue of which I understood nothing; I could feel all the threads vibrating, but could take hold of none of them by the end; but this poor wife seemed so troubled that she became interesting. I obeyed like a child, so imperious is real feeling, and we set ourselves to follow the two masks, one of which was evidently a man, the other a woman. They spoke in a low voice; the sounds reached our ears with difficulty.

" 'It is he!' she murmured; 'it is his voice; yes, yes, that is his figure—'

"The latter of the two dominoes began to laugh.

" 'That is his laugh,' said she; 'it is he, monsieur, it is he! The letter said true, O, mon Dieu, mon Dieu!'

"In the meanwhile the two masks kept on, and we followed them always. They went out of the hall, and we went out after them; they took the stairs leading to the boxes, and we ascended in their footsteps; they did not stop till they came to the boxes in the centre; we were like their two shadows. A little closed box was opened; they entered it; the door again closed upon them.

"The poor creature I was supporting on my arm frightened me by her excitement. I could not see her face, but crushed against me as she was, I could feel her heart beating, her body shivering, her limbs trembling. There was something uncanny in the way there came to me such knowledge of unheard-of suffering, the spectacle of which I had before my very eyes, of whose victim I knew nothing, and of the cause of which I was completely ignorant. Nevertheless, for nothing in this world would I have abandoned that woman at such a moment.

"As she saw the two masks enter the box and the box close upon them, she stopped still a moment, motionless, and as if overwhelmed. Then she sprang forward to the door to listen. Placed as she was her slightest movement would betray her presence and ruin her; I dragged her back violently by the arm, I lifted the latch of the adjoining box, I drew her in after me, I lowered the grille and pulled the door to.

" 'If you wish to listen,' I said to her, 'at least listen from here.'

"She fell upon one knee and flattened her ear against the partition, and I—I held myself erect on the opposite side, my arms crossed, my head bent and thoughtful.

"All that I had been able to observe of that woman seemed to me to indicate a type of beauty. The lower part of her face, which was not concealed by her mask, was youthful, velvety, and round; her lips were scarlet and delicate; her teeth, which the black velvet mask falling just above them made appear still whiter, were small, separated, and glistening; her hand was one to be modeled, her figure to be held between the fingers; her black hair, silky, escaped in profusion from beneath the hood of her domino, and the foot of a child, that played in and out under her skirt, looked as if it should have trouble in balancing her body, all lithe, all graceful, all airy as it was. Oh, what a marvelous piece of perfection must she be! Oh! he that should hold her in his arms, that should see every faculty of that spirit absorbed in loving him, that should feel the beating of her heart against his, her tremblings, her nervous palpitations, and that should be able to say: 'All of this, all of this, comes of love, of love for me, for me alone among all the millions of men, for me, angel predestined! Oh! that man!—that man!—'

"Such were my thoughts, when all at once I saw that woman rise, turn toward me, and say to me in a voice broken and fierce:

" 'Monsieur, I am beautiful, I swear it; I am young, I am but nineteen. Until now I have been white as an angel of the Creation—ah, well—' she threw both arms about my neck, '—ah, well, I am yours—take me!—'

"At the same instant I felt her lips pressed close to mine, and the effect of a bite, rather than that of a kiss, ran shuddering and dismayed through my whole body; over my eyes passed a cloud of flame.

"Ten minutes later I was holding her in my arms, in a swoon, half dead and sobbing.

"Slowly she came to herself; through her mask I made out how haggard were her eyes; I saw the lower part of her pale face, I heard her teeth chatter one upon the other, as in the chill of a fever. I see it all once more.

"She remembered all that taken place, and fell at my feet.

" 'If you have any compassion,' she said to me, sobbing, 'any pity, turn away your eyes from me, never seek to know me; let me go and forget me. I will remember for two!'

"At these words she rose again; quickly, like a thought that escapes us, she darted toward the door, opened it, and coming back again, 'Do not follow me, in heaven's name, Monsieur, do not follow me!' she said.

"The door pushed violently open, closed again between her and me, stole her from my sight, like an apparition. I have never seen her more!

"I have never seen her more! And ever since, ever since the six months that have glided by, I have sought her everywhere, at balls, at spectacles, at promenades. Every time I have seen from a distance a woman with lithe figure, with a foot like a child's, with black hair, I have followed her, I have drawn near to her, I have looked into her face, hoping that her blushes would betray her. Nowhere have I found her again, in no place have I seen her again—except at night, except in my dreams! Oh! there, there she reappears; there I feel her, I feel her embraces, her biting caresses so ardent, as if she had something of the devil in her; then the mask has fallen and a face most grotesque appeared to me at times blurred as if veiled in a cloud; sometimes brilliant, as if circled by an aureole; sometimes pale, with a skull white and naked, with eyes vanished from the orbits, with teeth chattering and few. In short, ever since that night, I have ceased to live; burning with mad passion for a woman I do not know, hoping always and always disappointed at my hopes. Jealous without the right to be so, without knowing of whom to be jealous, not daring to avow such madness, and all the time pursued, preyed upon, wasted away, consumed by her."

As he finished these words he tore a letter from his breast.

"Now that I have told you everything," he said to me, "take this letter and read it."

I took the letter and read:

"Have you perhaps forgotten a poor woman who has forgotten nothing and who dies because she can not forget?

"When you receive this letter I shall be no more. Then go to the cemetery of Père-Lachaise, tell the concierge to let you see among the newest graves one that bears on its stone the simple name 'Marie,' and when you are face to face with that grave, fall on your knees and pray."

"Ah, well!" continued Anthony, "I received that letter yesterday, and I went there this morning. The concierge conducted me to the grave, and I remained two hours on my knees there, praying and weeping. Do you understand? She was there, that woman. Her flaming spirit nad stolen away; the body consumed by it had bowed, even to breaking, beneath the burden of jealousy and of remorse; she was there, under my feet, and she had lived, and she had died, for me unknown; unknown!—and taking a place in my life as she had taken one in the grave; unknown!—and burying in my heart a corpse, cold and lifeless, as she had buried one in the sepulchre—Oh! Do you know anything to equal it? Do you know any event so appalling? Therefore, now, no more hope. I will see her again never. I would dig up her grave that I might recover, perhaps, some traces wherewithal to reconstruct her face; and I love her always! Do you understand, Alexandre? I love her like a madman, and I would kill myself this instant in order to rejoin her, if she were not to remain unknown to me for eternity, as she was unknown to me in this world."

With these words he snatched the letter from my hands, kissed it over and over again, and began to weep like a little child.

I took him in my arms, and not knowing what to say to him, I wept with him.

VALIA

BY LEONID ANDREIEV

VALIA

BY LEONID ANDREIEV

VALIA was reading a huge, very huge book, almost half as large as himself, with very black letters and pictures occupying the entire page. To see the top line Valia had to stretch out his neck, lean far over the table, kneeling in his chair, and putting his short chubby finger on the letters for fear they would be lost among the other ones like it, in which case it was a difficult task to find them again. Owing to these circumstances, unforeseen by the publishers, the reading advanced very slowly, notwithstanding the breath-catching interest of the book.

It was a story about a very strong boy whose name was Prince Bova, and who could, by merely grasping the legs or arms of other boys, wrench them away from the body.

But Valia was suddenly interrupted in his reading; his mother entered with some other woman.

"Here he is," said his mother, her eyes red with weeping. The tears had evidently been shed very recently as she was still crushing a white lace handkerchief in her hand.

"Valichka, darling!" exclaimed the other woman, and putting her arms about his head, she began to kiss his face and eyes, pressing her thin, hard lips to them. She did not fondle him as did his mother, whose kisses were soft and melting; this one seemed loath to let go of him. Valia accepted her pricking caresses with a frown and silence; he was very much displeased at being interrupted, and he did not at all like this strange woman, tall, with bony, long fingers upon which there was not even one ring. And she smelled so bad: a damp, moldly smell, while his mother always exhaled a fresh, exquisite perfume.

At last the woman left him in peace, and while he was wiping his lips she looked him over with that quick sort of glance which seemed to photograph one. His short nose with its indication of a future little hump, his thick, unchildish brows over dark eyes, and the general appearance of stern seriousness, recalled some one to her, and she began to cry. Even her weeping was unlike mama's: the face remained immovable while the tears quickly rolled down one after the other— before one had time to fall another was already chasing after it. Her tears ceased as suddenly as they had commenced, and she asked: "Valichka, do you know me?"—"No."

"I called to see you. Twice I called to see you."

Perhaps she had called upon him, perhaps she had called twice, but how should Valia know of it? With her questions she only hindered him from reading.

"I am your mama, Valia!" said the woman.

Valia looked around in astonishment to find his mama, but she was no longer in the room.

"Why, can there be two mamas?" he asked. "What nonsense you are telling me."

The woman laughed, but this laugh did not please Valia; it was evident that the woman did not wish to laugh at all, and did it purposely to fool him. For some moments they were both silent.

"And what book is it you are reading?"

"About Prince Bova," Valia informed her with serious self-esteem and an evident respect for the big book.

"Ach, it must be very interesting! Tell me, please!" the woman asked with an ingratiating smile.

And once more something unnatural and false sounded in this voice, which tried to be soft and round like the voice of his mother, but remained sharp and prickly. The same insincerity appeared also in all the movements of the woman; she turned on her chair and even stretched out her neck with a manner as if preparing for a long and attentive listening; and when Valia reluctantly began the story, she immediately retired within herself, like a dark-lantern on which the cover is suddenly thrown. Valia felt the offense toward himself and Prince Bova, but, wishing to be polite, he quickly finished the story and added: "That is all."

"Well, good-by, my dear, my dove!" said the strange woman, and once more pressed her lips to Valia's face. "I shall soon call again. Will you be glad?"

"Yes, come please," politely replied Valia, and to get rid of her more quickly he added: "I will be very glad."

The visitor left him, but hardly had Valia found in the book again the word at which he had been interrupted, when mama entered, looked at him, and she also began to weep. He could easily understand why the other woman should have wept; she must have been sorry that she was so unpleasant and tiresome—but why should his mama weep?

"Listen, mama," he said musingly, "how that woman bored me! She says that she is my mama. Why, could there be two mamas to one boy?"

"No, baby, there could not; but she speaks the truth; she is your mother."

"And what are you, then?"

"I am your auntie."

This was a very unexpected discovery, but Valia received it with unshakable indifference; auntie, well, let it be auntie—was it not just the same? A word did not, as yet, have the same meaning for him as it would for a grown person. But his former mother did not understand it, and began to explain why it had so happened that she had been a mother and had become an aunt. Once, long ago, when Valia was very little—

"How little? So?" Valia raised his hand about a quarter of a yard from the table. "Like Kiska?" Valia exclaimed, joyfully surprised, with mouth opened and brow lifted. He spoke of his kitten that had been presented to him.

"Yes."

Valia broke into a happy laugh, but immediately resumed his usual earnestness, and with the condescension of a grown person recalling the mistakes of his youth, he remarked: "How funny I must have been!"

When he was so very little and funny, like Kiska, he had been brought by that woman and given away forever, also like Kiska. And now, when he had become so big and clever, the woman wanted him.

"Do you wish to go to her?" asked his former mother and reddened with joy when Valia resolutely and sternly said: "No, she does not please me!" and once more took up his book.

Valia considered the affair closed, but he was mistaken. This strange woman, with a face as devoid of life as if all the blood had been drained out of it, who had appeared from no one knew where, and vanished without leaving a trace, seemed to have set the whole house in turmoil and filled it with a dull alarm. Mama-auntie often cried and repeatedly asked Valia if he wished to leave her; uncle-papa grumbled, patted his bald

pate so that the sparse, gray hair on it stood up,
and when auntie-mama was absent from the room
he also asked Valia if he would like to go to that
woman. Once, in the evening, when Valia was
already in his little bed but was not yet sleeping,
he heard his uncle and auntie speaking of him
and the woman. The uncle spoke in an angry
basso at which the crystal pendants of the chan-
delier gently trembled and sparkled with bluish
and reddish lights.

"You speak nonsense, Nastasia Philippovna.
We have no right to give the child away."

"She loves him, Grisha."

"And we! Do we not love him? You are
arguing very strangely, Nastasia Philippovna.
It seems as if you would be glad to get rid of the
child—"

"Are you not ashamed of yourself?"

"Well, well, how quick you are to take offense.
Just consider this matter cold-bloodedly and rea-
sonably. Some frivolous thing or other gives
birth to children, light-heartedly disposes of them
by placing them on your threshold, and afterward
says: 'Kindly give me my child, because, on account of my lover having abandoned me, I feel
lonesome. For theatres and concerts I have no
money, so give me the child to serve as a toy to
play with.' No, madam, be easy, we shall see
who wins in this case!"

"You are unjust to her, Grisha. You know
well how ill and lonely she is—"

"You, Nastasia Philippovna, can make even a saint lose patience, by God! And the child you seem to have forgotten? For you is it wholly immaterial whether he is brought up an honest man or a scoundrel? And I could bet my head that he would be brought up by her a scoundrel, rascal, and—scoundrel."

"Grisha!"

"I ask you, for God's sake, not to irritate me! And where did you get this devilish habit of contradicting? 'She is so lonely.' And are *we* not lonely? The heartless woman that you are, Nastasia Philippovna! And why did I marry you!"

The heartless woman broke into tears, and her husband immediately begged her pardon, declaring that only a born fool could pay any attention to the words of such an old ass as he was. Gradually she became calmer and asked: "What does Talonsky say?"

"And what makes you think that he is such a clever fellow?" Gregory Aristarchovich again flew into a passion. "He says that everything depends on how the court will look at it. . . Something new, is it not, as if we did not know without his telling that everything depends on how the court will look at it! Of course it matters little to him—what does he care?—he will have his bark and then safely go his way. If I had *my* way, it would go ill with all these empty talkers—"

But here Nastasia Philippovna shut the dining-room door and Valia did not hear the end of the conversation. But he lay for a long time with open eyes, trying to understand what sort of woman it was who wished to take him away from his home and ruin him.

On the next day he waited from early morning expecting his auntie to ask him if he wished to go to his mother; but auntie did not ask. Neither did his uncle. Instead of this, they both gazed at Valia as if he were dangerously ill and would soon die; they caressed him and brought him large books with colored pictures. The woman did not call any more, but it seemed to Valia that she must be lurking outside the door watching for him, and that as soon as he would pass the threshold she would seize him and carry him out into a black and dismal distance where cruel monsters were wriggling and breathing fire.

In the evenings while his uncle Gregory Aristarchovich was occupied in his study and Nastasia Philippovna was knitting something, or playing a game of solitaire, Valia read his books, in which the lines would grow gradually thicker and the letters smaller. Everything in the room was quiet, so quiet that the only thing to be heard was the rustling of the pages he turned, and occasionally the uncle's loud cough from the study, or the striking of the abacus counters. The lamp, with its blue shade, threw a bright light on the blue plush table-cover, but the corners of the room were full of a quiet, mysterious gloom

There stood large plants with curious leaves and roots crawling out upon the surface and looking very much like fighting serpents, and it seemed as if something large and dark was moving amidst them. Valia read, and before his wide-open eyes passed terrible, beautiful and sad images which awakened in him pity and love, but more often fear. Valia was sorry for the poor water-nymph who so dearly loved the handsome prince that for him she had given up her sisters and the deep, peaceful ocean; and the prince knew nothing of this love, because the poor water-nymph was dumb, and so he married a gay princess; and while great festivities in honor of the wedding were in full swing on board the ship, and music was playing and all were enjoying themselves, the poor water-nymph threw herself into the dark waves to die. Poor, sweet little water-nymph, so quiet and sad, and modest! But often terrible, cruel, human monsters appeared before Valia. In the dark nights they flew somewhere on their prickly wings, and the air whistled over their heads, and their eyes burned like red-hot coals. And afterward, they were surrounded by other monsters like themselves while a mysterious and terrible something was happening there. Laughter as sharp as a knife, long and pitiful wailing; strange weird dances in the purplish light of torches, their slanty, fiery tongues wrapped in the red clouds of smoke; and dead men with long, black beards— All this was the manifestation of a single enigmatic and cruel power, wishing to destroy man. Angry and mysterious spectres filled the air, hid among the plants, whispered something, and pointed their bony fingers at Valia; they gazed at him from behind the door of the adjoining unlit room, giggled and waited till he would go to bed, when they would silently dart around over his head; they peeped at him from out of the garden through the large, dark windows, and wailed sorrowfully with the wind.

In and out among all this vicious and terrible throng appeared the image of that woman who had come for Valia. Many people came and went in the house of Gregory Aristarchovich, and Valia did not remember their faces, but this face lived in his memory. It was such an elongated, thin, yellow face, and smiled with a sly, dissembling smile, from which two deep lines appeared at the two corners of the mouth. If this woman took Valia he would die.

"Listen," Valia once said to his aunt, tearing himself away from his book for a moment. "Listen," he repeated with his usual earnestness, and with a glance that gazed straight into the eyes of the person with whom he spoke: "I shall call you mama, not auntie. You talk nonsense when you say that the woman—is mama. You are mama, not she."

"Why?" asked Nastasia Philippovna, blushing like a young girl who had just received a com-

pliment. But along with her joy there could also
be heard in her voice the sound of fear for Valia.
He had become so strange of late, and timid;
feared to sleep alone, as he used to do, raved in
his sleep and cried.

"But, Valichka, it is true, she is your mother."

"I really wonder where you get this habit of
contradicting!" Valia said after some musing,
imitating the tone of Gregory Aristarchovich.

Nastasia Philippovna laughed, but while preparing for bed that night she spoke for a considerable time with her husband, who boomed like
a Turkish drum, abused the empty talkers, and
frivolous, hare-brained women, and afterward
went with his wife to see Valia.

They gazed long and silently into the face of
the sleeping child. The flame of the candle
swayed in the trembling hand of Gregory Aristarchovich and lent a fantastic, death-like coloring to the face of the boy, which was as white as
the pillows on which it rested. It seemed as if a
pair of stern, black eyes looked at them from the
dark hollows, demanding a reply and threaten-
ing them with misfortune and unknown sorrow,
and the lips twitched into a strange, ironic smile
as if upon his helpless child-head lay a vague reflection of those cruel and mysterious spectre
monsters that silently hovered over it.

"Valia!" whispered the frightened Nastasia.
The boy sighed deeply but did not move, as if
enchained in the sleep of death.

"Valia! Valia!" the deep, trembling voice of her husband was added to that of Nastasia Philippovna.

Valia opened his eyes, shaded by thick eyelashes; the light of the candle made him wink, and he sprang to his knees, pale and frightened. His uncovered, thin little arms, like a pearl necklace encircled his auntie's full, rosy neck, and hiding his little head upon her breast and screwing up his eyes tight as if fearing that they would open of themselves, he whispered: "I am afraid, mama, I am afraid! Do not go!"

That was a bad night for the whole household; when Valia at last fell asleep, Gregory Aristarchovich got an attack of asthma. He choked, and his full, white breast rose and fell spasmodically under the ice compresses. Toward morning he grew more tranquil, and the worn Nastasia fell asleep with the thought that her husband would not survive the loss of the child.

After a family council at which it was decided that Valia ought to read less and to see more of children of his own age, little girls and boys were brought to the house to play with him. But Valia from the first conceived a dislike for these foolish children who, in his eyes, were too noisy, loud and indecorous. They pulled flowers, tore books, jumped over chairs, and fought like little monkeys; and he, serious and thoughtful, looked on at their pranks with amazement and displeasure, and, going up to Nastasia Philippovna,

said: "They tire me! I would rather sit by you."
And in the evenings he once more took up his
book, and when Gregory Aristarchovich, grum-
bling at all the deviltry the child read about, and
by which he was losing his senses, gently tried to
take the book from Valia's hands, the child silently and irresolutely pressed it to himself. And
the improvised pedagogue beat a confused re-
treat and angrily scolded his wife:

"Is this what you call bringing up! No, Nastasia Philippovna, I see you are more fit to take
care of kittens than to bring up children. The
boy is so spoiled that one can not even take a book
away from him."

One morning while Valia was sitting at breakfast with Nastasia Philippovna, Gregory Aristarchovich suddenly came rushing into the dining-
room. His hat was tilted on the back of his head,
his face was covered with perspiration; while still
at the other side of the door he shouted joyfully
into the room:

"Refused! The court has refused!"

The diamond earrings in Nastasia Philippovna's ears began to sparkle, and the little knife
she held in her hand dropped to the plate.

"Is it true?" she asked, breathlessly.

Gregory Aristarchovich made a serious face,
just to show that he had spoken the truth, but
immediately forgetting his intention, his face became covered with a whole network of merry
wrinkles. Then once more remembering that he

lacked that earnestness of demeanor with which important news is usually imparted, he frowned, pushed a chair up to the table, placed his hat upon it, forgot that it was his hat, and thinking the chair to be already occupied by some one, threw a stern look at Nastasia Philippovna, then on Valia, winked his eye at Valia; and only after all these solemn preliminaries did he declare:

"I always said that Talonsky was a devilish clever fellow; can't fool him easily, Nastasia Philippovna."

"So it is true?"

"You are always ready with your eternal doubts. I said the case of Mme. Akimova is dismissed. Clever, is it not, little brother?" he turned to Valia and added in a stern, official tone: "And that said Akimova is to pay the costs."

"That woman will not take me, then?"

"I guess she won't, brother mine! Ach, I have entirely forgotten, I brought you some books!"

Gregory Aristarchovich rushed into the corridor, but halted on hearing Nastasia Philippovna's scream. Valia had fallen back on his chair in a faint.

A happy time began for the family. It was as if some one who had lain dangerously ill in the house had suddenly recovered and all began to breathe more easily and freely. Valia lost his fear of the terrible monsters and no longer suffered from nightmares. When the little monkeys, as he called the children, came to see

him again, he was the most inventive of the lot.
But even into the most fantastic plays he intro-
duced his habitual earnestness and staidness, and
when they played Indians, he found it indispen-
sable to divest himself of almost all his clothing
and cover his body with red paint.

In view of the businesslike manner in which
these games were conducted, Gregory Aristarchovich now found it possible to participate in
them, as far as his abilities allowed. In the rôle
of a bear he did not appear to great advantage,
but he had a great and well deserved success in
his rôle of elephant. And when Valia, silent and
earnest as a true son of the Goddess Kali, sat upon
his father's shoulders and gently tapped upon
his rosy bald pate with a tiny toy hammer, he
really reminded one of a little Eastern prince who
despotically reigns over people and animals.

The lawyer Talonsky tried to convey a hint to
Gregory Aristarchovich that all was not safe yet,
but the former could not comprehend how three
judges could reverse the decision of three other
judges, when the laws are the same here and
everywhere. And when the lawyer insisted,
Gregory Aristarchovich grew angry, and to prove
that there was nothing to be feared from the
higher court, he brought forward that same
Talonsky on whom he now implicitly relied:

"Why, are you not going to be present when
the case is brought before the court? Well, then
what is there to be talked about. I wish you,

Nastasia Philippovna, would make him ashamed of himself."

Talonsky smiled, and Nastasia Philippovna gently chided him for his purposeless doubts. They also spoke of the woman who had caused all the trouble, but now that she could menace them no more, and the court had decided that she must bear all the costs of the trial, they often dubbed her "poor woman."

Since the day Valia had heard that the woman had no longer any power to take him, she had lost in his eyes the halo of mysterious fear, which enveloped her like a mist and distorted the features of her thin face, and Valia began to think of her as he did of all other people. He now repeatedly heard that she was unhappy and could not understand why; but this pale bloodless face grew more simple, natural and near to him, the "poor woman," as they called her, began to interest him, and recalling other poor women of whom he had read, he felt a growing pity and a timid tenderness for her.

He imagined that she must sit alone in some dark room, fearing something and weeping, always weeping, as she had wept then when she had come to see him. And he felt sorry that he had not told her the story of Prince Bova better than he had at the time.

.   .   .   .

It appeared that three judges could, after all, disagree with the decision of three other judges.

VALIA

The higher court had reversed the decision of the district court, the child was adjudged to his real mother. And the appeal was not considered by the senate.

When the woman came to take Valia away with her, Gregory Aristarchovich was not at home, he was at Talonsky's house and was lying in Talonsky's bedroom, and only the bald, rosy pate was visible above the snow-white pillows.

Nastasia Philippovna did not leave her room, and the maid led Valia forth from it already dressed for the road. He wore a fur coat and tall overshoes in which he moved his feet with difficulty. From under his fur cap looked out a pale little face with a frank and serious expression in the dark eyes. Under his arm Valia carried a book in which was the story of a poor water-nymph.

The tall, gaunt woman pressed the boy to her shabby coat and sobbed out: "How you have grown, Valichka! You are unrecognizable," she said, trying to joke, but Valia adjusted his cap and, contrary to habit, did not look into the eyes of the one who from this day on was to be his mother, but into her mouth. It was large, but with beautiful, small teeth; the two wrinkles on the corners of the mouth were still on the same place where Valia had seen them first, only now they were deeper.

"You are not angry with me?" asked mama; but Valia, not replying to her question, said: "Let us be gone."

"Valichka!" came a pitiful scream from Nastasia Philippovna's room, and she appeared on the threshold with eyes swollen from weeping, and clasping her hands she rushed toward the child, sank on her knees, and put her head on his shoulder. She did not utter a sound, only the diamonds in her ears trembled.

"Come, Valia," sternly said the tall woman, taking his hand. "We must not remain any longer among people who have subjected your mother to such torture—such torture!"

Her dry voice was full of hatred and she longed to strike the kneeling woman with her foot.

"Ugh! heartless wretches! You would be glad to take even my only child from me!" she wrathfully whispered, and pulled Valia away by his hand. "Come! Don't be like your father, who abandoned me."

"Ta-ke ca-re of him," Nastasia called after them.

The hired sleigh which stood waiting for them flew softly and lightly over the snow and noiselessly carried Valia away from the quiet house with its wonderful plants and flowers, its mysterious fairy-tale world, immeasurable and deep as the sea, with its windows gently screened by the boughs of the tall trees of the garden. Soon the house was lost in the mass of other houses, as similar to each other as the letters in Valia's book, and vanished forever from Valia.

It seemed to him as if they were swimming in

a river, the banks of which were constituted of rows of lanterns as close to each other as beads on a string, but when they approached nearer, the beads were scattered, forming large, dark spaces and merging behind into just such a line of light. And then Valia thought that they were standing motionless on the very same spot; and everything began to be like a fairy tale—he himself and the tall woman who was pressing him to her, and everything around him.

The hand in which he carried his book was getting stiff with cold, but he would not ask his mother to take the book from him.

The small room into which Valia's mother had taken him was untidy and hot; in a corner neai the large bed stood a little curtained bed such as Valia had not slept in for a long, long time.

"You are frozen! Well, wait, we shall soon have some tea! Well, now you are with your mama. Are you glad?" his mother asked with the hard, unpleasant look of one who has been forced to smile beneath blows all her life long.

"No," Valia replied shyly, frightened at his own frankness.

"No? And I had bought some toys for you. Just look, there they are on the window.

Valia approached the window and examined the toys. They were wretched paper horses with straight, thick legs, Punch with a red cap on, with an idiotically grinning face and a large nose, and little tin soldiers with one foot raised in the air.

Valia had long ago given up playing with toys and did not like them, but from politeness he did not show it to his mother. "Yes, they are nice toys," he said.

She noticed the glance he threw at the window, and said with that unpleasant, ingratiating smile:

"I did not know what you liked, darling, and I bought them for you a long time ago."

Valia was silent, not knowing what to reply.

"You must know that I am all alone, Valia, all alone in the wide world; I have no one whose advice I could ask; I thought they would please you." Valia was silent.

Suddenly the muscles of the woman's face relaxed and the tears began to drop from her eyes, quickly, quickly, one after the other; and she threw herself on the bed which gave a pitiful squeak under the weight of her body, and with one hand pressed to her breast, the other to her temples, she looked vacantly through the wall with her pale, faded eyes, and whispered:

"He was not pleased! Not pleased!—"

Valia promptly approached the bed, put his little hand, still red with the cold, on the head of his mother, and spoke with the same serious staidness which distinguished this boy's speech:

"Do not cry, mama. I will love you very much. I do not care to play with toys, but I will love you ever so much. If you wish, I will read to you the story of the poor water-nymph."

THE LOST CHILD

BY FRANÇOIS ÉDOUARD JOACHIM COPPÉE

THE LOST CHILD

BY FRANÇOIS ÉDOUARD JOACHIM COPPÉE

O N that morning, which was the morning before Christmas, two important events happened simultaneously—the sun rose, and so did M. Jean-Baptiste Godefroy.

Unquestionably the sun, illuminating suddenly the whole of Paris with its morning rays, is an old friend regarded with affection by everybody. It is particularly welcome after a fortnight of misty atmosphere and gray skies, when the wind has cleared the air and allowed the sun's rays to reach the earth again. Besides all of which the sun is a person of importance. Formerly, he was regarded as a god, and was called Osiris, Apollyon, and I don't know what else. But do not imagine that because the sun is so important he is of greater influence than M. Jean-Baptiste Godefroy, millionaire banker, director of the *Comptoir Général de Crédit,* administrator of several big companies, deputy and member of the General Counsel of the Eure, officer of the Legion of Honor, etc., etc. And whatever opinion the sun may have about himself, he certainly has not a higher opinion than M. Jean-Baptiste

Translated by J. Matthewman   Copyright, 1894, by The Current Literature Publishing Company.

Godefroy has of *himself*. So we are authorized
to state, and we consider ourselves justified in
stating, that on the morning in question, at about
a quarter to eight, the sun and M. Jean-Baptiste
Godefroy rose.

Certainly the manner of rising of these two
great powers mentioned was not the same. The
good old sun began by doing a great many pretty
actions. As the sleet had, during the night, covered the bare branches of the trees in the boulevard Malesherbes, where the *hôtel* Godefroy is
situated, with a powdered coating, the great
magician sun amused himself by transforming
the branches into great bouquets of red coral. At
the same time he scattered his rays impartially on
those poor passers-by whom necessity sent out, so
early in the morning, to gain their daily bread.
He even had a smile for the poor clerk, who, in a
thin overcoat, was hurrying to his office, as well
as for the *grisette,* shivering under her thin, in-
sufficient clothing; for the workman carrying
half a loaf under his arm, for the car-conductor
as he punched the tickets, and for the dealer in
roast chestnuts, who was roasting his first panful.
In short, the sun gave pleasure to everybody in
the world. M. Jean-Baptiste Godefroy, on the
contrary, rose in quite a different frame of mind.
On the previous evening he had dined with the
Minister for Agriculture. The dinner, from the
removal of the *potage* to the salad, bristled with
truffles, and the banker's stomach, aged forty-

seven years, experienced the burning and biting of pyrosis. So the manner in which M. Jean-Baptiste Godefroy rang for his valet-de-chambre was so expressive that, as he got some warm water for his master's shaving, Charles said to the kitchen-maid:

"There he goes! The monkey is barbarously ill-tempered again this morning. My poor Gertrude, we're going to have a miserable day."

Whereupon, walking on tiptoe, with eyes modestly cast down, he entered the chamber of his master, opened the curtains, lit the fire, and made all the necessary preparations for the toilet with the discreet demeanor and respectful gestures of a sacristan placing the sacred vessels on the altar for the priest.

"What sort of weather this morning?" demanded M. Godefroy curtly, as he buttoned his undervest of gray swandown upon a stomach that was already a little too prominent.

"Very cold, sir," replied Charles meekly. "At six o'clock the thermometer marked seven degrees above zero. But, as you will see, sir, the sky is quite clear, and I think we are going to have a fine morning."

In stropping his razor, M. Godefroy approached the window, drew aside one of the hangings, looked on the boulevard, which was bathed in brightness, and made a slight grimace which bore some resemblance to a smile.

It is all very well to be perfectly stiff and correct, and to know that it is bad taste to show feeling of any kind in the presence of domestics, but the appearance of the roguish sun in the middle of December sends such a glow of warmth to the heart that it is impossible to disguise the fact. So M. Godefroy deigned, as before observed, to smile. If some one had whispered to the opulent banker that his smile had anything in common with that of the printer's boy, who was enjoying himself by making a slide on the pavement, M. Godefroy would have been highly incensed. But it really was so all the same; and during the space of one minute this man who was so occupied by business matters, this leading light in the financial and political worlds, indulged in the childish pastime of watching the passers-by, and following with his eyes the files of conveyances as they gaily rolled in the sunshine.

But pray do not be alarmed. Such a weakness could not last long. People of no account, and those who have nothing to do, may be able to let their time slip by in doing nothing. It is very well for women, children, poets, and riffraff. M. Godefroy had other fish to fry; and the work of the day which was commencing promised to be exceptionally heavy. From half-past eight to ten o'clock he had a meeting at his office with a certain number of gentlemen, all of whom bore a striking resemblance to M. Godefroy. Like him, they were very nervous; they had risen with the sun, they were all *blasés,* and they all had the same object in view—to gain money. After breakfast (which he took after the meeting), M. Godefroy had to leap into his carriage and rush to the Bourse, to exchange a few words with other gentlemen who had also risen at dawn, but who had not the least spark of imagination among them. (The conversations were always on the same subject—money.) From there, without losing an instant, M. Godefroy went to preside over another meeting of acquaintances entirely void of compassion and tenderness. The meeting was held round a baize-covered table, which was strewn with heaps of papers and well provided with ink-wells. The conversation again turned on money, and various methods of gaining it. After the aforesaid meeting he, in his capacity of deputy, had to appear before several commissions (always held in rooms where there were baize-covered tables and ink-wells and heaps of papers). There he found men as devoid of sentiment as he was, all utterly incapable of neglecting any occasion of gaining money, but who, nevertheless, had the extreme goodness to sacrifice several hours of the afternoon to the glory of France.

After having quickly shaved he donned a morning suit, the elegant cut and finish of which showed that the old beau of nearly fifty had not ceased trying to please. When he shaved he spared the narrow strip of pepper-and-salt beard round his chin, as it gave him the air of a trust-

worthy family man in the eyes of the Arrogants
and of fools in general. Then he descended to his
cabinet, where he received the file of men who
were entirely occupied by one thought—that of
augmenting their capital. These gentlemen discussed several projected enterprises, all of them
of considerable importance, notably that of a new
railroad to be laid across a wild desert. Another
scheme was for the founding of monster works
in the environs of Paris, another of a mine to be
worked in one of the South American republics.
It goes without saying that no one asked if the
railway would have passengers or goods to carry,
or if the proposed works should manufacture cot-
ton nightcaps or distil whisky; whether the mine
was to be of virgin gold or of second-rate cop-
per: certainly not. The conversation of M. Godefroy's morning callers turned exclusively upon
the profits which it would be possible to realize
during the week which should follow the issue of
the shares. They discussed particularly the values
of the shares, which they knew would be destined
before long to be worth less than the paper on
which they were printed in fine style.

These conversations, bristling with figures,
lasted till ten o'clock precisely, and then the director of the *Comptoir Général de Crédit,* who,
by the way, was an honest man—at least, as
honest as is to be found in business—courteously
conducted his last visitor to the head of the stair-
way. The visitor named was an old villain, as

rich as Crœsus, who, by a not uncommon chance, enjoyed the general esteem of the public; whereas, had justice been done to him, he would have been lodging at the expense of the State in one of those large establishments provided by a thoughtful government for smaller delinquents; and there he would have pursued a useful and healthy calling for a lengthy period, the exact length having been fixed by the judges of the supreme court. But M. Godefroy showed him out relentlessly, notwithstanding his importance —it was absolutely necessary to be at the Bourse at 11 o'clock—and went into the dining-room.

It was a luxuriously furnished room. The furniture and plate would have served to endow a cathedral. Nevertheless, notwithstanding that M. Godefroy took a gulp of bicarbonate of soda, his indigestion refused to subside, consequently the banker could only take the scantiest breakfast—that of a dyspeptic. In the midst of such luxury, and under the eye of a well-paid butler, M. Godefroy could only eat a couple of boiled eggs and nibble a little mutton chop. The man of money trifled with dessert—took only a crumb of Roquefort—not more than two cents' worth. Then the door opened and an overdressed but charming little child—young Raoul, four years old—the son of the company director, entered the room, accompanied by his German nursery governess.

This event occurred every day at the same hour

—a quarter to eleven, precisely, while the carriage which was to take the banker to the Bourse was awaiting the gentleman who had only a quarter of an hour to give to paternal sentiment. It was not that he did not love his son. He did love him—nay, he adored him, in his own particular way. But then, you know, business *is* business.

At the age of forty-two, when already worldly-wise and *blasé,* he had fancied himself in love with the daughter of one of his club friends—Marquis de Neufontaine, an old rascal—a nobleman, but one whose card-playing was more than open to suspicion, and who would have been expelled from the club more than once but for the influence of M. Godefroy. The nobleman was only too happy to become the father-in-law of a man who would pay his debts, and without any scruples he handed over his daughter—a simple and ingenuous child of seventeen, who was taken from a convent to be married—to the worldly banker. The girl was certainly sweet and pretty, but she had no dowry except numerous aristocratic prejudices and romantic illusions, and her father thought he was fortunate in getting rid of her on such favorable terms. M. Godefroy, who was the son of an avowed old miser of Andelys, had always remained a man of the people, and intensely vulgar. In spite of his improved circumstances, he had not improved. His entire lack of tact and refinement was painful to his young wife, whose tenderest feelings he ruthlessly and thoughtlessly trampled upon. Things were looking unpromising, when, happily for her, Madame Godefroy died in giving birth to her firstborn. When he spoke of his deceased wife, the banker waxed poetical, although had she lived they would have been divorced in six months. His son he loved dearly for several reasons—first, because the child was an only son; secondly, because he was a scion of two such houses as Godefroy and Neufontaine; finally, because the man of money had naturally great respect for the heir to many millions. So the youngster had golden rattles and other similar toys, and was brought up like a young Dauphin. But his father, overwhelmed with business worries, could never give the child more than fifteen minutes per day of his precious time—and, as on the day mentioned, it was always during "cheese"—and for the rest of the day the father abandoned the child to the care of the servants.

"Good morning, Raoul."

"Good morning, papa."

And the company director, having put his serviette away, sat young Raoul on his left knee, took the child's head between his big paws, and in stroking and kissing it actually forgot all his money matters and even his note of the afternoon, which was of great importance to him, as by it he could gain quite an important amount of patronage.

"Papa," said little Raoul suddenly, "will

Father Christmas put anything in my shoe to-night?"

The father answered with "Yes, if you are a good child." This was very striking from a man who was a pronounced freethinker, who always applauded every anti-clerical attack in the Chamber with a vigorous "Hear, hear." He made a mental note that he must buy some toys for his child that very afternoon.

Then he turned to the nursery governess with: "Are you quite satisfied with Raoul, Mademoiselle Bertha?"

Mademoiselle Bertha became as red as a peony at being addressed, as if the question were scarcely *comme il faut,* and replied by a little imbecile snigger, which seemed fully to satisfy M. Godefroy's curiosity about his son's conduct.

"It's fine to-day," said the financier, "but cold. If you take Raoul to Monceau Park, mademoiselle, please be careful to wrap him up well."

Mademoiselle, by a second fit of idiotic smiling, having set at rest M. Godefroy's doubts and fears on that essential point, he kissed his child, left the room hastily, and in the hall was enveloped in his fur coat by Charles, who also closed the carriage door. Then the faithful fellow went off to the café which he frequented, Rue de Miromesnil, where he had promised to meet the coachman of the baroness who lived opposite, to play a game of billiards, thirty up—and spot-barred, of course.

THE LOST CHILD

Thanks to the brown bay—for which a thou‑
sand francs over and above its value was paid by
M. Godefroy as a result of a sumptuous snail
supper given to that gentleman's coachman by
the horse-dealer—thanks to the expensive brown
bay which certainly went well, the financier was
able to get through his many engagements satis‑
factorily. He appeared punctually at the Bourse,
sat at several committee tables, and at a quarter
to five, by voting with the ministry, he helped to
reassure France and Europe that the rumors of
a ministerial crisis had been totally unfounded.
He voted with the ministry because he had suc‑
ceeded in obtaining the favors which he de‑
manded as the price of his vote.

After he had thus nobly fulfilled his duty to
himself and his country, M. Godefroy remem‑
bered what he had said to his child on the sub‑
ject of Father Christmas, and gave his coach‑
man the address of a dealer in toys. There he
bought, and had put in his carriage, a fantastic
rocking-horse, mounted on casters—a whip in
each ear; a box of leaden soldiers—all as exactly
alike as those grenadiers of the Russian regiment
of the time of Paul I, who all had black hair and
snub noses; and a score of other toys, all equally
striking and costly. Then, as he returned home,
softly reposing in his well-swung carriage, the
rich banker, who, after all, was a father, began to
think with pride of his little boy and to form
plans for his future.

When the child grew up he should have an education worthy of a prince, and he would be one, too, for there was no longer any aristocracy except that of money, and his boy would have a capital of about 30,000,000 francs.

If his father, a pettifogging provincial lawyer, who had formerly dined in the Latin Quarter when in Paris, who had remarked every evening when putting on a white tie that he looked as fine as if he were going to a wedding—if he had been able to accumulate an enormous fortune, and to become thereby a power in the republic; if he had been able to obtain in marriage a young lady, one of whose ancestors had fallen at Marignano, what an important personage little Raoul might become. M. Godefroy built all sorts of air-castles for his boy, forgetting that Christmas is the birthday of a very poor little child, son of a couple of vagrants, born in a stable, where the parents only found lodging through charity.

In the midst of the banker's dreams the coachman cried: "Door, please," and drove into the yard. As he went up the steps M. Godefroy was thinking that he had barely time to dress for dinner; but on entering the vestibule he found all the domestics crowded in front of him in a state of alarm and confusion. In a corner, crouching on a seat, was the German nursery-governess, crying. When she saw the banker she buried her face in her hands and wept still more copiously than before. M. Godefroy felt that some misfortune had happened.

"What's the meaning of all this? What's amiss? What has happened?"

Charles, the *valet de chambre*, a sneaking rascal of the worst type, looked at his master with eyes full of pity and stammered: "Mr. Raoul—"

"My boy?"

"Lost, sir. The stupid German did it. Since four o'clock this afternoon he has not been seen."

The father staggered back like one who had been hit by a ball. The German threw herself at his feet, screaming: "Mercy, mercy!" and the domestics all spoke at the same time.

Bertha didn't go to *parc Monceau*. She lost the child over there on the fortifications. We have sought him all over, sir. We went to the office for you, sir, and then to the Chamber, but you had just left. Just imagine, the German had a rendezvous with her lover every day, beyond the ramparts, near the gate of Asnières. What a shame! It is a place full of low gipsies and strolling players. Perhaps the child has been stolen. Yes, sir, we informed the police at once. How could we imagine such a thing? A hypocrite, that German! She had a rendezvous, doubtless, with a countryman—a Prussian spy, sure enough!"

His son lost! M. Godefroy seemed to have a torrent of blood rushing through his head. He sprang at Mademoiselle, seized her by the arms and shook her furiously.

"Where did you lose him, you miserable girl? Tell me the truth before I shake you to pieces. Do you hear? Do you hear?"

But the unfortunate girl could only cry and beg for mercy.

The banker tried to be calm. No, it was impossible. Nobody would dare to steal *his* boy. Somebody would find him and bring him back. Of that there could be no doubt. He could scatter money about right and left, and could have the entire police force at his orders. And he would set to work at once, for not an instant should be lost.

"Charles, don't let the horses be taken out. You others, see that this girl doesn't escape. I'm going to the Prefecture."

And M. Godefroy, with his heart thumping against his sides as if it would break them, his hair wild with fright, darted into his carriage, which at once rolled off as fast as the horses could take it. What irony! The carriage was full of glittering playthings, which sparkled every time a gaslight shone on them. For the next day was the birthday of the divine Infant at whose cradle wise men and simple shepherds alike adored.

"My poor little Raoul! Poor darling! Where is my boy?" repeated the father as in his anguish he dug his nails into the cushions of the carriage.

THE LOST CHILD

At that moment all his titles and decorations, his honors, his millions, were valueless to him. He had one single idea burning in his brain. "My poor child! Where is my child?"

At last he reached the Prefecture of Police. But no one was there—the office had been deserted for some time.

"I am M. Godefroy, deputy from L'Eure— My little boy is lost in Paris; a child of four years. I must see the Prefect." He slipped a louis into the hand of the *concièrge.*

The good old soul, a veteran with a gray mustache, less for the sake of the money than out of compassion for the poor father, led him to the Prefect's private apartments. M. Godefroy was finally ushered into the room of the man in whom were centred all his hopes. He was in evening dress, and wore a monocle; his manner was frigid and rather pretentious. The distressed father, whose knees trembled through emotion, sank into an armchair, and, bursting into tears, told of the loss of his boy—told the story stammeringly and with many breaks, for his voice was choked by sobs.

The Prefect, who was also father of a family, was inwardly moved at the sight of his visitor's grief, but he repressed his emotion and assumed a cold and self-important air.

"You say, sir, that your child has been missing since four o'clock?"

"Yes."

"Just when night was falling, confound it. He isn't at all precocious, speaks very little, doesn't know where he lives, and can't even pronounce his own name?"

"Unfortunately that is so."

"Not far from Asnières gate? A suspected quarter. But cheer up. We have a very intelligent *Commissaire de Police* there. I'll telephone to him."

. . . .

The distressed father was left alone for five minutes. How his temples throbbed and his heart beat!

Then, suddenly, the Prefect reappeared, smiling with satisfaction. "Found!"

Whereupon M. Godefroy rushed to the Prefect, whose hand he pressed till that functionary winced with the pain.

"I must acknowledge that we were exceedingly fortunate. The little chap is blond, isn't he? Rather pale? In blue velvet? Black felt hat, with a white feather in it?"

"Yes, yes; that's he. That's my little Raoul."

"Well, he's at the house of a poor fellow down in that quarter who had just been at the police office to make his declaration to the Commissaire. Here's his address, which I took down: *'Pierron, rue des Cailloux, Levallois-Perret.'* With good horses you may reach your boy in less than an hour. Certainly, you won't find him in an aristocratic quarter; his surroundings won't be of the highest. The man who found him is only a small dealer in vegetables."

But that was of no importance to M. Godefroy, who, having expressed his gratitude to the Prefect, leaped down the stairs four at a time, and sprang into his carriage. At that moment he realized how devotedly he loved his child. As he drove away he no longer thought of little Raoul's princely education and magnificent inheritance. He was decided never again to hand over the child entirely to the hands of servants, and he also made up his mind to devote less time to monetary matters and the glory of France and attend more to his own. The thought also occurred to him that France wouldn't be likely to suffer from the neglect. He had hitherto been ashamed to recognize the existence of an old-maid sister of his father, but he decided to send for her to his house. She would certainly shock his lackeys by her primitive manners and ideas. But what of that? She would take care of his boy, which to him was of much more importance than the good opinion of his servants. The financier, who was always in a hurry, never felt so eager to arrive punctually at a committee meeting as he was to reach the lost little one. For the first time in his life he was longing through pure affection to take the child in his arms.

The carriage rolled rapidly along in the clear, crisp night air down boulevard Malesherbes; and, having crossed the ramparts and passed the large houses, plunged into the quiet solitude of suburban streets. When the carriage stopped M. Godefroy saw a wretched hovel, on which was the number he was seeking; it was the house where Pierron lived. The door of the house opened immediately, and a big, rough-looking fellow with red mustache appeared. One of his sleeves was empty. Seeing the gentleman in the carriage, Pierron said cheerily: "So you are the little one's father. Don't be afraid. The little darling is quite safe," and, stepping aside in order to allow M. Godefroy to pass, he placed his finger on his lips with: "Hush! The little one is asleep!"

Yes, it was a real hovel. By the dim light of a little oil lamp M. Godefroy could just distinguish a dresser from which a drawer was missing, some broken chairs, a round table on which stood a beer-mug which was half empty, three glasses, some cold meat on a plate, and on the bare plaster of the wall two gaudy pictures—a bird's-eye view of the Exposition of 1889, with the Eiffel Tower in bright blue, and the portrait of General Boulanger when a handsome young lieutenant. This last evidence of weakness of the tenant of the house may well be excused, since it was shared by nearly everybody in France. The man took the lamp and went on tiptoe to the corner of the room where, on a clean bed, two little fellows were fast asleep. In the little one, around whom the other had thrown a protecting arm, M. Godefroy recognized his son.

"The youngsters were tired to death, and so sleepy," said Pierron, trying to soften his rough voice. "I had no idea when you would come, so gave them some supper and put them to bed, and then I went to make a declaration at the police office. Zidore generally sleeps up in the garret, but I thought they would be better here, and that I should be better able to watch them."

M. Godefroy, however, scarcely heard the explanation. Strangely moved, he looked at the two sleeping infants on an iron bedstead and covered with an old blanket which had once been used either in barracks or hospital. Little Raoul, who was still in his velvet suit, looked so frail and delicate compared with his companion that the banker almost envied the latter his brown complexion.

"Is he your boy?" he asked Pierron.

"No," answered he. "I am a bachelor, and don't suppose I shall ever marry, because of my accident. You see, a dray passed over my arm— that was all. Two years ago a neighbor of mine died, when that child was only five years old. The poor mother really died of starvation. She wove wreaths for the cemeteries, but could make nothing worth mentioning at that trade—not enough to live. However, she worked for the child for five years, and then the neighbors had to buy wreaths for her. So I took care of the youngster. Oh, it was nothing much, and I was soon repaid. He is seven years old, and is a sharp little fellow, so he helps me a great deal. On Sundays and Thursdays, and the other days after school, he helps me push my handcart. Zidore is a smart little chap. It was he who found your boy."

"What!" exclaimed M. Godefroy—"that child!"

"Oh, he's quite a little man, I assure you. When he left school he found your child, who was walking on ahead, crying like a fountain. He spoke to him and comforted him, like an old grandfather. The difficulty is, that one can't easily understand what your little one says— English words are mixed up with German and French. So we couldn't get much out of him, nor could we learn his address. Zidore brought him to me—I wasn't far away; and then all the old women in the place came round chattering and croaking like so many frogs, and all full of advice.

"'Take him to the police,'" said some.

But Zidore protested.

"That would scare him," said he, for like all Parisians, he has no particular liking for the police—"and besides, your little one didn't wish to leave him. So I came back here with the child as soon as I could. They had supper, and then off to bed. Don't they look sweet?"

When he was in his carriage, M. Godefroy had decided to reward the finder of his child hand-somely—to give him a handful of that gold so easily gained. Since entering the house he had seen a side of human nature with which he was formerly unacquainted—the brave charity of the poor in their misery. The courage of the poor girl who had worked herself to death weaving wreaths to keep her child; the generosity of the poor cripple in adopting the orphan, and above all, the intelligent goodness of the little street Arab in protecting the child who was still smaller than himself—all this touched M. Godefroy deeply and set him reflecting. For the thought had occurred to him that there were other cripples who needed to be looked after as well as Pierron, and other orphans as well as Zidore. He also debated whether it would not be better to employ his time looking after them, and whether money might not be put to a better use than merely gaining money. Such was his reverie as he stood looking at the two sleeping children. Finally, he turned round to study the features of the greengrocer, and was charmed by the loyal expression in the face of the man, and his clear, truthful eyes.

"My friend," said M. Godefroy, "you and your adopted son have rendered me an immense service. I shall soon prove to you that I am not ungrateful. But, for to-day—I see that you are not in comfortable circumstances, and I should like to leave a small proof of my thankfulness."

But the hand of the cripple arrested that of the banker, which was diving into his coat-pocket where he kept bank-notes.

"No, sir; no! Anybody else should have done just as we have done. I will not accept any recompense; but pray don't take offense. Certainly, I am not rolling in wealth, but please excuse my pride—that of an old soldier; I have the Tonquin medal—and I don't wish to eat food which I haven't earned."

"As you like," said the financier; "but an old soldier like you is capable of something better. You are too good to push a handcart. I will make some arrangement for you, never fear."

The cripple responded by a quiet smile, and said coldly: "Well, sir, if you really wish to do something for me—"

"You'll let me care for Zidore, won't you?" cried M. Godefroy, eagerly.

"That I will, with the greatest of pleasure," responded Pierron, joyfully. "I have often thought about the child's future. He is a sharp little fellow. His teachers are delighted with him."

Then Pierron suddenly stopped, and an expression came over his face which M. Godefroy at once interpreted as one of distrust. The thought evidently was: "Oh, when he has once left us he'll forget us entirely."

"You can safely pick the child up in your arms and take him to the carriage. He'll be better at home than here, of course. Oh, you needn't be afraid of disturbing him. He is fast asleep, and you can just pick him up. He must have his shoes on first, though."

Following Pierron's glance M. Godefroy perceived on the hearth, where a scanty coke fire was dying out, two pairs of children's shoes—the elegant ones of Raoul, and the rough ones of Zidore. Each pair contained a little toy and a package of bonbons.

"Don't think about that," said Pierron in an abashed tone. "Zidore put the shoes there. You know children still believe in Christmas and the child Jesus, whatever scholars may say about fables; so, as I came back from the *commissaire,* as I didn't know whether your boy would have to stay here to-night, I got those things for them both."

At which the eyes of M. Godefroy, the freethinker, the hardened capitalist, and *blasé* man of the world, filled with tears.

He rushed out of the house, but returned in a minute with his arms full of the superb mechanical horse, the box of leaden soldiers, and the rest of the costly playthings bought by him in the afternoon, and which had not even been taken out of the carriage.

"My friend, my dear friend," said he to the greengrocer, "see, these are the presents which Christmas has brought to my little Raoul. I want him to find them here, when he awakens, and to share them with Zidore, who will henceforth be his playmate and friend. You'll trust me now, won't you? I'll take care both of Zidore and of you, and then I shall ever remain in your debt, for not only have you found my boy, but you have also reminded me, who am rich and lived only for myself, that there are other poor who need to be looked after. I swear by these two sleeping children, I won't forget them any longer."

Such is the miracle which happened on the 24th of December of last year, ladies and gentlemen, at Paris, in the full flow of modern egotism. It doesn't sound likely—that I own; and I am compelled to attribute this miraculous event to the influence of the Divine Child who came down to earth nearly nineteen centuries ago to command men to love one another.

THE MAN WHO WOULD BE KING

BY RUDYARD KIPLING

THE MAN WHO WOULD
BE KING

BY RUDYARD KIPLING

"Brother to a Prince and fellow to a beggar if he be found worthy."

THE law, as quoted, lays down a fair conduct of life, and one not easy to follow. I have been fellow to a beggar again and again under circumstances which prevented either of us finding out whether the other was worthy. I have still to be brother to a Prince, though I once came near to kinship with what might have been a veritable King and was promised the reversion of a Kingdom—army, law-courts, revenue and policy all complete. But, to-day, I greatly fear that my King is dead, and if I want a crown I must go and hunt it for myself.

The beginning of everything was in a railway train upon the road to Mhow from Ajmir. There had been a Deficit in the Budget, which necessitated traveling, not Second-class, which is only half as dear as First-class, but by Intermediate, which is very awful indeed. There are no cushions in the Intermediate class, and the population are either Intermediate, which is Eurasian, or native, which for a long night journey is nasty, or Loafer, which is amusing though intoxicated. Intermediates do not patronize refreshment-rooms. They carry their food in bundles and pots, and buy sweets from the native sweetmeat-sellers, and drink the roadside water. That is why in the hot weather Intermediates are taken out of the carriages dead, and in all weathers are most properly looked down upon.

My particular Intermediate happened to be empty till I reached Nasirabad, when a huge gentleman in shirt-sleeves entered, and, following the custom of Intermediates, passed the time of day. He was a wanderer and a vagabond like myself, but with an educated taste for whiskey. He told tales of things he had seen and done, of out-of-the-way corners of the Empire into which he had penetrated, and of adventures in which he risked his life for a few days' food. "If India was filled with men like you and me, not knowing more than the crows where they'd get their next day's rations, it isn't seventy millions of revenue the land would be paying—it's seven hundred millions," said he; and as I looked at his mouth and chin I was disposed to agree with him. We talked politics—the politics of Loaferdom that sees thing from the underside where the lath and plaster is not smoothed off—and we talked postal arrangements because my friend wanted to send a telegram back from the next station to Ajmir, which is the turning-off place from the Bombay to the Mhow line as you travel

westward. My friend had no money beyond
eight annas which he wanted for dinner, and I
had no money at all, owing to the hitch in the
Budget before mentioned. Further, I was going
into a wilderness where, though I should resume
touch with the Treasury, there were no telegraph
offices. I was, therefore, unable to help him in
any way.

"We might threaten a Station-master, and
make him send a wire on tick," said my friend,
"but that'd mean inquiries for you and for me,
and I've got my hands full these days. Did you
say you are traveling back along this line within
any days?"

"Within ten," I said.

"Can't you make it eight?" said he. "Mine is
rather urgent business."

"I can send your telegram within ten days if
that will serve you," I said.

"I couldn't trust the wire to fetch him now I
think of it. It's this way. He leaves Delhi on
the 23d for Bombay. That means he'll be running through Ajmir about the night of the 23d.'

"But I'm going into the Indian Desert," I explained.

"Well *and* good," said he. "You'll be changing at Marwar Junction to get into Jodhpore
territory—you must do that—and he'll be coming through Marwar Junction in the early
morning of the 24th by the Bombay Mail.
Can you be at Marwar Junction on that time?

'Twon't be inconveniencing you because I know that there's precious few pickings to be got out of these Central India States,—even though you pretend to be correspondent of the *Backwoodsman.*"

"Have you ever tried that trick?" I asked.

"Again and again, but the Residents find you out, and then you get escorted to the Border before you've time to get your knife into them. But about my friend here. I *must* give him a word o' mouth to tell him what's come to me or else he won't know where to go. I would take it more than kind of you if you was to come out of Central India in time to catch him at Marwar Junction, and say to him:—'He has gone South for the week.' He'll know what that means. He's a big man with a red beard, and a great swell he is. You'll find him sleeping like a gentleman with all his luggage round him in a Second-class compartment. But don't you be afraid. Slip down the window, and say:—'He has gone South for the week,' and he'll tumble. It's only cutting your time of stay in those parts by two days. I ask you as a stranger—going to the West," he said, with emphasis.

"Where have *you* come from?" said I.

"From the East," said he, "and I am hoping that you will give him the message on the Square —for the sake of my Mother as well as your own."

Englishmen are not usually softened by appeals to the memory of their mothers, but for certain reasons, which will be fully apparent, I saw fit to agree.

"It's more than a little matter," said he, "and that's why I ask you to do it—and now I know that I can depend on you doing it. A Second-class carriage at Marwar Junction, and a red-haired man asleep in it. You'll be sure to remember. I get out at the next station, and I must hold on there till he comes or sends me what I want."

"I'll give the message if I catch him," I said, "and for the sake of your Mother as well as mine I'll give you a word of advice. Don't try to run Central India States just now as the correspondent of the *Backwoodsman*. There's a real one knocking about here, and it might lead to trouble."

"Thank you," said he, simply, "and when will the swine be gone? I can't starve because he's ruining my work. I wanted to get hold of the Degumber Rajah down here about his father's widow, and give him a jump."

"What did he do to his father's widow, then?"

"Filled her up with red pepper and slippered her to death as she hung from a beam. I found that out myself, and I'm the only man that would dare going into the State to get hush-money for it. They'll try to poison me, same as they did in Chortumna when I went on the loot there. But you'll give the man at Marwar Junction my message?"

He got out at a little roadside station, and I reflected. I had heard, more than once, of men personating correspondents of newspapers and bleeding small Native States with threats of exposure, but I had never met any of the caste before. They lead a hard life, and generally die with great suddenness. The Native States have a wholesome horror of English newspapers, which may throw a light on their peculiar methods of government, and do their best to choke correspondents with champagne, or drive them out of their mind with four-in-hand barouches. They do not understand that nobody cares a straw for the internal administration of Native States so long as oppression and crime are kept within decent limits, and the ruler is not drugged, drunk, or diseased from one end of the year to the other. Native States were created by Providence in order to supply picturesque scenery, tigers, and tall-writing. They are the dark places of the earth, full of unimaginable cruelty, touching the Railway and the Telegraph on one side, and, on the other, the days of Harun-al-Raschid. When I left the train I did business with divers Kings, and in eight days passed through many changes of life. Sometimes I wore dress-clothes and consorted with Princes and Politicals, drinking from crystal and eating from silver. Sometimes I lay out upon the

ground and devoured what I could get, from a
plate made of a flapjack, and drank the running
water, and slept under the same rug as my servant. It was all in the day's work.

Then I headed for the Great Indian Desert
upon the proper date, as I had promised, and
the night Mail set me down at Marwar Junction,
where a funny little, happy-go-lucky, native-
managed railway runs to Jodhpore. The Bombay Mail from Delhi makes a short halt at Marwar. She arrived as I got in, and I had just
time to hurry to her platform and go down the
carriages. There was only one Second-class on
the train. I slipped the window, and looked
down upon a flaming red beard, half covered by
a railway rug. That was my man, fast asleep,
and I dug him gently in the ribs. He woke with
a grunt, and I saw his face in the light of the
lamps. It was a great and shining face.

"Tickets again?" said he.

"No," said I. "I am to tell you that he is
gone South for the week. He is gone South for
the week!"

The train had begun to move out. The red
man rubbed his eyes. "He has gone South for
the week," he repeated. "Now that's just like
his impidence. Did he say that I was to give
you anything?—'Cause I won't."

"He didn't," I said, and dropped away, and
watched the red lights die out in the dark. It
was horribly cold, because the wind was blow-

ing off the sands. I climbed into my own train
—not an Intermediate Carriage this time—and
went to sleep.

If the man with the beard had given me a
rupee I should have kept it as a memento of a
rather curious affair. But the consciousness of
having done my duty was my only reward.

Later on I reflected that two gentlemen like
my friends could not do any good if they fore-
gathered and personated correspondents of newspapers, and might, if they "stuck up" one of
the little rat-trap states of Central India or
Southern Rajputana, get themselves into serious difficulties. I therefore took some trouble
to describe them as accurately as I could remember to people who would be interested in
deporting them; and succeeded, so I was later
informed, in having them headed back from
Degumber borders.

Then I became respectable, and returned to
an Office where there were no Kings and no
incidents except the daily manufacture of a newspaper. A newspaper office seems to attract
every conceivable sort of person, to the prejudice
of discipline. Zenana-mission ladies arrive, and
beg that the Editor will instantly abandon all
his duties to describe a Christian prize-giving in
a back-slum of a perfectly inaccessible village;
Colonels who have been over-passed for com-
mands sit down and sketch the outline of a series
of ten, twelve, or twenty-four leading articles on

Seniority *versus* Selection; missionaries wish to know why they have not been permitted to escape from their regular vehicles of abuse and swear at a brother missionary under special patronage of the editorial We; stranded theatrical companies troop up to explain that they cannot pay for their advertisements, but on their return from New Zealand or Tahiti will do so with interest; inventors of patent punkah-pulling machines, carriage couplings and unbreakable swords and axle-trees call with specifications in their pockets and hours at their disposal; tea-companies enter and elaborate their prospectuses with the office pens; secretaries of ball-committees clamor to have the glories of their last dance more fully expounded; strange ladies rustle in and say:—"I want a hundred lady's cards printed *at once,* please," which is manifestly part of an Editor's duty; and every dissolute ruffian that ever tramped the Grand Trunk Road makes it his business to ask for employment as a proof-reader. And, all the time, the telephone-bell is ringing madly, and Kings are being killed on the Continent, and Empires are saying—"You're another," and Mister Gladstone is calling down brimstone upon the British Dominions, and the little black copy-boys are whining, *"kaa-pi chay-ha-yeh"* (copy wanted) like tired bees, and most of the paper is as blank as Modred's shield.

But that is the amusing part of the year. There are other six months wherein none ever come to call, and the thermometer walks inch by inch up to the top of the glass, and the office is darkened to just above reading-light, and the press machines are red-hot of touch, and nobody writes anything but accounts of amusements in the Hill-stations or obituary notices. Then the telephone becomes a tinkling terror, because it tells you of the sudden deaths of men and women that you knew intimately, and the prickly-heat covers you as with a garment, and you sit down and write:—"A slight increase of sickness is reported from the Khuda Janta Khan District. The outbreak is purely sporadic in its nature, and, thanks to the energetic efforts of the District authorities, is now almost at an end. It is, however, with deep regret we record the death, etc."

Then the sickness really breaks out, and the less recording and reporting the better for the peace of the subscribers. But the Empires and the Kings continue to divert themselves as selfishly as before, and the Foreman thinks that a daily paper really ought to come out once in twenty-four hours, and all the people at the Hill-stations in the middle of their amusements say:—"Good gracious! Why can't the paper be sparkling? I'm sure there's plenty going on up here."

That is the dark half of the moon, and, as the advertisements say, "must be experienced to be appreciated."

THE MAN WHO WOULD BE KING

It was in that season, and a remarkably evil season, that the paper began running the last issue of the week on Saturday night, which is to say, Sunday morning, after the custom of a London paper. This was a great convenience, for immediately after the paper was put to bed, the dawn would lower the thermometer from 96° to almost 84° for half an hour, and in that chill—you have no idea how cold is 84° on the grass until you begin to pray for it—a very tired man could set off to sleep ere the heat roused him.

One Saturday night it was my pleasant duty to put the paper to bed alone. A King or courtier or a courtesan or a community was going to die or get a new Constitution, or do something that was important on the other side of the world, and the paper was to be held open till the latest possible minute in order to catch the telegram. It was a pitchy black night, as stifling as a June night can be, and the *loo,* the red-hot wind from the westward, was booming among the tinder-dry trees and pretending that the rain was on its heels. Now and again a spot of almost boiling water would fall on the dust with the flop of a frog, but all our weary world knew that was only pretence. It was a shade cooler in the press-room than the office, so I sat there, while the type clicked and clicked and the night-jars hooted at the windows, and the all but naked compositors wiped the sweat

from their foreheads and called for water.
The thing that was keeping us back, whatever
it was, would not come off, though the *loo*
dropped and the last type was set, and the
whole round earth stood still in the choking
heat, with its finger on its lip, to wait the event.
I drowsed, and wondered whether the telegraph was a blessing, and whether this dying
man, or struggling people, was aware of the
inconvenience the delay was causing. There
was no special reason beyond the heat and
worry to make tension, but, as the clock hands
crept up to three o'clock and the machines spun
their fly-wheels two and three times to see that
all was in order, before I said the word that
would set them off, I could have shrieked
aloud.

Then the roar and rattle of the wheels shivered the quiet into little bits. I rose to go away,
but two men in white clothes stood in front of
me. The first one said:—"It's him!" The
second said:—"So it is!" And they both laughed
almost as loudly as the machinery roared, and
mopped their foreheads. "We see there was a
light burning across the road and we were sleeping in that ditch there for coolness, and I said
to my friend here, 'The office is open. Let's come
along and speak to him as turned us back from
the Degumber State,'" said the smaller of the
two. He was the man I had met in the Mhow
train, and his fellow was the red-bearded man of

Marwar Junction. There was no mistaking the
eyebrows of the one or the beard of the other.

I was not pleased, because I wished to go to
sleep, not to squabble with loafers. "What do
you want?" I asked.

"Half an hour's talk with you cool and comfortable, in the office," said the red-bearded
man. "We'd *like* some drink—the Contrack
doesn't begin yet, Peachey, so you needn't look
—but what we really want is advice. We don't
want money. We ask you as a favor, because
you did us a bad turn about Degumber."

I led from the press-room to the stifling
office with the maps on the walls, and the red-
haired man rubbed his hands. "That's something like," said he. "This was the proper shop
to come to. Now, Sir, let me introduce to you
Brother Peachey Carnehan, that's him, and
Brother Daniel Dravot, that is *me,* and the less
said about our professions the better, for we have
been most things in our time. Soldier, sailor,
compositor, photographer, proof-reader, street-
preacher, and correspondents of the *Backwoodsman* when we thought the paper wanted one.
Carnehan is sober, and so am I. Look at us
first and see that's sure. It will save you cutting
into my talk. We'll take one of your cigars
apiece, and you shall see us light."

I watched the test. The men were absolutely
sober, so I gave them each a tepid peg.

"Well *and* good," said Carnehan of the eye-

brows, wiping the froth from his moustache.
"Let me talk now, Dan. We have been all over
India, mostly on foot. We have been boiler-
fitters, engine-drivers, petty contractors, and
all that, and we have decided that India isn't
big enough for such as us."

They certainly were too big for the office.
Dravot's beard seemed to fill half the room and
Carnehan's shoulders the other half, as they sat
on the big table. Carnehan continued: "The
country isn't half worked out because they that
governs it won't let you touch it. They spend
all their blessed time in governing it, and you
can't lift a spade, nor chip a rock, nor look for
oil, nor anything like that without all the Government saying—'Leave it alone and let us govern.' Therefore, such as it is, we will let it alone,
and go away to some other place where a man
isn't crowded and can come to his own. We are
not little men, and there is nothing that we are
afraid of except Drink, and we have signed a
Contrack on that. *Therefore,* we are going away
to be Kings."

"Kings in our own right," muttered Dravot.

"Yes, of course," I said. "You've been
tramping in the sun, and it's a very warm night,
and hadn't you better sleep over the notion?
Come to-morrow."

"Neither drunk nor sunstruck," said Dravot.
"We have slept over the notion half a year, and
require to see Books and Atlases, and we have

decided that there is only one place now in the world that two strong men can Sar-a-*whack*. They call it Kafiristan. By my reckoning it's the top right-hand corner of Afghanistan, not more than three hundred miles from Peshawur. They have two and thirty heathen idols there, and we'll be the thirty-third. It's a mountainous country, and the women of those parts are very beautiful."

"But that is provided against in the Contrack," said Carnehan. "Neither Women nor Liqu-or, Daniel."

"And that's all we know, except that no one has gone there, and they fight, and in any place where they fight, a man who knows how to drill men can always be a King. We shall go to those parts and say to any King we find—'D' you want to vanquish your foes?' and we will show him how to drill men; for that we know better than anything else. Then we will subvert that King and seize his Throne and establish a Dy-nasty."

"You'll be cut to pieces before you're fifty miles across the Border," I said. "You have to travel through Afghanistan to get to that country. It's one mass of mountains and peaks and glaciers, and no Englishman has been through it. The people are utter brutes, and even if you reached them you couldn't do anything."

"That's more like," said Carnehan. "If you

could think us a little more mad we would be more pleased. We have come to you to know about this country, to read a book about it, and to be shown maps. We want you to tell us that we are fools and to show us your books." He turned to the bookcases.

"Are you at all in earnest?" I said.

"A little," said Dravot, sweetly. "As big a map as you have got, even if it's all blank where Kafiristan is, and any books you've got. We can read, though we aren't very educated."

I uncased the big thirty-two-miles-to-the-inch map of India, and two smaller Frontier maps, hauled down volume INF-KAN of the *Encyclopaedia Britannica,* and the men consulted them.

"See here!" said Dravot, his thumb on the map. "Up to Jagdallak, Peachey and me know the road. We was there with Roberts's Army. We'll have to turn off to the right at Jagdallak through Laghmann territory. Then we get among the hills—fourteen thousand feet—fifteen thousand—it will be cold work there, but it don't look very far on the map."

I handed him Wood on the *Sources of the Oxus.* Carnehan was deep in the *Encyclopaedia.*

"They're a mixed lot," said Dravot, reflectively; "and it won't help us to know the names of their tribes. The more tribes the more they'll fight, and the better for us. From Jagdallak to Ashang. H'mm!"

"But all the information about the country is as sketchy and inaccurate as can be," I protested. "No one knows anything about it really. Here's the file of the *United Services' Institute.* Read what Bellew says."

"Blow Bellew!" said Carnehan. "Dan, they're an all-fired lot of heathens, but this book here says they think they're related to us English."

I smoked while the men pored over *Raverty, Wood,* the maps, and the *Encyclopaedia.*

"There is no use your waiting," said Dravot, politely. "It's about four o'clock now. We'll go before six o'clock if you want to sleep, and we won't steal any of the papers. Don't you sit up. We're two harmless lunatics and if you come, to-morrow evening, down to the Serai we'll say good-bye to you."

"You *are* two fools," I answered. "You'll be turned back at the Frontier or cut up the minute you set foot in Afghanistan. Do you want any money or a recommendation down-country? I can help you to the chance of work next week."

"Next week we shall be hard at work ourselves, thank you," said Dravot. "It isn't so easy being a King as it looks. When we've got our Kingdom in going order we'll let you know, and you can come up and help us to govern it."

"Would two lunatics make a Contrack like that?" said Carnehan, with subdued pride, showing me a greasy half-sheet of note-paper

on which was written the following. I copied
it, then and there, as a curiosity:

*This Contract between me and you persuing witnesseth in the
name of God—Amen and so forth.*

(One)   *That me and you will settle this matter together: i. e.,
to be Kings of Kafiristan.*

(Two)   *That you and me will not, while this matter is being
settled, look at any Liquor, nor any Woman, black,
white or brown, so as to get mixed up with one or the
other harmful.*

(Three) *That we conduct ourselves with dignity and discretion
and if one of us gets into trouble the other will stay
by him.*

   Signed by you and me this day.
   Peachey Taliaferro Carnehan.
   Daniel Dravot.
   Both Gentlemen at Large.

"There was no need for the last article,"
said Carnehan, blushing modestly; "but it looks
regular. Now you knew the sort of men that
loafers are—we *are* loafers, Dan, until we get
out of India—and *do* you think that we would
sign a Contrack like that unless we was in earnest? We have kept away from the two things
that make life worth having.'

"You won't enjoy your lives much longer if
you are going to try this idiotic adventure.
Don't set the office on fire," I said, "and go away
before nine o'clock."

I left them still poring over the maps and
making notes on the back of the "Contrack."
"Be sure to come down to the Serai to-morrow,"
were their parting words.

The Kumharsen Serai is the great four-square
sink of humanity where the strings of camels and

horses from the North load and unload. All the
nationalities of Central Asia may be found there,
and most of the folk of India proper. Balkh
and Bokhara there meet Bengal and Bombay,
and try to draw eyeteeth. You can buy ponies,
turquoises, Persian pussy-cats, saddle-bags, fat-
tailed sheep and mush in the Kumharsen Serai,
and get many strange things for nothing. In
the afternoon I went down there to see whether
my friends intended to keep their word or were
lying about drunk.

A priest attired in fragments of ribbons and
rags stalked up to me, gravely twisting a child's
paper whirligig. Behind was his servant bending under the load of a crate of mud toys. The
two were loading up two camels, and the inhabitants of the Serai watched them with shrieks of
laughter.

"The priest is mad," said a horse-dealer to
me. "He is going up to Kabul to sell toys to
the Amir. He will either be raised to honor or
have his head cut off. He came in here this
morning and has been behaving madly ever
since."

"The witless are under the protection of God,"
stammered a flat-cheeked Usbeg in broken
Hindi. "They foretell future events."

"Would they could have foretold that my
caravan would have been cut up by the Shin-
waris almost within shadow of the Pass!"
grunted the Eusufzai agent of a Rajputana

trading-house whose goods had been feloniously diverted into the hands of other robbers just across the Border, and whose misfortunes were the laughing-stock of the bazar. "Ohé, priest, whence come you and whither do you go?"

"From Roum have I come," shouted the priest, waving his whirligig; "from Roum, blown by the breath of a hundred devils across the sea! O thieves, robbers, liars, the blessing of Pir Khan on pigs, dogs, and perjurers! Who will take the Protected of God to the North to sell charms that are never still to the Amir? The camels shall not gall, the sons shall not fall sick, and the wives shall remain faithful while they are away, of the men who give me place in their caravan. Who will assist me to slipper the King of the Roos with a golden slipper with a silver heel? The protection of Pir Khan be upon his labors!" He spread out the skirts of his gaberdine and pirouetted between the lines of tethered horses.

"There starts a caravan from Peshawur to Kabul in twenty days, *Huzrut*," said the Eusufzai trader. "My camels go therewith. Do thou also go and bring us good-luck."

"I will go even now!" shouted the priest. "I will depart upon my winged camels, and be at Peshawur in a day! Ho! Hazar Mir Khan," he yelled to his servant, "drive out the camels, but let me first mount my own."

He leaped on the back of his beast as it knelt, and, turning round to me, cried:—"Come thou also, Sahib, a little along the road, and I will sell thee a charm—an amulet that shall make thee King of Kafiristan."

Then the light broke upon me, and I followed the two camels out of the Serai till we reached open road and the priest halted.

"What d' you think o' that?" said he in English. "Carnehan can't talk their patter, so I've made him my servant. He makes a handsome servant. 'Tisn't for nothing that I've been knocking about the country for fourteen years. Didn't I do that talk neat? We'll hitch on to a caravan at Peshawur till we get to Jagdallak, and then we'll see if we can get donkeys for our camels, and strike into Kafiristan. Whirligigs for the Amir, O Lor'! Put your hand under the camel-bags and tell me what you feel."

I felt the butt of a Martini, and another and another.

"Twenty of 'em," said Dravot, placidly. "Twenty of 'em, and ammunition to correspond, under the whirligigs and the mud dolls."

"Heaven help you if you are caught with those things!" I said. "A Martini is worth her weight in silver among the Pathans."

"Fifteen hundred rupees of capital—every rupee we could beg, borrow, or steal—are invested on these two camels," said Dravot. "We won't get caught. We're going through the Khaiber with a regular caravan. Who'd touch a poor mad priest?"

"Have you got everything you want?" I asked, overcome with astonishment.

"Not yet, but we shall soon. Give us a memento of your kindness, *Brother*. You did me a service yesterday, and that time in Marwar. Half my Kingdom shall you have, as the saying is." I slipped a small charm compass from my watch-chain and handed it up to the priest.

"Good-bye," said Dravot, giving me his hand cautiously. "It's the last time we'll shake hands with an Englishman these many days. Shake hands with him, Carnehan," he cried, as the second camel passed me.

Carnehan leaned down and shook hands. Then the camels passed away along the dusty road, and I was left alone to wonder. My eye could detect no failure in the disguises. The scene in Serai attested that they were complete to the native mind. There was just the chance, therefore, that Carnehan and Dravot would be able to wander through Afghanistan without detection. But, beyond, they would find death, certain and awful death.

Ten days later a native friend of mine, giving me the news of the day from Peshawur, wound up his letter with:—"There has been much laughter here on account of a certain mad priest who is going in his estimation to sell petty gauds and insignificant trinkets which he ascribes as great charms to H. H. the Amir of Bokhara. He passed through Peshawur and associated himself to the Second Summer caravan that goes to Kabul. The merchants are pleased, because through superstition they imagine that such mad fellows bring good-fortune."

The two, then, were beyond the Border. I would have prayed for them, but, that night, a real King died in Europe, and demanded an obituary notice.

. . . .

The wheel of the world swings through the same phases again and again. Summer passed and winter thereafter, and came and passed again. The daily paper continued and I with it, and upon the third summer there fell a hot night, a night-issue, and a strained waiting for something to be telegraphed from the other side of the world, exactly as had happened before. A few great men had died in the past two years, the machines worked with more clatter, and some of the trees in the Office garden were a few feet taller. But that was all the difference.

I passed over to the press-room, and went through just such a scene as I have already described. The nervous tension was stronger than it had been two years before, and I felt the heat more acutely. At three o'clock I cried, "Print off," and turned to go, when there crept to my chair what was left of a man. He was bent into a circle, his head was sunk between his shoulders, and he moved his feet one over the other like a bear. I could hardly see whether he walked or crawled—this rag-wrapped, whining cripple who addressed me by name, crying that he was come back. "Can you give me a drink?" he whimpered. "For the Lord's sake, give me a drink!"

I went back to the office, the man following with groans of pain, and I turned up the lamp.

"Don't you know me?" he gasped, dropping into a chair, and he turned his drawn face, surmounted by a shock of grey hair, to the light.

I looked at him intently. Once before had I seen eyebrows that met over the nose in an inch-broad black band, but for the life of me I could not tell where.

"I don't know you," I said, handing him the whiskey. "What can I do for you?"

He took a gulp of the spirit raw, and shivered in spite of the suffocating heat.

"I've come back," he repeated; "and I was the King of Kafiristan—me and Dravot—crowned Kings we was! In this office we settled it—you setting there and giving us the books. I am Peachey—Peachey Taliaferro Carnehan, and you've been setting here ever since—O Lord!"

I was more than a little astonished, and expressed my feelings accordingly.

"It's true," said Carnehan, with a dry cackle, nursing his feet, which were wrapped in rags. "True as gospel. Kings we were, with crowns upon our heads—me and Dravot—poor Dan—oh, poor, poor Dan, that would never take advice, not though I begged of him!"

"Take the whiskey," I said, "and take your own time. Tell me all you can recollect of every-thing from beginning to end. You got across the border on your camels, Dravot dressed as a mad priest and you his servant. Do you remember that?"

"I ain't mad—yet, but I shall be that way soon. Of course I remember. Keep looking at me, or maybe my words will go all to pieces. Keep looking at me in my eyes and don't say anything."

I leaned forward and looked into his face as steadily as I could. He dropped one hand upon the table and I grasped it by the wrist. It was twisted like a bird's claw, and upon the back was a ragged, red, diamond-shaped scar.

"No, don't look there. Look at *me*," said Carnehan.

"That comes afterward, but for the Lord's sake don't distrack me. We left with that cara-van, me and Dravot playing all sorts of antics to amuse the people we were with. Dravot used to make us laugh in the evenings when all the people was cooking their dinners—cooking their dinners, and . . . what did they do then? They lit little fires with sparks that went into Dravot's beard, and we all laughed—fit to die. Little red fires they was, going into Dravot's big red beard —so funny." His eyes left mine and he smiled foolishly.

"You went as far as Jagdallak with that caravan," I said, at a venture, "after you had lit those fires. To Jagdallak, where you turned off to try to get into Kafiristan."

"No, we didn't neither. What are you talking about? We turned off before Jagdallak, because we heard the roads was good. But they wasn't good enough for our two camels—mine and Dravot's. When we left the caravan, Dravot took off all his clothes and mine too, and said we would be heathen, because the Kafirs didn't allow Mohammedans to talk to them. So we dressed betwixt and between, and such a sight as Daniel Dravot I never saw yet nor expect to see again. He burned half his beard, and slung a sheep-skin over his shoulder, and shaved his head into patterns. He shaved mine, too, and made me wear outrageous things to look like a heathen. That was in a most mountaineous country, and our camels couldn't go along any more because of the mountains. They were tall and black, and coming home I saw them fight like wild goats—there are lots of goats in Kafiristan. And these mountains, they never keep still, no more than goats. Always fighting they are, and don't let you sleep at night."

"Take some more whiskey," I said, very slowly. "What did you and Daniel Dravot do when the camels could go no further because of the rough roads that led into Kafiristan?"

"What did which do? There was a party called Peachey Taliaferro Carnehan that was with Dravot. Shall I tell you about him? He died out there in the cold. Slap from the bridge fell old Peachey, turning and twisting in the air like a penny whirligig that you can sell to the Amir—No; they was two for three ha'-pence, those whirligigs, or I am much mistaken and woful sore. And then these camels were no use, and Peachey said to Dravot—'For the Lord's sake, let's get out of this before our heads are chopped off,' and with that they killed the camels all among the mountains, not having anything in particular to eat, but first they took off the boxes with the guns and the ammunition, till two men came along driving four mules. Dravot up and dances in front of them, singing—'Sell me four mules.' Says the first man—'If you are rich enough to buy, you are rich enough to rob;' but before ever he could put his hand to his knife, Dravot breaks his neck over his knee, and the other party runs away. So Carnehan loaded the mules with the rifles that was taken off the camels, and together we starts forward into those bitter cold mountaineous parts, and never a road broader than the back of your hand."

He paused for a moment, while I asked him if he could remember the nature of the country through which he had journeyed.

"I am telling you as straight as I can, but my head isn't as good as it might be. They drove nails through it to make me hear better how Dravot died. The country was mountaineous and the mules were most contrary, and the inhabitants was dispersed and solitary. They went up and up, and down and down, and that other party, Carnehan, was imploring of Dravot not to sing and whistle so loud, for fear of bringing down the tremenjus avalanches. But Dravot says that if a King couldn't sing it wasn't worth being King, and whacked the mules over the rump, and never took no heed for ten cold days. We came to a big level valley all among the mountains, and the mules were near dead, so we killed them, not having anything in special for them or us to eat. We sat upon the boxes, and played odd and even with the cartridges that was jolted out.

"Then ten men with bows and arrows ran down that valley, chasing twenty men with bows and arrows, and the row was tremenjus. They was fair men—fairer than you or me—with yellow hair and remarkable well built. Says Dravot, unpacking the guns—'This is the beginning of the business. We'll fight for the ten men,' and with that he fires two rifles at the twenty men, and drops one of them at two hundred yards from the rock where we was sitting. The other men began to run, but Carnehan and Dravot sits on the boxes picking them off at all ranges, up and down the valley. Then we goes up to the ten men that had run across the snow too, and they fires a footy little arrow at us. Dravot he shoots above their heads and they all falls down flat. Then he walks over and kicks them, and then he lifts them up and shakes hands all round to make them friendly like. He calls them and gives them the boxes to carry, and waves his hand for all the world as though he was King already. They takes the boxes and him across the valley and up the hill into a pine wood on the top, where there was half a dozen big stone idols. Dravot he goes to the biggest—a fellow they call Imbra —and lays a rifle and a cartridge at his feet, rubbing his nose respectful with his own nose, patting him on the head, and saluting in front of it. He turns round to the men and nods his head, and says—'That's all right. I'm in the know too, and all these old jim-jams are my friends.' Then he opens his mouth and points down it, and when the first man brings him food, he says—'No;' and when the second man brings him food, he says—'No;' but when one of the old priests and the boss of the village brings him food, he says— 'Yes;' very haughty, and eats it slow. That was how we came to our first village, without any trouble, just as though we had tumbled from the skies. But we tumbled from one of those damned rope-bridges, you see, and you couldn't expect a man to laugh much after that."

"Take some more whiskey and go on," I said. "That was the first village you came into. How did you get to be King?"

"I wasn't King," said Carnehan. "Dravot he was the King, and a handsome man he looked

with the gold crown on his head and all. Him
and the other party stayed in that village, and
every morning Dravot sat by the side of old
Imbra, and the people came and worshipped.
That was Dravot's order. Then a lot of men
came into the valley, and Carnehan and Dravot
picks them off with the rifles before they knew
where they was, and runs down into the valley
and up again the other side, and finds another
village, same as the first one, and the people all
falls down flat on their faces, and Dravot says—
'Now what is the trouble between you two villages?' and the people points to a woman, as fair
as you or me, that was carried off, and Dravot
takes her back to the first village and counts up
the dead—eight there was. For each dead man
Dravot pours a little milk on the ground and
waves his arms like a whirligig and 'That's all
right,' says he. Then he and Carnehan takes the
big boss of each village by the arm and walks
them down into the valley, and shows them how
to scratch a line with a spear right down the valley, and gives each a sod of turf from both sides
o' the line. Then all the people comes down and
shouts like the devil and all, and Dravot says—
'Go and dig the land, and be fruitful and mul-
tiply,' which they did, though they didn't understand. Then we asks the names of things in their
lingo—bread and water and fire and idols and
such, and Dravot leads the priest of each village
up to the idol, and says he must sit there and

judge the people, and if anything goes wrong he is to be shot.

"Next week they was all turning up the land in the valley as quiet as bees and much prettier, and the priests heard all the complaints and told Dravot in dumb show what it was about. 'That's just the beginning,' says Dravot. 'They think we're Gods.' He and Carnehan picks out twenty good men and shows them how to click off a rifle, and form fours, and advance in line, and they was very pleased to do so, and clever to see the hang of it. Then he takes out his pipe and his baccy-pouch and leaves one at one village and one at the other, and off we two goes to see what was to be done in the next valley. That was all rock, and there was a little village there, and Carnehan says,—'Send 'em to the old valley to plant,' and takes 'em there and gives 'em some land that wasn't took before. They were a poor lot, and we blooded 'em with a kid before letting 'em into the new Kingdom. That was to impress the people, and then they settled down quiet, and Carnehan went back to Dravot, who had got into another valley, all snow and ice and most moun-taineous. There was no people there, and the Army got afraid, so Dravot shoots one of them, and goes on till he finds some people in a village, and the Army explains that unless the people wants to be killed they had better not shoot their little matchlocks; for they had matchlocks. We makes friends with the priest and I stays there

alone with two of the Army, teaching the men
how to drill, and a thundering big Chief comes
across the snow with kettle-drums and horns
twanging, because he heard there was a new God
kicking about. Carnehan sights for the brown
of the men half a mile across the snow and wings
one of them. Then he sends a message to the
Chief that, unless he wished to be killed, he must
come and shake hands with me and leave his arms
behind. The Chief comes alone first, and Carnehan shakes hands with him and whirls his arms
about, same as Dravot used, and very much surprised that Chief was, and strokes my eyebrows.
Then Carnehan goes alone to the Chief, and asks
him in dumb show if he had an enemy he hated.
'I have,' says the Chief. So Carnehan weeds out
the pick of his men, and sets the two of the Army
to show them drill, and at the end of two weeks
the men can manœuvre about as well as Volun-
teers. So he marches with the Chief to a great
big plain on the top of a mountain, and the
Chief's men rushes into a village and takes it; we
three Martinis firing into the brown of the enemy.
So we took that village too, and I gives the Chief
a rag from my coat and says, 'Occupy till I
come;' which was scriptural. By way of a re-
minder, when me and the Army was eighteen hundred yards away, I drops a bullet near him standing on the snow, and all the people falls flat on
their faces. Then I sends a letter to Dravot,
wherever he be by land or by sea."

At the risk of throwing the creature out of train I interrupted,—"How could you write a letter up yonder?"

"The letter?—Oh!—The letter! Keep looking at me between the eyes, please. It was a string-talk letter, that we'd learned the way of it from a blind beggar in the Punjab."

I remember that there had once come to the office a blind man with a knotted twig and a piece of string which he wound round the twig according to some cipher of his own. He could, after the lapse of days or hours, repeat the sentence which he had reeled up. He had reduced the alphabet to eleven primitive sounds; and tried to teach me his method, but failed.

"I sent that letter to Dravot," said Carnehan; "and told him to come back because this Kingdom was growing too big for me to handle, and then I struck for the first valley, to see how the priests were working. They called the village we took along with the Chief, Bashkai, and the first village we took, Er-Heb. The priests at Er-Heb was doing all right, but they had a lot of pending cases about land to show me, and some men from another village had been firing arrows at night. I went out and looked for that village and fired four rounds at it from a thousand yards. That used all the cartridges I cared to spend, and I waited for Dravot, who had been away two or three months, and I kept my people quiet.

"One morning I heard the devil's own noise

of drums and horns, and Dan Dravot marches down the hill with his Army and a tail of hundreds of men, and, which was the most amazing —a great gold crown on his head. 'My Gord, Carnehan,' says Daniel, 'this is a tremenjus business, and we've got the whole country as far as it's worth having. I am the son of Alexander by Queen Semiramis, and you're my younger brother and a God too! It's the biggest thing we've ever seen. I've been marching and fighting for six weeks with the Army, and every footy little village for fifty miles has come in rejoiceful; and more than that, I've got the key of the whole show, as you'll see, and I've got a crown for you! I told 'em to make two of 'em at a place called Shu, where the gold lies in the rock like suet in mutton. Gold I've seen, and turquoise I've kicked out of the cliffs, and there's garnets in the sands of the river, and here's a chunk of amber that a man brought me. Call up all the priests and, here, take your crown.'

"One of the men opens a black hair bag and I slips the crown on. It was too small and too heavy, but I wore it for the glory. Hammered gold it was—five pound weight, like a hoop of a barrel.

"'Peachey,' says Dravot, 'we don't want to fight no more. The Craft's the trick, so help me!" and he brings forward that same Chief that I left at Bashkai—Billy Fish we called him afterward, because he was so like Billy Fish that drove the big tank-engine at Mach on the Bolan in the old days. 'Shake hands with him,' says Dravot, and I shook hands and nearly dropped, for Billy Fish gave me the Grip. I said nothing, but tried him with the Fellow Craft Grip. He answers, all right, and I tried the Master's Grip, but that was a slip. 'A Fellow Craft he is!' I says to Dan. 'Does he know the word?' 'He does,' says Dan, 'and all the priests know. It's a miracle! The Chiefs and the priests can work a Fellow Craft Lodge in a way that's very like ours, and they've cut the marks on the rocks, but they don't know the Third Degree, and they've come to find out. It's Gord's Truth. I've known these long years that the Afghans knew up to the Fellow Craft Degree, but this is a miracle. A God and a Grand-Master of the Craft am I, and a Lodge in the Third Degree I will open, and we'll raise the head priests and the Chief's of the villages.'

" 'It's against all the law,' I says, 'holding a Lodge without warrant from any one; and we never held office in any Lodge.'

" 'It's a master-stroke of policy,' says Dravot. 'It means running the country as easy as a four-wheeled bogy on a down grade. We can't stop to inquire now, or they'll turn against us. I've forty Chiefs at my heel, and passed and raised according to their merit they shall be. Billet these men on the villages and see that we run up a Lodge of some kind. The temple of Imbra will do for the Lodge-room. The women must make

aprons as you show them. I'll hold a levee of
Chiefs to-night and Lodge to-morrow.'

"I was fair run off my legs, but I wasn't such
a fool as not to see what a pull this Craft business
gave us. I showed the priests' families how to
make aprons of the degrees, but for Dravot's
apron the blue border and marks was made of
turquoise lumps on white hide, not cloth. We took
a great square stone in the temple for the Master's
chair, and little stones for the officers' chairs, and
painted the black pavement with white squares,
and did what we could to make things regular.

"At the levee which was held that night on
the hillside with big bonfires, Dravot gives out
that him and me were Gods and sons of Alexander, and Past Grand-Masters in the Craft, and
was come to make Kafiristan a country where
every man should eat in peace and drink in quiet,
and specially obey us. Then the Chiefs come
round to shake hands, and they was so hairy and
white and fair it was just shaking hands with old
friends. We gave them names acording as they
was like men we had known in India—Billy Fish,
Holly Wilworth, Pikky Kergan that was Bazar-
master when I was at Mhow, and so on and so on.

"The most amazing miracle was at Lodge next
night. One of the old priests was watching us
continuous, and I felt uneasy, for I knew we'd
have to fudge the Ritual, and I didn't know what
the men knew. The old priest was a stranger
come in from beyond the village of Bashkai. The

minute Dravot puts on the Master's apron that
the girls had made for him, the priest fetches a
whoop and a howl, and tries to overturn the stone
that Dravot was sitting on. 'It's all up now,' I
says. 'That comes of meddling with the Craft
without warrant!' Dravot never winked an eye,
not when ten priests took and tilted over the
Grand-Master's chair—which was to say the
stone of Imbra. The priest begins rubbing the
bottom end of it to clear away the black dirt, and
presently he shows all the other priests the Master's Mark, same as was on Dravot's apron, cut
into the stone. Not even the priests of the temple
of Imbra knew it was there. The old chap falls
flat on his face at Dravot's feet and kisses 'em.
'Luck again,' says Dravot, across the Lodge to
me, 'they say it's the missing Mark that no one
could understand the why of. We're more than
safe now.' Then he bangs the butt of his gun
for a gavel and says:—'By virtue of the authority
vested in me by my own right hand and the help
of Peachey, I declare myself Grand-Master of all
Freemasonry in Kafiristan in this the Mother
Lodge o' the country, and King of Kafiristan
equally with Peachey!' At that he puts on his
crown and I puts on mine—I was doing Senior
Warden—and we opens the Lodge in most ample
form. It was a amazing miracle! The priests
moved in Lodge through the first two degrees
almost without telling, as if the memory was
coming back to them. After that, Peachey and

Dravot raised such as was worthy—high priests and Chiefs of far-off villages. Billy Fish was the first, and I can tell you we scared the soul out of him. It was not in any way according to Ritual, but it served our turn. We didn't raise more than ten of the biggest men, because we didn't want to make the Degree common. And they was clamoring to be raised.

" 'In another six months,' says Dravot, 'we'll hold another Communication and see how you are working.' Then he asks them about their villages, and learns that they was fighting one against the other and were fair sick and tired of it. And when they wasn't doing that they was fighting with the Mohammedans. 'You can fight those when they come into our country,' says Dravot. 'Tell off every tenth man of your tribes for a Frontier guard, and send two hundred at a time to this valley to be drilled. Nobody is going to be shot or speared any more so long as he does well, and I know that you won't cheat me because you're white people—sons of Alexander—and not like common, black Mohammedans. You are *my* people and by God,' says he, running off into English at the end—'I'll make a damned fine Nation of you, or I'll die in the making!'

"I can't tell all we did for the next six months because Dravot did a lot I couldn't see the hang off, and he learned their lingo in a way I never could. My work was to help the people plough

and now and again go out with some of the Army
and see what the other villages were doing, and
make 'em throw rope-bridges across the ravines
which cut up the country horrid. Dravot was
very kind to me, but when he walked up and
down in the pine wood pulling that bloody red
beard of his with both fists I knew he was thinking plans I could not advise him about, and I just
waited for orders.

"But Dravot never showed me disrespect before the people. They were afraid of me and the
Army, but they loved Dan. He was the best of
friends with the priests and the Chiefs; but any
one could come across the hills with a complaint
and Dravot would hear him out fair, and call four
priests together and say what was to be done. He
used to call in Billy Fish from Bashkai, and
Pikky Kergan from Shu, and an old Chief we
called Kafuzelum—it was like enough to his real
name—and hold councils with 'em when there was
any fighting to be done in small villages. That
was his Council of War, and the four priests of
Bashkai, Shu, Khawak, and Madora was his
Privy Council. Between the lot of 'em they sent
me, with forty men and twenty rifles, and sixty
men carrying turquoises, into the Ghorband country to buy those hand-made Martini rifles, that
come out of the Amir's workshops at Kabul,
from one of the Amir's Herati regiments that
would have sold the very teeth out of their mouths
for turquoises.

"I stayed in Ghorband a month, and gave the Governor there the pick of my baskets for hush-money, and bribed the Colonel of the regiment some more, and, between the two and the tribes-people, we got more than a hundred hand-made Martinis, a hundred good Kohat Jezails that'll throw to six hundred yards, and forty man-loads of very bad ammunition for the rifles. I came back with what I had, and distributed 'em among the men that the Chiefs sent to me to drill. Dravot was too busy to attend to those things, but the old Army that we first made helped me, and we turned out five hundred men that could drill, and two hundred that knew how to hold arms pretty straight.

"Even those cork-screwed, hand-made guns was a miracle to them. Dravot talked big about powder-shops and factories, walking up and down in the pine wood when the winter was coming on.

"'I won't make a Nation,' says he. 'I'll make an Empire! These men aren't niggers; they're English! Look at their eyes—look at their mouths. Look at the way they stand up. They sit on chairs in their own houses. They're the Lost Tribes, or something like it, and they've grown to be English. I'll take a census in the spring if the priests don't get frightened. There must be a fair two million of 'em in these hills. The villages are full o' little children. Two million people—two hundred and fifty thousand

fighting men—and all English! They only want
the rifles and a little drilling. Two hundred and
fifty thousand men, ready to cut in on Russia's
right flank when she tries for India! Peachey,
man,' he says, chewing his beard in great hunks,
'we shall be Emperors—Emperors of the Earth!
Rajah Brooke will be a suckling to us. I'll treat
with the Viceroy on equal terms. I'll ask him to
send me twelve picked English—twelve that I
know of—to help us govern a bit. There's
Mackray, Sergeant-pensioner at Segowli —
many's the good dinner he's given me, and his
wife a pair of trousers. There's Donkin, the
Warder of Tounghoo Jail; there's hundreds that
I could lay my hand on if I was in India. The
Viceroy shall do it for me. I'll send a man
through in the spring for those men, and I'll
write for a dispensation from the Grand-Lodge
for what I've done as Grand-Master. That—
and all the Sniders that'll be thrown out when the
native troops in India take up the Martini.
They'll be worn smooth, but they'll do for fighting in these hills. Twelve English, a hundred
thousand Sniders run through the Amir's country in driblets—I'd be content with twenty thousand in one year—and we'd be an Empire. When
everything was shipshape, I'd hand over the
crown—this crown I'm wearing now—to Queen
Victoria on my knees, and she'd say: "Rise up,
Sir Daniel Dravot." Oh, it's big! It's big, I
tell you! But there's so much to be done in every

place—Bashkai, Khawak, Shu, and everywhere else.'

" 'What is it?' I says. 'There are no more men coming in to be drilled this autumn. Look at those fat, black clouds. They're bringing the snow.'

" 'It isn't that,' says Daniel, putting his hand very hard on my shoulder; 'and I don't wish to say anything that's against you, for no other living man would have followed me and made me what I am as you have done. You're a first-class Commander-in-Chief, and the people know you; but—it's a big country, and somehow you can't help me, Peachey, in the way I want to be helped.'

" 'Go to your blasted priests, then!' I said, and I was sorry when I made that remark, but it did hurt me sore to find Daniel talking so superior when I'd drilled all the men, and done all he told me.

" 'Don't let's quarrel, Peachey,' says Daniel, without cursing. 'You're a King, too, and the half of this Kingdom is yours; but can't you see, Peachey, we want cleverer men than us now—three or four of 'em, that we can scatter about for our Deputies. It's a hugeous great State, and I can't always tell the right thing to do, and I haven't time for all I want to do, and here's the winter coming on and all.' He put half his beard into his mouth, and it was as red as the gold of his crown.

" 'I'm sorry, Daniel,' says I. 'I've done all I

could. I've drilled the men and shown the people how to stack their oats better; and I've brought in those tinware rifles from Ghorband—but I know what you're driving at. I take it Kings always feel oppressed that way.'

" 'There's another thing too,' says Dravot, walking up and down. 'The winter's coming and these people won't be giving much trouble and if they do we can't move about. I want a wife.'

" 'For Gord's sake leave the women alone!' I says. 'We've both got all the work we can, though I *am* a fool. Remember the Contrack, and keep clear o' women.'

" 'The Contrack only lasted till such time as we was Kings; and Kings we have been these months past,' says Dravot, weighing his crown in his hand. 'You go get a wife too, Peachey— a nice, strappin', plump girl that'll keep you warm in the winter. They're prettier than English girls, and we can take the pick of 'em. Boil 'em once or twice in hot water, and they'll come as fair as chicken and ham.'

" 'Don't tempt me!' I says. 'I will not have any dealings with a woman not till we are a dam' side more settled than we are now. I've been doing the work o' two men, and you've been doing the work o' three. Let's lie off a bit, and see if we can get some better tobacco from Afghan country and run in some good liquor; but no women.'

" 'Who's talking o' *women?*' says Dravot. 'I

said *wife*—a Queen to breed a King's son for the King. A Queen out of the strongest tribe, that'll make them your blood-brothers, and that'll lie by your side and tell you all the people thinks about you and their own affairs. That's what I want.'

" 'Do you remember that Bengali woman I kept at Mogul Serai when I was a plate-layer?' says I. 'A fat lot o' good she was to me. She taught me the lingo and one or two other things; but what happened? She ran away with the Station-master's servant and half my month's pay. Then she turned up at Dadur Junction in tow of a half-caste, and had the impidence to say I was her husband—all among the drivers in the running-shed!'

" 'We've done with that,' says Dravot. 'These women are whiter than you or me, and a Queen I will have for the winter months.'

" 'For the last time o' asking, Dan, do *not*,' I says. 'It'll only bring us harm. The Bible says that Kings ain't to waste their strength on women, 'specially when they've got a new raw Kingdom to work over.'

" 'For the last time of answering, I will,' said Dravot, and he went away through the pine-trees looking like a big red devil. The low sun hit his crown and beard on one side and the two blazed like hot coals.

"But getting a wife was not as easy as Dan thought. He put it before the Council, and there was no answer till Billy Fish said that he'd better ask the girls. Dravot damned them all round. 'What's wrong with me?' he shouts, standing by the idol Imbra. 'Am I a dog or am I not enough of a man for your wenches? Haven't I put the shadow of my hand over this country? Who stopped the last Afghan raid?' It was me really, but Dravot was too angry to remember. 'Who brought your guns? Who repaired the bridges? Who's the Grand-Master of the sign cut in the stone?' and he thumped his hand on the block that he used to sit on in Lodge, and at Council, which opened like Lodge always. Billy Fish said nothing, and no more did the others. 'Keep your hair on, Dan,' said I; 'and ask the girls. That's how it's done at Home, and these people are quite English.'

" 'The marriage of the King is a matter of State,' says Dan, in a white-hot rage, for he could feel, I hope, that he was going against his better mind. He walked out of the Council-room, and the others sat still, looking at the ground.

" 'Billy Fish,' says I to the Chief of Bashkai, 'what's the difficulty here? A straight answer to a true friend.' 'You know,' says Billy Fish. 'How should a man tell you who know everything? How can daughters of men marry Gods or Devils? It's not proper.'

"I remembered something like that in the Bible; but if, after seeing us as long as they had, they still believed we were Gods, it wasn't for me to undeceive them.

373

" 'A God can do anything,' says I. 'If the King is fond of a girl he'll not let her die.' 'She'll have to,' said Billy Fish. 'There are all sorts of Gods and Devils in these mountains, and now and again a girl marries one of them and isn't seen any more. Besides, you two know the Mark cut in the stone. Only the Gods know that. We thought you were men till you showed the sign of the Master.'

"I wished then that we had explained about the loss of the genuine secrets of a Master-Mason at the first go-off; but I said nothing. All that night there was a blowing of horns in a little dark temple half-way down the hill, and I heard a girl crying fit to die. One of the priests told us that she was being prepared to marry the King.

" 'I'll have no nonsense of that kind,' says Dan. 'I don't want to interfere with your customs, but I'll take my own wife.' 'The girl's a little bit afraid,' says the priest. 'She thinks she's going to die, and they are a-heartening of her up down in the temple.'

" 'Hearten her very tender, then,' says Dravot, 'or I'll hearten you with the butt of a gun so that you'll never want to be heartened again.' He licked his lips, did Dan, and stayed up walking about more than half the night, thinking of the wife that he was going to get in the morning. I wasn't any means comfortable, for I knew that dealings with a woman in foreign parts, though you was a crowned King twenty times over, could not but be risky. I got up very early in the morning while Dravot was asleep, and I saw the priests talking together in whispers, and the Chiefs talking together too, and they looked at me out of the corners of their eyes.

" 'What is up, Fish?' I says to the Bashkai man, who was wrapped up in his furs and looking splendid to behold.

" 'I can't rightly say,' says he; 'but if you can induce the King to drop all this nonsense about marriage, you'll be doing him and me and yourself a great service.'

" 'That I do believe,' says I. 'But sure, you know, Billy, as well as me, having fought against and for us, that the King and me are nothing more than two of the finest men that God Almighty ever made. Nothing more, I do assure you.'

" 'That may be,' says Billy Fish, 'and yet I should be sorry if it was.' He sinks his head upon his great fur cloak for a minute and thinks. 'King,' says he, 'be you man or God or Devil, I'll stick by you to-day. I have twenty of my men with me, and they will follow me. We'll go to Bashkai until the storm blows over.'

"A little snow had fallen in the night, and everything was white except the greasy fat clouds that blew down and down from the north. Dravot came out with his crown on his head, swinging his arms and stamping his feet, and looking more pleased than Punch.

"'For the last time, drop it, Dan,' says I, in a whisper. 'Billy Fish here says that there will be a row.'

"'A row among my people!' says Dravot. 'Not much. Peachey, you're a fool not to get a wife too. Where's the girl?' says he, with a voice as loud as the braying of a jackass. 'Call up all the Chiefs and priests, and let the Emperor see if his wife suits him.'

"There was no need to call any one. They were all there leaning on their guns and spears round the clearing in the centre of the pine wood. A deputation of priests went down to the little temple to bring up the girl, and the horns blew up fit to wake the dead. Billy Fish saunters round and gets as close to Daniel as he could, and behind him stood his twenty men with match-locks. Not a man of them under six feet. I was next to Dravot, and behind me was twenty men of the regular Army. Up comes the girl, and a strapping wench she was, covered with silver and turquoises, but white as death, and looking back every minute at the priests.

"'She'll do,' said Dan, looking her over. 'What's to be afraid of, lass? Come and kiss me.' He puts his arm round her. She shuts her eyes, gives a bit of a squeak, and down goes her face in the side of Dan's flaming red beard.

"'The slut's bitten me!' says he, clapping his hand to his neck, and, sure enough, his hand was red with blood. Billy Fish and two of his matchlock-men catches hold of Dan by the shoulders and drags him into the Bashkai lot, while the priests howl in their lingo — 'Neither God nor Devil, but a man!' I was all taken aback, for a priest cut at me in front, and the Army behind began firing into the Bashkai men.

" 'God A-mighty!' says Dan. 'What is the meaning o' this?'

" 'Come back! Come away!' says Billy Fish. 'Ruin and Mutiny is the matter. We'll break for Bashkai if we can.'

"I tried to give some sort of orders to my men —the men o' the regular Army—but it was no use, so I fired into the brown of 'em with an English Martini and drilled three beggars in a line. The valley was full of shouting, howling creatures, and every soul was shrieking, 'Not a God nor a Devil, but only a man!' The Bashkai troops stuck to Billy Fish all they were worth, but their matchlocks wasn't half as good as the Kabul breech-loaders, and four of them dropped. Dan was bellowing like a bull, for he was very wrathy; and Billy Fish had a hard job to prevent him running out at the crowd.

" 'We can't stand,' says Billy Fish. 'Make a run for it down the valley! The whole place is against us.' The matchlock-men ran, and we went down the valley in spite of Dravot's protestations. He was swearing horribly and crying out that he was a King. The priests rolled great stones on us, and the regular Army fired hard, and there wasn't more than six men, not counting Dan, Billy Fish, and Me, that came down to the bottom of the valley alive.

"Then they stopped firing and the horns in the temple blew again. 'Come away—for Gord's sake come away!' says Billy Fish. 'They'll send runners out to all the villages before ever we get to Bashkai. I can protect you there, but I can't do anything now.'

"My own notion is that Dan began to go mad in his head from that hour. He stared up and down like a stuck pig. Then he was all for walking back alone and killing the priests with his bare hands; which he could have done. 'An Emperor am I,' says Daniel, 'and next year I shall be a Knight of the Queen.'

" 'All right, Dan,' says I; 'but come along now while there's time.'

" 'It's your fault,' says he, 'for not looking after your Army better. There was mutiny in the midst and you didn't know—you damned engine-driving, plate-laying, missionary's-pass-hunting hound!' He sat upon a rock and called me every foul name he could lay tongue to. I was too heart-sick to care, though it was all his foolishness that brought the smash.

" 'I'm sorry, Dan,' says I, 'but there's no accounting for natives. This business is our Fifty-Seven. Maybe we'll make something out of it yet, when we've got to Bashkai.'

" 'Let's get to Bashkai, then,' says Dan, 'and,

by God, when I come back here again I'll sweep the valley so there isn't a bug in a blanket left!'

"We walked all that day, and all that night Dan was stumping up and down on the snow, chewing his beard and muttering to himself.

" 'There's no hope o' getting clear,' said Billy Fish. 'The priests will have sent runners to the villages to say that you are only men. Why didn't you stick on as Gods till things was more settled? I'm a dead man,' says Billy Fish, and he throws himself down on the snow and begins to pray to his Gods.

"Next morning we was in a cruel bad country —all up and down, no level ground at all, and no food either. The six Bashkai men looked at Billy Fish hungry-wise as if they wanted to ask something, but they said never a word. At noon we came to the top of a flat mountain all covered with snow, and when we climbed up into it, behold, there was an Army in position waiting in the middle!

" 'The runners have been very quick,' says Billy Fish, with a little bit of a laugh. 'They are waiting for us.'

"Three or four men began to fire from the enemy's side, and a chance shot took Daniel in the calf of the leg. That brought him to his senses. He looks across the snow at the Army, and sees the rifles that we had brought into the country.

" 'We're done for,' says he. 'They are Eng-

lishmen, these people—and it's my blasted nonsense that has brought you to this. Get back,
Billy Fish, and take your men away; you've done
what you could, and now cut for it. Carnehan,'
says he, 'shake hands with me and go along with
Billy. Maybe they won't kill you. I'll go and
meet 'em alone. It's me that did it. Me, the
King!'

"'Go!' says I. 'Go to Hell, Dan. I'm with
you here. Billy Fish, you clear out, and we two
will meet those folk.'

"'I'm a Chief,' says Billy Fish, quite quiet.
'I stay with you. My men can go.'

"The Bashkai fellows didn't wait for a second
word, but ran off, and Dan and Me and Billy
Fish walked across to where the drums were
drumming and the horns were horning. It was
cold—awful cold. I've got that cold in the back
of my head now. There's a lump of it there."

The punkah-coolies had gone to sleep. Two
kerosene lamps were blazing in the office, and the
perspiration poured down my face and splashed
on the blotter as I leaned forward. Carnehan
was shivering, and I feared that his mind might
go. I wiped my face, took a fresh grip of the
piteously mangled hands, and said: "What happened after that?"

The momentary shift of my eyes had broken
the clear current.

"What was you pleased to say?" whined
Carnehan. "They took them without any sound.

Not a little whisper all along the snow, not
though the King knocked down the first man that
set hand on him—not though old Peachey fired
his last cartridge into the brown of 'em. Not a
single solitary sound did those swines make.
They just closed up tight, and I tell you their
furs stunk. There was a man called Billy Fish, a
good friend of us all, and they cut his throat, Sir,
then and there, like a pig; and the King kicks up
the bloody snow and says:—'We've had a dashed
fine run for our money. What's coming next?
But Peachey, Peachey Taliaferro, I tell you, Sir,
in confidence as betwixt two friends, he lost his
head, Sir. No, he didn't neither. The King lost
his head, so he did, all along o' one of those cunning rope-bridges. Kindly let me have the paper-
cutter, Sir. It tilted this way. They marched
him a mile across that snow to a rope-bridge over
a ravine with a river at the bottom. You may
have seen such. They prodded him behind like
an ox. 'Damn your eyes!' says the King. 'D'you
suppose I can't die like a gentleman?' He turns
to Peachey—Peachey that was crying like a
child. 'I've brought you to this, Peachey,' says
he. 'Brought you out of your happy life to be
killed in Kafiristan, where you was late Commander-in-Chief of the Emperor's forces. Say you
forgive me, Peachey.' 'I do,' says Peachey. Fully
and freely do I forgive you, Dan.' 'Shake hands,
Peachey,' says he. 'I'm going now.' Out he
goes, looking neither right nor left, and when he

was plumb in the middle of those dizzy dancing ropes, 'Cut, you beggars,' he shouts; and they cut, and old Dan fell, turning round and round and round twenty thousand miles, for he took half an hour to fall till he struck the water, and I could see his body caught on a rock with the gold crown close beside.

"But do you know what they did to Peachey between two pine trees? They crucified him, Sir, as Peachey's hand will show. They used wooden pegs for his hands and his feet; and he didn't die. He hung there and screamed, and they took him down next day, and said it was a miracle that he wasn't dead. They took him down—poor old Peachey that hadn't done them any harm—that hadn't done them any. . . ."

He rocked to and fro and wept bitterly, wiping his eyes with the back of his scarred hands and moaning like a child for some ten minutes.

"They was cruel enough to feed him up in the temple, because they said he was more of a God than old Daniel that was a man. Then they turned him out on the snow, and told him to go home, and Peachey came home in about a year, begging along the roads quite safe; for Daniel Dravot he walked before and said:—'Come along, Peachey. It's a big thing we're doing.' The mountains they danced at night, and the mountains they tried to fall on Peachey's head, but Dan he held up his hand, and Peachey came along bent double. He never let go of Dan's hand, and he never let go of Dan's head. They gave it to him as a present in the temple, to remind him not to come again, and though the crown was pure gold, and Peachey was starving, never would Peachey sell the same. You knew Dravot, Sir! You knew Right Worshipful Brother Dravot! Look at him now!"

He fumbled in the mass of rags round his bent waist; brought out a black horsehair bag embroidered with silver thread; and shook therefrom on to my table—the dried, withered head of Daniel Dravot! The morning sun that had long been paling the lamps struck the red beard and blind, sunken eyes; struck, too, a heavy circlet of gold studded with raw turquoises, that Carnehan placed tenderly on the battered temples.

"You behold now," said Carnehan, "the Emperor in his habit as he lived—the King of Kafiristan with his crown upon his head. Poor old Daniel that was a monarch once!"

I shuddered, for, in spite of defacements manifold, I recognized the head of the man of Marwar Junction. Carnehan rose to go. I attempted to stop him. He was not fit to walk abroad. "Let me take away the whiskey, and give me a little money," he gasped. "I was a King once. I'll go to the Deputy Commissioner and ask to set in the Poorhouse till I get my health. No, thank you, I can't wait till you get a carriage for me. I've urgent private affairs—in the south— at Marwar."

He shambled out of the office and departed in the direction of the Deputy Commissioner's house. That day at noon I had occasion to go down the blinding hot Mall, and I saw a crooked man crawling along the white dust of the roadside, his hat in his hand, quavering dolorously after the fashion of street-singers at Home. There was not a soul in sight, and he was out of all possible earshot of the houses. And he sang through his nose, turning his head from right to left:

> "The Son of Man goes forth to war,
>   A golden crown to gain;
>   His blood-red banner streams afar—
>   Who follows in his train?"

I waited to hear no more, but put the poor wretch into my carriage and drove him off to the nearest missionary for eventual transfer to the Asylum. He repeated the hymn twice while he was with me, whom he did not in the least recognize, and I left him singing it to the missionary.

Two days later I inquired after his welfare.

"He was admitted suffering from sunstroke. He died early yesterday morning," said the Superintendent. "Is it true that he was half an hour bareheaded in the sun at midday?"

"Yes," said I, "but do you happen to know if he had anything upon him by any chance when he died?"

"Not to my knowledge," said the Superintendent.

And there the matter rests.